ASTEROID: DESTRUCTION

The Asteroid Series
Book Three

A novel by

Bobby Akart

Copyright Information

PRAISE FOR *THE ASTEROID TRILOGY*

"Akart draws you into a story in such a way that you'll be anxiously casting your eyes to the sky in nervous anticipation."

"Not since *Lucifer's Hammer* have readers' imaginations been captured by the very real threats that imperil our planet from space."

"Hollywood got it wrong. NASA has to rethink their intergalactic tactics because these global killers are far tougher than we think. Akart's research lays open the fact that we're wholly unprepared for an extinction-level event caused by a devastating asteroid impact."

"America needs a real hero, and Akart gave us Gunner Fox!"

Other Works by Amazon Top 50 Author, Bobby Akart

The Asteroid Series
Discovery
Diversion
Destruction

The Doomsday Series
Apocalypse
Haven
Anarchy
Minutemen
Civil War

The Yellowstone Series
Hellfire
Inferno
Fallout
Survival

The Lone Star Series
Axis of Evil
Beyond Borders
Lines in the Sand
Texas Strong
Fifth Column
Suicide Six

The Pandemic Series
Beginnings
The Innocents
Level 6
Quietus

The Blackout Series
36 Hours
Zero Hour
Turning Point
Shiloh Ranch
Hornet's Nest
Devil's Homecoming

The Boston Brahmin Series
The Loyal Nine
Cyber Attack
Martial Law
False Flag
The Mechanics
Choose Freedom
Patriot's Farewell
Seeds of Liberty (Companion Guide)

The Prepping for Tomorrow Series
Cyber Warfare
EMP: Electromagnetic Pulse
Economic Collapse

DEDICATIONS

For many years, I have lived by the following premise:

Because you never know when the day before
is the day before, prepare for tomorrow.

My friends, I study and write about the threats we face, not only to both entertain and inform you, but because I am constantly learning how to prepare for the benefit of my family as well. There is nothing more important on this planet than my darling wife, Dani, and our two girls, Bullie and Boom. One day the apocalypse will be upon us, and I'll be damned if I'm gonna let it stand in the way of our life together.

The Asteroid series is dedicated to the love and support of my family. I will always protect you from anything that threatens us.

ACKNOWLEDGEMENTS

Writing a book that is both informative and entertaining requires a tremendous team effort. Writing is the easy part. For their efforts in making the Asteroid series a reality, I would like to thank Hristo Argirov Kovatliev for his incredible cover art, Pauline Nolet for her editorial prowess, Stef Mcdaid for making this manuscript decipherable in so many formats, Chris Abernathy for his memorable performance in narrating this novel, and the Team—Denise, Joe, Jim, Shirley, and Kenda—whose advice, friendship and attention to detail is priceless.

You'll be introduced to two characters in this story who, through their generous donations to charities my family supports, won the right to have a character named after them. One is a gentleman named Sparky Newsome in Washington, Georgia who bid at a local Rotary Club auction. As it happened, Sparky is the editor and owner of the local newspaper, *The News-Reporter*. This changed the trajectory of my story's outline considerably, and for the better.

The use of Mr. Newsome in the Asteroid trilogy, led to incorporating Washington, Georgia as a location, which then led me to the Deerlick Astronomy Village in nearby Crawfordville. Founded by two astronomers in 2005, the DAV is considered one of the darkest locations in the Eastern United States by DarkSiteFinder.com.

Jackie Holcombe, who donated to a special program at Village Veterinary Medical Center in Farragut, Tennessee that supports people who can't afford extraordinary medical procedures for their pets, was also a named character in the series. She earned a prominent role in the story, alongside Mr. Newsome, as you will see. A huge thank you to both of them for their generosity and allowing me to include them in this series.

The research associated with this project surpassed that of the Yellowstone series. In fact, the premise for this story resulted from my conversations with the team of scientists at NASA's Jet Propulsion Laboratory at CalTech over a year ago.

As I dug into the science, once again, source material and research papers were heaped upon my shoulders. My email inbox was put into circuit overload as so many folks from around the globe contributed to my research. One thing is certain—astrophysicists are uniform in their desire to inform the public as to the threats we face from near-Earth objects, especially those that are recently discovered, or remain undiscovered.

There are so many people and organizations to thank, so let me name a few.

I was fortunate enough to be introduced to some brilliant members of our military at Wright-Patterson Air Force Base in Ohio. The USAF's Aeronautical Systems Division, the ASD, provided me invaluable insight into America's future fighting aircraft. They told me what are capabilities are today, and where they'd likely be ten years from now, and beyond. Literally, the sky's the limit for these folks. Don't be surprised that one day, we'll be flying fighter jets in space.

Also, a great source for the technical descriptions of the aircraft of our adversaries was provided by the US Naval Institute's Military Database in Arlington, Virginia. A big thank you to Melissa Cartwright for helping me navigate through a sea of information. Let me add, anyone who thinks we should be cutting our defense budget is short-sighted, or uninformed. The military capabilities of Russia and China will astound you.

As I've already mentioned, my research regarding the Yellowstone Caldera started with the work of Dr. Brian H. Wilcox, an aerospace engineer at the Jet Propulsion Laboratory in Pasadena, California. Although his proposition that our greatest threat to humankind may not necessarily come from above, in the form of a near-Earth object, but rather, from below, as an eruption from the Yellowstone Supervolcano, he has cautioned that it's the newly discovered asteroids that have the potential to be planet killers. Frankly, I don't know how Dr. Wilcox sleeps at night.

Lastly, I must make mention of the team at NASA's Planetary Defense Coordination Office. The PDCO employs a variety of ground and space-based telescopes to search for near-Earth objects, determines their orbits, and measures their physical characteristics in order to accurately assess the threat to our planet. Their functions including warning our government of the threats, suggesting mitigation techniques to alter the course of an incoming object, and acts to coordinate with multiple agencies as an emergency response is formulated. Thank you to Linda Billings and others in the Public Communications office at the PDCO; Patricia Talbert in the Professional Outreach department; and of course, Lindley Johnson, the Program Executive of the PDCO.

Without their efforts, this story could not be told.

Thank you all!

ABOUT THE AUTHOR

Bobby Akart

Author Bobby Akart has been ranked by Amazon as #50 on the Amazon Charts list of most popular, bestselling authors. He has achieved recognition as the #1 bestselling Horror Author, #2 bestselling Science Fiction Author, #3 bestselling Religion & Spirituality Author, #6 bestselling Action & Adventure Author, #7 bestselling Historical Author and #10 bestselling Thriller Author.

He has written over thirty international bestsellers, in nearly fifty fiction and nonfiction genres, including the chart-busting Yellowstone series, the thought-provoking Doomsday series, the reader-favorite Lone Star series, the critically acclaimed Boston Brahmin series, the bestselling Blackout series, the frighteningly realistic Pandemic series, his highly cited nonfiction Prepping for Tomorrow series, and his latest project—the Asteroid series, a scientific thriller that will remind us all that life on Earth may have begun, and might well end, with something from space.

His novel *Yellowstone: Fallout* reached the Top 50 on the Amazon bestsellers list and earned him two Kindle All-Star awards for most pages read in a month and most pages read as an author. The Yellowstone series vaulted him to the #1 bestselling horror author on Amazon, and the #2 bestselling science fiction author.

Bobby has provided his readers a diverse range of topics that are both informative and entertaining. His attention to detail and impeccable research has allowed him to capture the imaginations of his readers through his fictional works and bring them valuable knowledge through his nonfiction books.

SIGN UP for Bobby Akart's mailing list to receive special offers, bonus content, and you'll be the first to receive news about new releases in the Asteroid series:

Visit Bobby Akart's website for informative blog entries on preparedness, writing, and a behind-the-scenes look into his novels.

BobbyAkart.com

VISIT Amazon.com/BobbyAkart, a dedicated feature page created by Amazon for his work, to view more information on his thriller fiction novels and post-apocalyptic book series, as well as his nonfiction Prepping for Tomorrow series.

Author's Introduction to the Asteroid Series

June 13, 2019
I want you to imagine how vast our solar system is ...

For those of us stuck on Earth, we might gaze up into the night sky and marvel at the size of our solar system, but we'll never get the opportunity to get a closer look. We take for granted the Sun that brightens our day, or the mysterious Moon that appears at night. The trained eye can pick out constellations and even other planets, if one knows where to look.

But just how big is our solar system? Before you can appreciate its vastness, let's consider the units of measurement that give it a sense of scale. Distances are so large that measurements like feet and miles are irrelevant. Most distances are defined in astronomical units, or AUs. One AU, based upon the distance from the Earth to the Sun, is roughly equal to ninety-three-million-miles.

To put that into perspective, if you flew around our planet, you'd cover twenty-five thousand miles. If you traveled to the moon, you'd cover about ten times that, or two-hundred-forty-thousand miles. To reach the sun, we're looking at almost forty times the distance to the moon. And finally, to reach the outer limits of our solar system, where the Oort Cloud is located, is over one-hundred-thousand AUs, or nearly two light years away.

Now, that's a lot of space, pardon the pun. It would take our fastest spacecraft thirty-seven thousand years to get there.

That said, however, space objects travel the vast openness of our solar system with regularity. Over many millions of years, these objects, both large and small, wander the solar system. Some remain within the gravitational orbit of larger bodies, or within the asteroid belt that exists between Mars and Jupiter.

Others, the wayward nomads who are looking for a larger object's gravity to become attached to, float aimlessly, and mostly harmlessly, through space for years and years and years. Until …

They collide with other objects.

Asteroids are typically material left over from the period of planetary formation four-and-a-half billion years ago. They're the remains of what didn't form into planets in the inner solar system, or often the result of collisions in the past.

They vary in size from only a few feet to the big daddy of them all—*Ceres*, which measures about one-fourth the size of our moon. At almost six-hundred-miles wide, Ceres is about the size of Texas.

This story focuses on the threats our planet faces from a collision with a near-Earth object, or NEO. If you consider an asteroid can be as small as a few feet across, there are an estimated five-hundred-million of them considered to be near-Earth—between us and the Sun. If you limit the number to potentially hazardous asteroids, those within four-and-a-half million miles, then the number is reduced to around twenty-thousand.

That's a lot of traffic in our neighborhood, and yet only ninety percent are accounted for. While NASA and other space agencies around the globe do an admirable job of identifying and tracking these NEOs, the fact of the matter is that they only have identified ninety percent of the threats. That leaves a one-in-ten-chance that an object remains undiscovered.

The big uncertainty is that we haven't discovered many near-Earth asteroids, so we don't know if they are on a collision course with Earth. Now, there is comfort in knowing that the vastness of space might make the odds in our favor that one of these wandering nomads doesn't hit us.

However, because of the size of our planet, and the gravity associated with Earth, asteroids can be pulled toward us. It's happened before, on many occasions.

NEO impact events have played a significant role in the evolution of our solar system since its formation. Major impact events have significantly shaped Earth's history, have been implicated in the formation of the Earth–Moon system, the evolutionary history of life, the origin of water on Earth and several mass extinctions. The famous prehistoric Chicxulub (cheek-sha-loob) impact, sixty-six million years ago, is believed to be the cause of the Cretaceous–Paleogene extinction event that resulted in the demise of the dinosaurs.

Could it happen again? Absolutely. When? Nobody knows. At present, there are only a few potentially close-shaves in our future, at least, that we know of. It's the ones that we haven't discovered that keep astrophysicists and amateur astronomers up at night, watching the skies.

Thank you for reading and I know you'll enjoy the Asteroid series, a Gunner Fox trilogy.

REAL-WORLD NEWS EXCERPTS

A Massive Asteroid Got Extremely Close to Earth and Scientists Didn't Know Until it Was Only Days Away ~ *Yahoo News, July 28, 2019*

The 427 foot wide asteroid got within 45,000 miles of Earth last week. That's only twenty percent of the distance between the Earth and the Moon, that qualifies as a pretty narrow miss.

Dubbed a "city-killer", it was classified because it would strike the planet with the force of multiple nuclear bombs capable of destroying America's largest cities.

How did they miss this?

While NASA and other agencies have technology to track objects like this, there isn't enough funding to observe every single one. NASA manages to track less than one third of the major asteroids.

"City Killer" asteroid misses Earth and Scientists had no idea ~ *CBS News, June 29, 2019*

Asteroid 2019 OK came hurtling toward Earth at a speed of 15 miles a second, according to NASA. It came as close as forty-five-thousand miles from our planet. The asteroid, about the size of a large boulder, only became visible a few days ago.

Astronomy professor, Alan Duffy, said it would have hit with over thirty times the energy of the atomic blast at Hiroshima during World War II.

There are twenty thousand near-Earth asteroids and they do occasionally make an appearance. In 2013, one slammed into Russia, injuring sixteen-hundred people and caused millions in damages.

The same-day notice provided in the case of 2019 MO illustrates the weakness in preparing for a much bigger asteroid smacking into the Earth's atmosphere.

How the Space Force would help protect Earth from Future Asteroid Threats ~ *Tariq Malik, SPACE.com, June 20, 2018*

If the Space Force like the one proposed by President Donald Trump becomes a reality, odds are, it would play a role in defending Earth from an incoming asteroid.

In a report released today (June 20, 2018), NASA and other federal officials unveiled what the United States should do over the next 10 years to safeguard Earth from potential asteroid impacts. That 18-page plan, called the "The National Near-Earth Object Preparedness Strategy and Action Plan," would involve work from agencies across the federal government, White House officials said — even, potentially, Trump's proposed Space Force.

The U.S. currently has three possible methods for deflecting any potentially hazardous asteroid from hitting Earth:

•A "gravity tractor" that would park a spacecraft near the asteroid and let the gravitational attraction of the two objects nudge the asteroid off course.
•A "kinetic impactor" that would slam a spacecraft into an asteroid to knock it off course.
•A nuclear strike aimed at vaporizing the surface of an asteroid, creating jet of material that would push the asteroid off course.

All three of those options would require at least a 10-year lead time before a potential asteroid impact, NASA Planetary Defense Officer Lindley Johnson told reporters at the teleconference.

Johnson even suggested that civilians, like amateur astronomers or the B612 Foundation for asteroid awareness, could play a response role.

"Planetary defense is a team sport," Johnson said. "We welcome capability wherever it comes."

You can download the full National Near-Earth Object Preparedness Strategy and Action Plan here from the White House Office of Science and Technology Policy.

Epigraph

"Up until now Congressional appropriators and senior NASA officials are mostly relying on luck to keep us safe from catastrophic fatalities resulting from the surprise impact of an unseen asteroid. So far, luck and the odds are on our side as evidenced by both the 1908 Siberian Tunguska impact and the 2013 Chelyabinsk airburst occurring in relatively remote areas of our planet. However, luck is not a plan."

~ Professor Richard P. Binzel,
Massachusetts Institute of Technology
*****

"Asteroid detection, tracking, and defense of our planet is something that NASA, its interagency partners, and the global community take very seriously."

~ John M. Grunsfeld, American physicist
and former NASA astronaut
*****

"NASA and Congress criticized for proposed budget cuts."

~ SpaceNews.com, March 13, 2019
*****

"Sooner or later, NASA will need to save us by detecting and deflecting an incoming asteroid. By most estimates, the mortality risk posed by an asteroid impact is put at about the same risk as flying a commercial airliner. However, you have to remember that the entirety of the human race would be riding on that plane, making an impact event one of the few risks that really could wipe us all out."

~ Nathan Myhrvold, former Chief Technology Officer at Microsoft

ASTEROID: DESTRUCTION

The Asteroid Series
Book Three

PROLOGUE

Eight Years Prior
Unknown Location

Gunner Fox was blindfolded and unable to see any of his surroundings. His body felt hot, sweaty, as if he'd been locked in a one-hundred-twenty-degree steam room. He was beginning to feel the effects of dehydration.

His eyes felt like they were sinking back into his head. The lack of sleep from the heavy metal music piped into the dark, hot box of a cell was causing him to be disoriented. Dizziness had taken over and he felt faint.

Gunner tried to roll over on occasion, hoping to get away from the vomit he attempted to keep confined to one corner of the windowless cell. But his sleepiness, lack of energy, and confusion left him lying in it nonetheless.

Suddenly, a light appeared, barely discernible through the black cloth that was wrapped over his eyes and around his head. A clank indicated a small observation panel had been opened briefly and then forced shut. Gunner steeled his nerves, waiting to be tortured again. For days, as many as four, although he'd lost count, he'd been subjected to mental and physical abuse.

No food. No water. No opportunity to see his captors. They'd brought him to the brink of death and insanity.

A loud thump, followed by the sounds of metallic locks turning outside his prison cell sent him a message that his brutal captors were back. *Would it be more of the same? Beatings, electric shock, and verbal abuse?* Gunner prepared himself mentally, but physically, his strength and ability to survive the ongoing assault was waning.

"Get the stinking bastard up!" The leader spoke in English but with a heavy Russian accent. Two men grabbed Gunner under the arms and attempted to bring him to his feet.

His legs buckled underneath him, causing him to collapse against one of the guards, rubbing his puke-covered clothes against the man.

The guard let out a series of curses in Russian. Words that Gunner couldn't understand, but the anger in the man's voice was apparent.

Gunner's face was smashed against the concrete wall, drawing blood from a gash in his forehead that had been received on day one when he refused to answer their questions. At the time, his reaction, a toothy grin followed by spitting blood that resulted from a punch by his captors, felt good to him. He was resisting them. He was denying them the satisfaction of breaking him.

They, in turn, stepped up their tortuous game. Now, after several days, Gunner was beginning to question whether he would survive his captivity. The men were sadistic. Enjoying the torture being administered on their prisoner. Stretching out their tactics to have a maximum psychological and physical effect on the man held in solitary confinement, away from the other prisoners.

"Strip him down!" the Russian bellowed. "He stinks like a rat in a sewer!"

The guards quickly obliged. Gunner heard the sounds of switchblade knives opening. The men weren't careful in their quick motions to tear his clothes off him. As his shirt was cut open, so was a long, thin line of flesh, causing more of his blood to begin running down the center of his chest.

His jeans were torn apart with a series of slices of the sharp blades, jabbing into the fleshy part of his butt and also slightly puncturing his right thigh. The pain caused him to wince and bite his tongue. But he didn't yell. He wouldn't give them that satisfaction.

They stood Gunner up, the salty sweat beginning to seep into the new cuts in his skin. Suddenly, the guards were forcibly shaking him. This was followed by an open-handed slap across his face, a sucker punch that he could never see coming.

"Are you listening to me, *Amerikanskiy*? Are you?" The

interrogator demanded Gunner's attention.

Gunner said nothing, which earned him a hard slap to the stomach. The pain raced through his body. His captors were expert at inflicting suffering and discomfort upon him without causing internal damage. They wanted him to stay alive.

He was dragged out of the cell and his arms were yoked above his head. The guards clamped his wrists into large, three-inch-wide handcuffs attached to a chain. He was now suspended in the air, stretched upward, completely nude.

"Do it!" screamed the man in his Russian accent.

Gunner knew what to expect, so he braced his body. He waited. Listening for the wheel to crank. Mustering the strength to stand on his toes, for hours, knowing that if he failed, both of his arms would be pulled out of his shoulder sockets.

Gunner had been stretched to his limit, physically and mentally. But he held on. He kept visions of Heather in the forefront of his mind. Typically, when on a mission, he tried to block her out of his consciousness. He felt guilty about that, as he loved her more than life. But a soldier who was obsessed with the person he loved couldn't perform as a hardened warrior on the battlefield. Heather understood this, allowing Gunner to ease his guilt.

This, however, was different. He needed her strength. He had to focus on their love to keep his sanity. He needed a vision of Heather, and her voice in his head, to endure the suffering he was going through.

"Are you prepared to answer my questions, *Amerikanskiy?*"

Gunner remained silent, as he had throughout the ordeal. No name. No rank. No serial number. They would get nothing out of him, not even an acknowledgment that they existed.

It infuriated his captors. He was certain of it. They had a job to do—make him talk, break him, and then declare victory as he begged for mercy. Gunner Fox had no intention of giving them that satisfaction. On the contrary, all he could think about was surviving, escaping, and getting home to Heather. After he killed them all, of course.

Gunner was holding on, but his mind was slipping. It had been hours since the interrogator made his final efforts to get Gunner to talk.

"It's time," the interrogator bellowed. "I am tired of coddling this *Amerikanskiy* asshole!"

The crank was turned and Gunner was lowered to the ground in a heap. He was unable to move his arms at first, stiff from the hours of being suspended above his head.

Gunner attempted to cover his genitals as the men kicked him in the thighs and back several times. He curled up in a fetal position, allowing his body to relax as the kicks continued.

"I will kill you right now if you don't tell us what we want!" The man was screaming in Russian. Gunner couldn't understand what he was saying, but the tone of the maniac's voice spoke volumes.

Then the man became eerily calm. A massive swing in emotions that caught Gunner off guard. For the first time, he truly expected to die.

A calm American accent appeared among his captors for the first time. "He won't talk unless we make him. Let's get on with it."

Two guards abruptly grabbed Gunner and began to drag him across the rough concrete floor. His body went limp as the hard surface ripped the skin off his knees and the tops of his feet.

They lifted him up and rolled him over onto a wooden board. Two other sets of hands quickly bound his wrists and ankles with leather straps. Gunner fought them, writhing back and forth in a futile attempt to avoid the restraints. Somehow, he knew what was coming.

First, he heard the water. The sound of a towel being dipped into a sink or bucket, being sloshed around to soak it thoroughly. He prepared himself for the ultimate form of human torture—waterboarding.

His captor leaned over Gunner's face and hissed—the sadistic man's hot breath felt in his nostrils. "You will break. You will not make me look like a fool. I will give you this one last chance. Speak, or prepare to die."

Gunner did not give in. Instead, he spontaneously smiled. *Give it your best shot, pal.*

And the man did. He forced the soaking wet towel over Gunner's nose and mouth. One of the guards slowly began to pour water over Gunner's face, further saturating the towel. The dousing lasted around fifteen seconds, during which time Gunner tried to turn his head away from the onslaught of water. It took three men to hold him still until it was time to assess their progress.

Gunner was still smiling.

"Talk! Talk, dammit!"

Gunner refused. He lay perfectly still, his eyes wide open, staring at the black cloth that had become part of his body since his arrival.

The interrogator reapplied the towel and the process continued. Waterboarding was first used during the fifteenth century. The Spanish Inquisition, instituted by Catholic monarchs in Spain, was intended to ensure converts to the faith of Christianity from Judaism and Islam remained true to their new Christian faith. A similar technique to waterboarding was just one of the many tools used by the monarchy. For some, simply burning the heretics at the stake was a more favored option.

The former Soviet Union perfected the art of waterboarding. It was often used against American spies during the height of the Cold War. The KGB found that sleep deprivation, exposure to extreme heat and cold, and hours upon hours of placing their captives in uncomfortable, stress-filled environs was effective at breaking a spy.

When the normal tactics didn't work, the Soviets adopted waterboarding as a technique. At first, the interrogators let their emotions get in the way of the task at hand. Many spies were killed by the torture. The technique was intended to create a feeling of suffocation. In practice, prisoners were drowning.

Gunner's captor, however, was a professional. He knew how much torture to administer to break a prisoner. He'd saved the best for last—waterboarding.

Yet it wasn't working, causing the leader to become increasingly frustrated. On the last attempts, the bucket of water turned into two, and then to three. For nearly a minute, water was poured over Gunner's face, and, at times, he was certain the interrogator loosened the pressure on the towel so water could find its way into Gunner's mouth and nose.

He wants to drown me!

Gunner was at his lowest point. His hope was almost lost, but he didn't outwardly manifest it to his captors.

Frustrated, the interrogator ripped the towel away from Gunner's face and slapped the last bucket, sending it careening across the concrete floor.

The man's frustration got the better of him, and his fit of rage gave Gunner an opening. His blindfold had been moved so that he could see the floor and the feet of his captors. He also could sense a glimmer of hope, which gave him newfound strength.

"Take him back!" the Russian yelled in English.

The guards brusquely unstrapped Gunner, who played the role of faint, semiconscious prisoner. As they had done for days, they dragged his lifeless body over the concrete floor and down the hallway toward his cell.

The farther he traveled into the bowels of the prison, the less he could hear the voice of the interrogator. After past torture sessions, he'd counted in his head each time he was returned to this cell.

One Mississippi. Two Mississippi. Three Mississippi.

It was a throwback to his days as a kid when his friends, including Cam, would get together to play a pickup football game in the backyard. The rule was that the defense couldn't rush the passer for three seconds—counted out in *Mississippi*s.

Gunner knew it took about thirty seconds to be returned to his cell. Despite his sleep-starved brain preventing him from thinking clearly, he'd remained singularly focused on one task—escape.

It was a prisoner's duty.

Now he could see the floor. He could study and anticipate the guards' movements. He'd prepared for that moment, that brief opening in which one of the guards would release his grip on Gunner to prepare the door to be locked while the other carried the burden of shoving Gunner into the cell.

Gunner's body tensed, a change in his demeanor that was noticed by the guard. But it was too late. Gunner spun and thrust the palm of his hand upward, striking the guard in the throat. He was immediately released, and without hesitation, he spun around and kicked the other guard's legs out from under him.

Both men groaned in pain, a guttural noise that could be heard down the all-concrete hallway. At this distance, to the interrogator and the unknown American in the torture room, it sounded no different than Gunner's usual moans after a brutal session of abuse.

He ripped the blindfold off and quickly adjusted to the light, thankful that the hallway was dimly lit. He pounced on top of the first guard, who was holding his throat in agony. Gunner reared back and slammed his fist into the side of the man's head, instantly knocking him unconscious.

He turned his attention to the other guard. He clamped his hand over the man's mouth. The guard's eyes grew wide at the sight of Gunner. He hadn't shaved in a week. His hair was matted with vomit. His naked body reeked of bodily fluids and feces. Gunner was more animal than human.

And the formerly caged animal's eyes were maniacal. He felt along the man's utility belt for a weapon. There was nothing. His captors must've anticipated Gunner's capabilities, knowing it would be a deadly mistake to have a gun or knife in his presence at any time.

Attached to the guard's belt, Gunner found a key ring—a large brass oval that held skeleton keys and vehicle fobs. He ripped it from the Velcro attachment and forced the skeleton key, the one used to open and close his cell, toward the guard's eye.

"You can either shut up, or lose your eyes, or you can die. Your choice."

The man couldn't speak. He shook his head violently from side to side to avoid the key jabbing toward his right eye.

"I need your uniform, asshole," hissed Gunner as he dragged the man into the cell. The guard was much thinner than his chubby partner, and his uniform would fit Gunner just about right.

7

Gunner turned the man around with his hand clamped over his mouth. The man began to unbutton the Russian military uniform and quickly dropped the clothes to the floor.

Gunner then gathered the strength to administer a choke hold. He looped his right arm around the guard's neck and began to squeeze. He lifted his left arm and pressed against the side of the guard's head, creating a *figure-four* appearance.

Then he squeezed. He resisted the urge to kill the man. He wanted to, but didn't. Cutting off the blood flow to the man's brain was sufficient to render him unconscious, thus giving Gunner the opportunity to escape.

With the man incapacitated, Gunner quickly dressed and dragged both guards into his cell, making sure to dump their bodies in the pools of urine and vomit on the floor. After checking the other man for weapons, a radio, or anything else of use, Gunner gently locked the cell door and eased down the hallway.

He could no longer hear the voices of the interrogator and the American who had witnessed the torture. As he gathered himself, he contemplated his next move. He wanted to inflict the kind of pain he'd endured on them. On everyone.

However, his need to escape took precedence. Gunner slowly made his way through the concrete hallways of the building where he was being held. He searched frantically for an exit. Any door that led to the outside.

Finally, a steel door with a single window that was eight inches square appeared at the end of another darkened hallway. There were other cell doors on both sides. His mind raced.

Are there other prisoners? Are they being tortured like I was? Should I take the time to save them?

Gunner took the skeleton key and began to unlock the doors one by one. Each cell was empty, spotlessly clean, with the fresh smell of Lysol.

Puzzled, Gunner shook his head and made his way to the door. He slowly glanced through the window and saw a stand of trees. A faint streetlight illuminated a portion of the woods. After surveilling the surroundings for a moment, gauging the activity of any perimeter security, Gunner took a chance and opened the door.

A rush of cold air enveloped his body, an environment that stood in stark contrast to the hot, humid cell he'd become accustomed to. It was refreshing and odd at the same time.

Reinvigorated by the prospect of freedom, he glanced around the outside of the building and dashed into the woods. Minutes later, he was walking alone down a dark road under a canopy of trees, wondering where the hell he was and how in the world he would make his way home.

PART ONE

Friday, April 27

The Best Day Ever...

CHAPTER 1

Present Day
April 27
Unknown Location

Gunner Fox tried to fight his way back to consciousness. He was alive, or at least he thought he was. He looked for a sign that he wasn't dreaming. A sound. Movement. Anything familiar that would bring him into the present.

For a while, his surroundings were deathly silent, as if some large control knob had turned down the volume of life on Earth. Then, gradually, a concert of humming, buzzing, and chirping sounds filled the air. An orchestra consisting of frogs, cicadas, howler monkeys, and tropical birds performed their songs over one another, completely ignoring the conductor, if there was one.

His eyes opened a narrow slit, allowing just enough sunlight in to let him see his surroundings. The sudden light stung his irises, forcing him to blink several times, trying to open them fully yet squinting in a futile attempt to shield the brightness.

He rolled his head back and forth, as if to confirm that it was still attached. His brain was pounding from the trauma it had suffered during the crash. The movement of his neck sent a sharp, stabbing pain through his body. Gunner became alarmed as he instantly thought of partial paralysis. He checked his extremities—fingers, wrists, toes, and ankles. All intact, all moving on command.

A sense of relief washed over him. Nothing appeared to be broken, yet he felt beat all to hell. He dared reach up to his forehead, using the flat of his hand to feel for a fever. His temperature was normal, but the thick, sticky liquid that covered his scalp was not.

Finally, his eyes adjusted, allowing in the initial glimpses of his surroundings. The first thing he saw was a tree branch—twisting and slicing through the air. Gunner tilted his head to study it. Ordinarily, something as commonplace wouldn't garner a second glance, but as his eyes continued to shift from side to side, allowing the light to illuminate this foreign environment, he noticed how odd it was.

The bark was smooth, gray-green in color, almost as if it belonged to a large hairless creature. Gunner closed his eyes and visualized a green hippopotamus with smooth, tentacle-like features. He shook his head, trying to remove the absurd notion from his consciousness.

The sun was rising, beginning to reveal itself through the black palm trees that surrounded him. He muttered the words, "Chunga palm." He'd seen them before, in Southeast Asia, on a mission with Cam and Bear.

Or was it in Venezuela? His mind raced, trying to make sense of it all. *Where am I?*

Gunner forced himself to focus. His head was throbbing and his body felt like it had been pummeled by a herd of buffalo. Nonetheless, he was pleased that he had remembered Cam and Bear. His memory loss was only temporary. Their words filled his head.

Day by day. Minute by minute. Ride or die. We stick together.

He wished they were with him.

Gunner was still strapped in his seat. Something tickled his hand. It was small, but it was clearly walking up his fingers and toward the underside of his wrist, where it hovered for a moment at his ulnar artery, the main blood vessel providing oxygenated blood to his hand.

He flexed his fingers in an attempt to remove the creature, whatever it was, from his body. It was too large to be an ant. It was cold, bug-like, not like a mammal.

It moved again. In Gunner's semiconscious state, his mental acuity was somewhat stifled, but he knew the feeling of a bug on his skin. His mind processed the sensation, and he recalled being stung by a jungle scorpion while on a mission. Most were extremely painful and some could be deadly.

He was in enough pain without a scorpion bite. He flailed his arm about, shaking the creature off his wrist until it was flung off his body. The interaction revealed to Gunner that he was in a dangerous place.

He felt around and found part of the Starhopper's controls. He reached above his head and grasped for the ceiling of the cockpit. He stretched his fingers, wiggling them in an effort to find the top, but it was gone. The command center had been ripped in half, the top torn to shreds as it had rolled over and over during the crash back to Earth.

"I'm still in the spaceship," he muttered aloud, though no one could hear him.

He glanced to his left and saw Chief Rawlings's lifeless body slumped over, held in place by the commander's seat restraints. A feeling of remorse washed over him as he remembered what had happened to the man who'd mentored him throughout the mission. It was starting to come back to him now.

Gunner tried to get his bearings, and then he was distracted by warmth dripping onto his face. *More blood?*

He touched the moisture as it rolled down his cheeks. He blinked several times, willing his eyes to work, pushing back the pain of his head that wanted to force him back into a deep sleep.

Mesmerized, Gunner studied the blood on his fingertips. Like a gardener checking the dipstick on his push mower, he wiped it off on his clothing and began to feel his head, desperately searching for the wound that was causing him to bleed.

He became puzzled. Now using both hands, he ran his fingers all over his face and scalp in search of the source of his bleeding.

Nothing. A pounding headache, to be sure. But no cut wounds that caused bleeding.

Drip. Drip. Drip.

Again the blood began to smack him on the cheek. He looked upward, and several drops fell onto his forehead, threatening to drip into his eyes. Tiny rivulets of dark moisture that tortured him, not because of the volume of blood, but because he couldn't discern its source.

He feverishly wiped the blood off his face and searched for the source. He focused his attention on the branch. It was still above him, yet somehow, impossibly, it was much closer.

And it was swelling. Pulsating as if it were an artery of a gigantic heart. Only, it was green.

"Come on, Gunner. Get your shit together." He bemoaned his inability to fully regain consciousness. His mind was in some kind of drug-induced stupor not unlike what LSD did to the hippies of the sixties. Everything was real, yet nothing was as it seemed.

More blood dripped onto him, awakening him somewhat. The sun was brighter, so his vision improved. At first, he looked down to the pair of khakis and the white, long-sleeve NASA shirt he'd changed into before he initiated the attack on the asteroid. There was blood splatter, and the sleeves on his shirt were torn slightly, but no gaping wounds. *Where is this blood coming from?*

He looked skyward, through a luminous jungle canopy that shimmered in hues of yellow, green and, beyond the tropical foliage, the light blue sky.

And at the branch.

Except it wasn't a branch. It was a thing. It was alive.

And it was eating the corpse of the Russian commander, Sokolov.

CHAPTER 2

Unknown Tropical Jungle

Suddenly, Gunner became keenly aware of his surroundings. His survival instincts forced his mind to function and his senses to awaken. He no longer had the luxury of observing the wonders of his unknown location through the prism of a semiconscious state. He was in mortal danger.

He'd spent countless days in the jungles of the world. From the Amazon in South America to the Congo of Africa to the rainforests of the Malay peninsula. Each were unique in their geologic makeup, but they all shared a common characteristic—they were a vast expanse of vegetation inhabited by tens of thousands of forms of wildlife.

The tropical jungles and rainforests of the world feature few large animals. There were no herds of plodding elephants, stampeding zebras, or foraging wildebeests. In the rainforests, in particular, one didn't have to fear roaming prides of lions or cackles of hyenas.

Rather, the underbelly of the tropical foliage was teeming with Jurassic-like creatures rarely seen by man, including large predators that were lying in wait—patiently waiting to ambush their next meal. These predators were seldom seen until it was too late.

There was nowhere on Earth that so aptly demonstrates survival of the fittest—the grim reality of the great horror of life that in order to live, all things must devour each other. It was a monstrous, unrelenting killing spree from which there was no means of escape. For the animal kingdom, there was no refuge in a higher being. There was no justice. There was only survival.

Behind the dense screens of vegetation or below the surface of ponds and rivers lay millions of species of insects, birds, spiders, rodents, frogs, tortoises, lizards, and bats. They all fed on one another, in the hierarchy of supremacy established over the millennia. At the top end of the food chain, of course, was man. Man reigned supreme in his ability to kill other animals for sustenance.

Unless, of course, man wandered off the beaten path. When man stepped out of his comfort zone, all bets were off. Because in the jungle, there existed threats large and small. From the toxin of the poison dart frog to the sting of the fat-tailed *Androctonus* scorpion, small reptiles were ready to inflict death upon even the top of the food chain when the opportunity presented itself.

As were the larger reptiles like crocodiles and snakes.

Snakes, like the green anaconda.

Gunner's eyes grew wide in wonder. The twenty-foot anaconda that he'd mistaken for a tree branch easily weighed five hundred pounds, plus the body weight of Commander Sokolov, who was now halfway consumed by the snake.

He was gripped with fear at first, and then he became enthralled at the sight. The female anaconda, much larger than her male counterparts, was slowly swallowing parts of the Russian's body. The activity defied all logic as the much smaller reptile gulped first Sokolov's head and then slowly took in his torso.

Gunner had seen larger snakes during his exploits, most notably a thirty-foot python he'd come across in Myanmar during a mission to rescue some Baptist missionaries in the country formerly known as Burma. He steered clear of the massive creature then, and now wished he could run as fast as he could from the anaconda.

He struggled with his harnesses, which had been pulled and tugged during his crash back to Earth. He subconsciously reached down for his knife that was always strapped to his leg during one of his special operations. But he wasn't on a mission. Not that kind, anyway.

There were no weapons on the Starhopper other than the four nuclear missiles that he'd used to destroy 2029 IM86. Most of it, anyway. He glanced upward at the light show. Meteors were burning up in the atmosphere. They were the smaller remnants of the blasted asteroid that had led the way on the trip back to Earth.

Gunner, however, knew there was more to come. As he'd raced the debris field toward the planet, he'd passed the larger chunks, the remains of the asteroid that would likely cause the most damage. These meteorites would be undeterred by Earth's atmosphere. Their progress wouldn't even be slowed by the thousands of man-made satellites orbiting the planet in low-Earth orbit.

Soon, within hours, Earth's surface would be pummeled by the debris, wreaking havoc all across the Northern Hemisphere.

But he had bigger fish to fry at the moment, as they say. If he didn't free himself from these harnesses, he was likely to join his Russian adversary in the belly of the anaconda.

Gunner lifted his legs so he could push off the control panel in an effort to change the dynamic of the multipoint harness that strapped him to the seat. The device that kept him alive during the tumble through the jungle now acted as a spiderweb that captured the five-hundred-pound snake's next meal.

He twisted and pulled the straps. The harness buckles had been pulled so hard during the crash that they refused to release. He searched for something to cut through the webbing of the straps. He felt beneath his seat, grasping for anything that might help free him.

"Yes!" he shouted, causing some nearby howler monkeys to let loose their cacophonous cries.

Gunner ignored the blood gushing out of the palm of his hand, rejoicing in the fact that he'd found a sharp piece of metal that could be used to cut the harnesses. Cut wounds could heal. Having one's head swallowed by a giant anaconda was another story.

He ignored the pain and began to saw away at the strap around his waist. Soon, his waist was free, allowing him more wiggle room in his seat. Then he went to work on the shoulder straps. He glanced up to the snake and saw that Sokolov was almost gone. His lower legs had already been severed during the crash, likely by the same sharp metal Gunner was using to free himself of the harnesses.

Gunner didn't know anything about the feeding habits of the

anaconda. In a brief moment of lightheartedness, he wondered if anacondas got *full*, or did they move on to their next option for *second helpings?*

He didn't plan on sticking around to find out. He subtly glanced over at Chief Rawlings, instantly feeling guilty that the famed astronaut would most likely be *seconds.*

Gunner continued to saw at the straps and finally freed himself. He quickly glanced around his surroundings in search of his blue duffle bag, but it wasn't there.

He gathered what was left of his strength, shifted his weight, then stood up to make his way behind the pilot's seat, putting a little distance and an obstacle between him and the anaconda. She'd finished her first course and was likely to make a move toward her next option if she was still hungry.

Fully coherent and assessing his options, Gunner took in his surroundings. Green and greenery obliterated all other colors. The tropical foliage was all unique, yet the same. Colors of ferns, moss, jade, asparagus, lettuce, and iridescent green velvet consumed his vision. Not that he was surprised. He'd thought a snake was a tree branch.

The first thing he did was unstrap the body of Chief Rawlings. He was a great man who hadn't deserved to die. He most certainly didn't deserve to suffer the same fate as Sokolov.

Gunner hoisted his mentor's body on his shoulder and looked around. He turned to look toward the rear of the Starhopper, which was no longer there. What was once a hundred-foot-plus example of man's greatest technological achievement was now a half-mile-long debris field that had cut a two-hundred-foot-wide swath through a jungle.

A remote jungle that could be anywhere on Earth.

CHAPTER 3

Unknown Tropical Jungle

Gunner stepped onto the jungle floor, his boots sinking into the moist undergrowth, which immediately gave him visions of the creatures that might be observing his ankles. He had to put that out of his mind as he considered what to do.

The crash didn't produce spontaneous fires as was typical in a debris field such as this one. Jet fuel burned and was subject to combustion. Rocket fuel was much different.

Jet engines were air breathers. Jets take in air needed for combustion, mix it with fuel, burn it to increase pressure, and exhaust the spent gases out the back of the aircraft at a high rate of speed.

Spacecraft contain separate tanks of hydrogen and oxygen that are mixed in the liquid-fuel rocket engines, burned, and expelled out the nozzles. This enables a rocket to fly in the vacuum of space where jets cannot.

It also makes for a cleaner crash site. Gunner knew what a combat jet crash site looked like. He'd seen them firsthand, on multiple occasions.

He was surrounded by twisted palm fronds and fallen trees. Over a slight rise, amidst the tree canopy, lay the remains of the Starhopper chaotically scattered about, various parts of its magnificent technology strewn in all directions.

Off in the distance, there was a flattened stretch of jungle, an overgrown tangled thicket shrouded in a light fog. Occasionally, a tall palm tree still stood, emerging from the jungle floor with its fronds shredded. Other palms were bizarrely bent, gnarled husks of their former self, crushed to the ground by the impact of the spacecraft.

Gunner studied the carnage, and then, in a moment of extreme clarity, he took in the beauty that surrounded him. Amidst the twisted wreckage, the debris of metal and electronics and body parts, was a garden of Eden complete with ferns, mosses, and gorgeous orchids and bromeliads that looked like they were in a hanging garden. Patches of vibrant colors stood out against the dark-green, misty background of the jungle.

He blinked several times and turned completely around in an effort to confirm it was all real. The searing pain from the simple movement convinced him he wasn't dreaming.

He adjusted the weight of Chief Rawlings's body draped over his shoulder. Carrying the additional load made the task of walking through the thick undergrowth more difficult. After several laborious steps, he sadly realized he couldn't attempt to bring the dead man out of the jungle.

He surveyed his surroundings, looking for options. Off to the side, a large piece of the parachute that had deployed during the crash hung from a palm frond. It appeared sufficient enough to swaddle the smaller man's body.

Gunner spread out the parachute remnant and lovingly wrapped Chief's body in it. Then he carried it away from the Starhopper, hoping that the anaconda would move on to another location, or meal.

Satisfied that he was safe, but uncertain whether the parachute material would deter animals from feeding on the body, he placed Chief Rawlings well above ground on the slick outer shell of the Starhopper and said a brief prayer.

With a sigh and a heavy heart, he stepped back onto the jungle floor and began walking through the flattened foliage. His first task was to find his duffle bag. It contained his lifeline to the world in the form of the satellite phone sent to him by Ghost while he was training in Houston's Building 9. Whether operating on a hunch or out of an abundance of caution, Ghost had felt the need for Gunner to have the communications device. Like a talisman cherished for its good luck, the satellite phone might be the only thing that got Gunner home.

Methodically, and taking every step forward under the assumption a dangerous creature was in his path, Gunner made his way through the dense underbrush that had been partially crushed to the jungle floor by the tumbling spacecraft. He was unsteady at first, but eventually found his Earth legs. Only a few days in space had caused his brain to think differently about mundane tasks like walking with the aid of gravity.

Gunner stopped for a moment and frowned. There were so many questions swirling in his mind, but the suddenness of the crash clouded his thinking. He consciously shook his head in an effort to clear it of the clutter associated with his reentry into Earth's atmosphere.

With the resurgence of the jungle's normal activities, Gunner became keenly aware of the threats his surroundings posed to him. He had to focus, or he could die.

He moved slowly through the jungle, searching for the blue duffle bearing his name. He abruptly stopped when he heard the faint shifting of leaves and cracking of twigs to his left. Gunner lowered himself to a crouch. The animals of the jungle could be dangerous, but so could man.

Not knowing where he was played a factor in his heightened state of awareness. His concerns weren't for the indigenous tribes of the world's remote jungles, such as the Pygmies of Central Africa or the Penan of Sarawak in Indonesia. He was more concerned with the Indonesian military, the rebels conducting guerilla warfare in the Congo, and the Colombian drug cartels. An American of Gunner's stature would be considered a prized possession and garner a huge ransom.

Gunner froze and listened. He called upon all of his senses to determine the location of the potential threat. He slowly scanned the terrain around him, looking for any signs of movement.

Suddenly, several crimson-backed tanagers flew out of the underbrush near the palm trees to his left. A tapir, in this case a nursing sow followed closely by a pair of striped juveniles, emerged from the palm thicket. A tapir was a fairly large herbivore resembling a pig except it had a snout shaped like a shortened elephant trunk.

He knew tapirs to be highly protective of their young and aggressive toward other animals, and humans, much the same way a wild hog was in Tate's Hell Forest near Dog Island. Whether she was a *mama grizzly*, or a tapir that happened to be a nursing mother, Gunner had nothing to fight her off with if she came for him.

He slowly inched backward, avoiding the large mammal's path. She stuck her nose trunk in the air and smelled Gunner. She glanced at him and emitted a grunting sound, a warning to stay back or suffer the consequences.

Gunner froze. Tapirs had a renowned unpredictability, and he didn't want to make any sudden moves that might be seen as hostile toward her calves.

The strong, rhino-like animal bared her teeth and uttered a long guttural sound. She turned toward Gunner and opened her mouth, emitting a hiss from the back of her throat. Her teeth were mostly intact, showing only a couple of broken chisel-shaped incisors. She lunged toward Gunner, snarling as she approached, before suddenly stopping. She was warning him off, ostensibly saying by her actions, *I don't want a fight, but I will if you don't back away.*

Gunner obliged without hesitation, stepping back several paces and looking at the ground to avoid eye contact that might be viewed as a challenge.

This appeared to satisfy the mother, who glanced back at her young and moved along. After the three-hundred-fifty-pound creature moseyed past, he continued on his quest for the duffle bag.

From time to time, Gunner looked skyward, where a meteor would catch his eye. He tried to recall his briefings during training. It was his understanding that the remnants of the asteroid were expected to hit farther north. At least away from any known rainforests. He'd attempted to ditch the Starhopper in the Caribbean Sea and had obviously overshot his landing area. But in the confusion and chaos associated with navigating the spacecraft through battered satellites and space rocks crashing toward Earth at thirty thousand miles per hour, Gunner was beginning to question where he was.

He needed to find some evidence of humanity, but as was always the case, he admonished himself to proceed with caution if, and when, he found someone.

CHAPTER 4

North American Aerospace Defense Command (NORAD)
Cheyenne Mountain, Colorado

Decades ago, during the Cold War, as nuclear threats loomed from Russia, and later Iran and North Korea, the United States created a series of fortified, state-of-the-art bunkers across the country. Part of the continuity-of-government plans, they were built to house the president and key officials of the government.

Locations included Raven Rock Mountain in Pennsylvania, Peters Mountain in the heart of the Appalachian Mountains, and of course, the most well-known of them all—Cheyenne Mountain. Located outside Colorado Springs, the military's North American Aerospace Defense Command, NORAD, was never kept secret from the public.

NORAD included the command post responsible for defending both Canada and the U.S. from air attacks such as Russian bombers or North Korean missiles. The project started in the 1950s as our government tested nuclear weapons in the Pacific Ocean. The race with the old Soviet Union to obtain bigger and more powerful nuclear warheads led to a certain amount of fear and paranoia in Washington.

Over time, our scientists began to learn the devastation that could be inflicted by a nuclear warhead carrying an electromagnetic pulse, commonly referred to as an EMP. An EMP, detonated at an altitude high enough over the United States, would send out a massive pulse of highly charged electrons. This burst of energy would overwhelm the electronics of America, causing computers to crash, critical infrastructure to fail, and have a devastating effect on the world economy.

With this threat looming, Congress, and the president through executive action, established a continuity-of-government plan. There were specific procedures and protocols to be followed in a variety of catastrophic events. Whether a nuclear war, as was envisioned in the fifties, or in the case of a catastrophic global pandemic, as many feared today, Cheyenne Mountain was there to keep the U.S. government operating.

Nature abhors a vacuum, as they say. For any government to function, the possibility of a vacant post or unfilled position at the highest levels of succession goes against the laws of physics and nature. More importantly, it goes against the laws of political power.

The continuity-of-government plan was sound in principle, and Cheyenne Mountain, in addition to the other facilities, insured the government would still be standing following the crisis.

President Mack Watson had never visited the Cheyenne Mountain complex. Only a hundred days into his presidency, it hadn't even crossed his mind. Yet here he was, facing an existential crisis that could mean the extinction of life on Earth.

Colonel Travis Moreno, the Command Center deputy director for NORAD, walked with President Watson and his chief of staff, Maggie Fielding, the former U.S. Navy commander who was fiercely loyal to the president. Colonel Moreno commented on the facility as he led them to a conference room for the morning briefing.

"Mr. President, while this facility was built in 1958, it's still probably the safest place in the world. At seventy years old, Cheyenne Mountain is considered a wonder of technology and engineering."

The president studied the walls and ceiling as they walked. "This appears to be solid granite."

"That's correct, sir. Tons upon tons of it. That in and of itself is sufficient to sustain almost any nuclear blast. In addition, the two blast doors that you entered the complex through last night weigh twenty-three tons, each."

"Amazing," observed the president. "While my motorcade was paused inside, I turned to watch them close. It took less than a minute."

"Yes, sir, very efficient."

"What about these springs?" asked the president, pointing to large coils that were found intermittently along the walkway.

"Sir, if there were an attempt to drop a nuke on Cheyenne Mountain, the force would have a kinetic effect upon any stationary structures. As a precaution, all of the buildings within the complex sit on these enormous springs. They're designed to provide a cushioning effect from the shock of the blast, protecting the people and the electronics inside."

"America's fortress," added Fielding.

"Yes, ma'am, that's correct," said Moreno. "Sitting two thousand feet below solid granite, hidden deep within the mountain, it was designed to withstand any type of threat."

"Including a massive asteroid?" President Watson asked the question that was on the mind of all seventy-two Americans who currently resided within Cheyenne Mountain.

Moreno hesitated and then stopped to survey his surroundings. "Yes, sir. We believe so."

The president managed a smile and caught Fielding's eye. He didn't think she shared Moreno's confidence, but this was their only option.

"Colonel, let me ask you about the supplies," the president began. "Based upon our current staffing levels and families, how long can Cheyenne Mountain remain self-sustainable?"

"Sir, we have sufficient food, water, power, and sewage facilities to survive for an extended period of time."

"How long?" asked Fielding.

"Eighteen months, ma'am."

"Air supply?" asked the president.

Moreno nodded, appearing to understand the concerns of the president and chief of staff. "Sir, sometimes we refer to the complex as *Mole City*. Everything is self-contained. Including our air supply.

You might notice there appears to be a slight breeze throughout the facility. It's purposefully overpressurized so radioactive or bio-particles won't seep inside."

"What about fuel to run the generators?" asked Fielding.

"We have a variety of storage reservoirs carved into the mountain, ma'am," replied Moreno. On average, we have six million gallons of water stored, which is replenished through our recycling processes, as well as half a million gallons of diesel fuel. The diesel is sufficient to run the six generators, supplemented by the ten-and-a-half megawatt power plant, for many years. In fact, the door entering the power control center is just ahead."

The three walked up a slight incline until they reached an oversized door. An inscription was carved into the granite.

The president read it aloud. "Without power, it's just a cave."

"That's right, sir. But it's more than a cave. It's a place where we can ensure that the United States of America will continue to exist despite the threats she faces. That's what we do here. For decades, the men and women of Cheyenne Mountain stay vigilant, preparing for the worst-case scenario. Frankly, if I were to list the top threats we anticipated facing—nuclear bombs, electromagnetic pulse weapons, solar flares, or a global pandemic—the concept of a direct hit by an asteroid seemed far-fetched. I would've ranked the eruption of the Yellowstone Caldera ahead of IM86."

"Yet here we are, right, Colonel?" asked the president.

"Yes, sir."

The colonel led them through a set of double doors and up two levels of staircases. He continued the tour.

"Spin classes? Really?" asked Fielding, pointing to a large workout room that, due to the circumstances, was empty.

"Yes, ma'am. Exercise is critical for the full-time staff here at Cheyenne Mountain. We encourage people to spend at least an hour a day in the gym. The Peloton bikes are extremely popular."

"It's empty today," observed the president, before asking, "And why are they rearranging everything?"

Moreno paused to explain. "Sir, on a normal day the gym would be full of our personnel doing cardio, lifting weights, or participating in a yoga class. But if there is a threat that requires a call to stations, especially something of this magnitude, this exercise room morphs into a hospital. These curtains along the windows can be pulled closed to create medical bays. If damage comes to the facility and our personnel are injured, um, frankly, we have to patch them up and get them back in the game. There's no room for excess at Cheyenne Mountain, and that means people, too."

Fielding glanced at the president and grimaced. He knew what she was thinking before she spoke. He'd ordered her to bring her husband to Cheyenne Mountain, and she'd reluctantly complied.

"Colonel, what about your families?" she asked.

Moreno sighed. He began to describe his wife and family, who lived in nearby Colorado Springs. They'd come to accept the fact that his career required him to be here. "In case of an *event*, as we call it, they're on their own. They know I have to be in the mountain to do my duty for my country. I love them dearly, but they understand the rules."

A wave of sadness overcame the president. The people who were assigned to Cheyenne Mountain left for work every day knowing if a catastrophic event befell America, the families and friends they left outside the blast doors could burn up in a nuclear explosion, succumb to a deadly pandemic, or suffer the wrath of the asteroid—IM86.

Moreno continued along the hallways until they reached the conference room overlooking the operations center. This was the nerve center of NORAD, a place in which the airmen were typically focused on detecting and tracking incoming nuclear threats to the United States. Their task was to give the nation's defense network the maximum response time available to counteract nuclear missiles fired by North Korea, Russia, China and, now, Iran.

There was not, however, a defense against the onslaught of space rocks headed toward Earth.

"Here we are," announced Moreno as he led the president and his chief of staff into the glass-enclosed conference room. The president's national security team, as well as scientists from NASA and the Jet Propulsion Laboratory, awaited him. "Mr. President, we refer to this room as the battle cab. It's a dedicated command center and meeting room for your use and senior members of your team. It's also available to our personnel to provide you briefings or continuous updates. Sir, the operations center to our right is akin to the brain stem. Information is gathered from a variety of resources around the globe, both terrestrial and from low-Earth orbit satellites. Once the data is gathered and analyzed, it comes here. To the battle cab, which is, for all intents and purposes, the brain of Cheyenne Mountain in a time of crisis. We will give you all the information available to make an informed decision on any issue."

The president smiled, thanked Colonel Moreno and dismissed him. He took a deep breath and turned to his chief of staff. "Well, it's time to hitch 'em up."

Fielding smiled in return. "Consider them hitched, sir."

CHAPTER 5

NORAD
Cheyenne Mountain, Colorado

The president entered the battle cab, where several officials were already standing, and those who were seated quickly rose to attention. It was standing room only in the conference room, as the president had insisted everyone attend this initial briefing.

"Good morning," he greeted them as he entered. "Please take a seat so we can get started."

Chairs shuffled and a few whispered words were exchanged between members of his cabinet as Fielding began to hand out the daily briefing report. The morning briefing might not have been at the White House, but it was an essential part of the government's daily operations nonetheless.

As chief of staff, she began conducting the briefing. "Naturally, the bulk of our time this morning will be spent discussing IM86 and the status of our mission to divert or destroy it. However, there are two topics the president would like to address first. One is the status of our military readiness." She turned to the chairman of the Joint Chiefs and nodded.

He began. "Mr. President, Mrs. Fielding, for weeks, we have redeployed most of our troops and support personnel abroad back to the United States. Coordinating with the Secretary of State's office, we have greatly increased our troop levels in Australia, the Philippines, and Guam. These are the southernmost military installations available to us that can maintain our naval vessels as well as quick reaction forces, if need be."

"Well," added the president, "NASA advised us that the Northern

Hemisphere was expected to bear the brunt of the space debris from this asteroid, and I suppose, in a moment, we'll know if that's still the case." The president thumbed through the daily briefing binder, pausing as he studied the information.

"Mr. President, may I add one additional comment?" asked the chairman of the Joint Chiefs.

Without looking up, President Watson gestured for him to continue.

"Sir, we have also redeployed our carrier strike groups and amphibious ready groups to points farther south throughout the world. In the western Pacific, the *Ronald Reagan* Carrier Strike Group was relocated from the Philippine Sea to a position off the coast of Australia in the Coral Sea.

"We have also relocated the *Abraham Lincoln* Carrier Strike Group out of the Gulf of Oman to the south side of the Saudi peninsula. The *Lincoln* CSG will remain in the Gulf of Aden, awaiting further orders."

The president looked up over his glasses. "I realize that much is to be determined about the scope and breadth of the destruction this asteroid's remnants will have on the planet, but the free flow of oil out of the Middle East is always a matter of vital interest to our nation. By moving the *Lincoln*, are we ceding control of the Persian Gulf to the Iranians and their pals in Moscow?"

The chairman of the Joint Chiefs was ready with his response. "I understand your concern, sir, and we've addressed it in advance. We've left behind the *Boxer* Amphibious Ready Group. Led by the USS *Boxer*, together with the USS *Harper's Ferry* and the USS *John Murtha*. Sir, forty-five hundred sailors and Marines with the 11th Marine Expeditionary Unit are ready to defend the Persian Gulf if need be. Between the Harriers and the SuperCobra attack choppers, we'll wear the Iranian naval forces out like yellow jackets chasing a wayward skunk."

"Thank you, Mr. Chairman, I have no doubt about it," said the president. He took a deep breath and remove his glasses. "I want to believe that our adversaries will focus their efforts on protecting their own people. But, as history has shown us, the weak use opportunities like this one to vanquish the strong. In the past, America has been the world's protector, always being the first to step up in a crisis. For the foreseeable future, we've got to focus on our own. However, maintaining a military presence abroad is a critical part of our national defense. It also sends a clear message that no nation, large or small, should challenge us. We'll use all of our resources to take care of American citizens, but we'll also stand ready to respond to any threat from our adversaries. Like yellow jackets, to use your analogy."

The president was satisfied with the nation's military readiness, so Fielding moved on to the next topic.

"We have representatives from NASA and the Jet Propulsion Laboratory with us this morning to provide us the current status of IM86. Before we get into the details, the president would like to know the whereabouts of our brave astronauts that piloted the Starhopper on this mission. Ms. Taylor, would you brief the president on this?"

Nola Taylor, the head of the Space Technology Mission Directorate, addressed the chief of staff. She'd met Fielding during the early briefings following the discovery of IM86. She stepped forward from the back of the conference room. "Good morning, Mr. President. As we disclosed in yesterday's briefing, we lost communications with the Starhopper crew several hours before their scheduled intercept of 2029 IM86. Communications were never restored, but we are prepared to call their mission a success. We repositioned our telescopes from their usual duties to focus on the incoming asteroid. We detected four massive explosions in fairly rapid succession, sir. We are prepared to affirmatively state they were a direct result of nuclear detonations, the last of which struck directly at the core of one of the asteroids."

A puzzled look came over President Watson's face. "There was more than one?"

"Yes, sir, based on our analysis of the explosions, and the fact that IM86 is much closer to Earth now, we've determined that this asteroid was peanut-shaped—two asteroids fused together by a collision many millions of years ago."

"Okay," interrupted the president. "I want to get back to that in a moment. Where are our people?"

Director Taylor sighed and made eye contact with Fielding. She furrowed her brow, then responded, "Sir, as I said, the last detonation was directly at one of the cores. Um, sir, we've had no contact with the Starhopper, nor have there been any visual sightings since."

The president leaned forward in his seat; a look of genuine concern washed over his face. "What are you saying?"

"Sir, the crew knew the risks. Um, we don't believe, based upon the size of the nuclear missiles used, and the proximity to the center …" Her voice trailed off as she couldn't bring herself to say the words.

The president rubbed his temples. "Are you saying they didn't make it out?"

Director Taylor shook her head. "Not likely, Mr. President."

CHAPTER 6

Fort Mills
Near Delta, Alabama

Pop nervously paced the floor. He'd grown increasingly frustrated with their inability to get any news on the whereabouts of Gunner. Telecommunications satellites were down, leaving news coverage spotty. Cell phone networks were overwhelmed or were rendered inoperable due to the loss of satellites as they were destroyed by the remnants of the asteroid.

Cam's satellite phone was capable of accessing multiple satellites in geosynchronous orbit above the equator. This was their only means of communication with NASA and Ghost, who remained at Fort Belvoir with the Jackal.

During the last phone call to Mission Control in Houston, Pop had exploded on Director Mark Foster when he was told Houston had no communication with the Starhopper following a series of nuclear detonations on the surface of the asteroid.

Pop refused to believe that Gunner had perished in the attacks, although the odds were very high that he did. Foster offered no hope whatsoever, an attitude that angered Cam and Bear as well. If he didn't know with a certainty as to the fate of Gunner, at least he could've showed some empathy to his grieving father.

"Hey, Pop, come sit with me for a minute," Cam offered as she slowly sat down on the couch. She too was distraught, but she tried to keep her emotions in check for Pop's benefit.

"Nah, I can't, Cam," he responded to her offer. "I'd be too fidgety and I'd be up pacing the floor again in less than a minute." He walked up to the front windows of the twelve-hundred-foot cabin and looked across the lake.

"Okay, since you won't sit, will you at least listen?" asked Cam.

"Sure, of course." Pop turned around and leaned against the windowsill. He hadn't slept since Wednesday and his eyes were surrounded by dark circles.

Cam was about to administer some tough love and sound advice. "Pop, I get it. Bear and I are frustrated, too. But one thing I can promise you is that we aren't giving up on Gunner. He's got more lives than a nine-life tomcat."

"And bigger balls, too," said Bear with a laugh. "But, Pop, he ain't stupid. I don't care what that joker in Houston said. If he took that last shot, it was calculated and thoroughly thought out. Gunner doesn't go anywhere without an exit plan."

Pop sighed and looked to the cabin's plank flooring. He mindlessly kicked at a nail that was popping up through the wood. "I've been worried about him ever since Heather's death. There were times when I questioned his will to live."

"You can't do that, Pop," Cam countered. "We know him. Sure, he broods a lot and puts on the appearance that he doesn't give a shit anymore. But that's not him. He loves you, and believe it or not, he has a loyalty to us. We're a team. We ride or die together. He'd never check out. Trust me on this."

Pop began to pace the floor again. "Okay, maybe you're right. No, I'm sure you're right. But all of that said, come on. He drove a spaceship with four nukes strapped on toward an asteroid. He let 'em all fly, according to that idiot Foster. They haven't seen or heard from him since."

Cam stood and approached Pop. She put her arms around him and then leaned back to speak to his face. "Listen to me. Foster doesn't know anything for certain. We've talked to Ghost about the difficulties tracking the Starhopper's return to Earth in the middle of that debris. It's like trying to track a gnat in a sandstorm. It's near impossible."

Pop smiled at the analogy. "Okay, but how about their tracking devices or whatever. It's a rocket ship, for Pete's sake. Doesn't it give off a signal of some kind?"

"Yes, sort of, Pop," replied Bear. "The problem is Earth's network of satellites is getting busted up by the debris. A lot of those five thousand satellites are space junk now."

Cam took over the pep talk. "We've gotta believe in Gunner. He'll make it back and then Ghost will get him to us."

Pop wasn't so sure. "What if he dropped down somewhere else? You know, besides Vandenberg. He'd make his way to Dog Island and then wonder where the hell we are. I think we should go there to wait."

Cam shook her head, dispelling the notion. "It's too early, Pop. This thing is just starting. The larger chunks of the asteroid will be hitting later this evening and into tomorrow morning. It's just not safe by the water yet."

Pop walked toward the front door, opened it and stepped out onto the porch. He looked skyward and viewed the incredible light show as the smaller meteors and parts of destroyed satellites burned up in Earth's atmosphere.

He turned and asked another question through the doorway. "What about the satellite phone Ghost sent him in Houston? Who's monitoring that?"

Cam joined him on the porch and glanced up as well. The continuous light show was a constant reminder that at any moment, one of the space rocks could manage to pass through the atmosphere unscathed and land right on their heads.

"The Jackal has been on a constant vigil, watching for any signs of activity on the phone. She's prepared to track its whereabouts as soon as she gets a ping on the comms network. Even if Gunner can't call, once the satphone is powered on, she can track it."

Somewhat satisfied, Pop relaxed. "I really could use some sleep," he began as he teared up. "It's hard, Cam. He's my son. Heather was my daughter, just like I look at you two as my kids. I can't stand the thought of harm coming to any of you."

Cam hugged the only father she had now that her parents were gone. She allowed herself a moment to cry with Pop. "Don't give up, Pop. Gunner would kick both of our asses if he saw us bawling like this."

Pop nodded and sniffled. Then he managed a laugh. "You're right. We've gotta be strong for him. The last thing I want to do is put it out there that he's, you know, gone."

"Exactly right! I've gotta say one more thing to you, okay?"

Pop nodded, so Cam continued. "We don't know what to expect over the next twenty-four to forty-eight hours, but things could get ugly. And I don't just mean from what the asteroid can do to us. We need to be strong, mentally and physically. So I'm gonna mother you for a minute."

"Oh boy," interjected Bear. "You're about to get a dose of what Cam gives me hell about."

Cam laughed. "No, Bear. The hell I give you is a different sort of hell. You deserve everything I dish out. Pop needs to eat and rest. So, I, Major-now-doctor Cameron Mills, hereby order you to the mess hall for some grub and then straight to bed for some shut-eye. Got it, Sergeant Fox?"

"Yes, Major," said Pop with a laugh. It was the lighthearted moment he needed to take his mind off Gunner, even for a short time.

CHAPTER 7

NORAD
Cheyenne Mountain, Colorado

"From what I'm reading here, the first wave of meteorite activity is focused farther south toward the lower latitudes and equator, am I right?" asked President Watson as the morning briefing continued.

Director Nola Taylor was prepared to field his questions. "That's correct, sir. Thus far, we've had reports of impact events throughout Latin America, Northern Africa, and Southeast Asia. The initial strikes have been minor compared to what's to come."

The president looked toward the director of Homeland Security. "How are FEMA and NASA coordinating their efforts?"

"Fortunately, Mr. President, as a result of the mission to divert the asteroid, there has been a delay in the impact events effecting the U.S. Every hour provides our national, state, and local responders additional time to coordinate disaster mitigation and response activities. Our planning has always used an initial assumption that the consequences of any NEO impact event would mirror the consequences of a major earthquake, tsunami, and hurricane occurring at the same time. Frankly, it's not unlike what we've designed in the event we have to implement an FIOP for an improvised nuclear devise."

"FIOP?" The president asked for clarification.

"Yes, sir. My apologies. Federal Interagency Operational Plan. The National Preparedness System outlines an organized process for responding to catastrophic events, which coordinates across all governmental agencies, including the military."

The president then asked, "What about public information? I'm sure folks are scared out of their wits. Food and supply deliveries have ceased. We've been dealing with looting for weeks."

The director of Homeland Security responded, "Sir, in the past, all of our theoretical exercises and assumptions involved an asteroid threat that allowed us years to prepare and warn the public. This came upon us very suddenly without an accurate prediction of the areas of impact. As a result, we focused our public messaging via media PSAs and direct text messaging to all operable cellular telephones in the country. Let me add, sir, that the risk to our citizens is more than just the direct hit from the asteroid or its debris field. It's also the potential loss of electricity and other critical infrastructure. We're already experiencing telecommunications outages in the public sector. Naturally, the military installations around the country utilize a buried, hardwired network, so our communications are fully operable."

President Watson turned his attention back to Nola Taylor from NASA. "You left us dangling with the words *compared to what's to come.* Please expound on this."

"Sir, based upon the limited data we have available to us on the success of the Starhopper mission, it appears that IM86 has been sufficiently destroyed to avoid an extinction-level event."

"Well, there's some good news," interjected the president. "However, I sense there's a *but* coming."

"Well, yes, sir," Taylor continued. "The timing of the attack by the Starhopper crew and the speed with which the combat pilot recruited for this task fired on the asteroid played a significant role in how the resulting debris field effected Earth." She hesitated for a moment and referred to her notes.

"Please continue," said the president.

"Of course, sir. My apologies. Because 2029 IM86 was a binary system, the gravitational pull of its two cores made it impossible to destroy it completely without further nuclear strikes. While Major Fox was apparently successful in obliterating the core at the front of the peanut-shaped asteroid, the second half remained, as did its gravitational pull."

"What does this mean?" the president asked.

"The asteroid was able to reconstitute itself to an extent. Granted, it isn't a solid space rock as it was before, but it nonetheless managed to stick together sufficiently enough to create a dense cluster of meteors similar to the Taurid swarm that crosses the Earth's orbit every thousand years."

The president leaned forward and rested his elbows on the conference table. He clasped his fingers together and studied Taylor. "Explain to me what the Taurid swarm is, and when did it occur last? More importantly, how does it relate to what we're dealing with today?"

"Sir, in 1908, the Earth's orbit and the Taurid swarm, which is the leftover debris of a comet, crossed trajectories. The comet's dust barreled through our atmosphere at sixty-five thousand miles per hour. Most of the debris burned up in Earth's atmosphere, similar to what we're experiencing today. However, some of the larger meteorites made it through. One in particular, known as the Siberian Tunguska Asteroid, a misnomer, actually, leveled eighty million trees over an eight-hundred-square-mile area in Russia. It packed a punch equal to fifteen megatons of TNT—a thousand times greater than the bomb dropped on Hiroshima in 1945."

"Are we looking at something like that now?" asked the president.

"Yes, sir, potentially. But more than just one. We could experience similar impact events around the globe, times a thousand."

The attendees burst into a low-level uproar as they began to discuss the destructive possibilities of that many explosions hitting Earth in a short period of time.

The president absorbed her revelation and then continued his questioning. "Now, Director Taylor, has there been any indication that this asteroid, or the remains of it, has been knocked off course? Do we have any hope that the rest of this asteroid might skirt by us, you know, since the present activity is closer to the equator?"

Director Taylor sighed and nodded her head. "Sir, through the efforts of the Starhopper crew, it's possible that North America could avoid a direct hit, with the bulk of the debris field striking the lower latitudes around the equator. We're assessing all of the probabilities at NASA and the JPL, and I have Dr. Brian Zahn here to explain more on that."

The president leaned back in his chair and motioned for the scientist from CalTech to stand. "Go ahead, Dr. Zahn."

"Thank you, sir," said the portly young man. "Mr. President, we may have a keyhole affecting the debris field of IM86."

"A what?" asked Fielding.

"A gravitational keyhole. It's a small section of Earth's gravitational region in which gravity can alter the orbit of NEOs. Now, this theory was most recently applied to the trajectory of 99942 Apophis that is scheduled for a flyby in 2036, but the same concept can be applied here. The keyhole can alter an asteroid's trajectory for the worse, as is the case with Apophis, or the better, which may be happening with IM86."

"I don't know anything about Apophis, so we'll worry about it after we survive this threat," interjected the president. "Tell me how this gravitational keyhole may benefit us."

"Mr. President, based upon our analysis, the Starhopper crew not only found the precise location to strike the asteroid, but they did so quickly. We believe this effort has forced IM86 off its trajectory enough so that it might strike closer to the North Pole."

The president was perplexed. "Wait, the reports we're receiving indicate the equatorial regions are currently in the line of fire."

"That's true, Mr. President, under current conditions, the smallish debris is striking near the equator. However, as the larger chunks of space rock approach later, they'll naturally be drawn, thanks to the keyhole effect, toward the poles, where Earth's gravitational field is strongest."

"Brian, Mr. President, if I may clarify something," interrupted Director Taylor.

"Yes, of course," said the president.

"The relationship between the gravitational keyhole, the North Pole, and Earth's true magnetic north is complicated. For several decades, the Earth has experienced the beginning of a pole shift that has accelerated of late."

"Shift to where?" asked the president.

Dr. Zahn replied, "Well, sir, eventually the poles will flip such that up is down and down is up. For the time being, due to this rapid change, the true magnetic north is moving closer to Russia. Therefore, the gravitational keyhole is moving along with it."

The president was intrigued by the science and inwardly promised to look into this pole shift theory at a later time. "Are you saying this keyhole may draw the debris field toward Russia and farther away from North America."

"Yes, sir. Our models are indicating that," replied Dr. Zahn.

"Sir, I must caution that this doesn't mean the United States mainland will be spared," added Director Taylor. "We simply have increased our chances of avoiding cataclysmic damage thanks to the efforts of the Starhopper crew."

President Watson was feeling better with this news, but he still needed to prepare the nation for a significant impact event.

"Dr. Zahn, Director Taylor, thank you both for this somewhat good news. Now, give me the worst-case scenario."

CHAPTER 8

Unknown Tropical Jungle

Gunner stopped and stood atop a fallen palm tree to get a better view of the surrounding thicket. Bits and pieces of shiny aluminum, the outer shell of the Starhopper, could be seen for hundreds of yards ahead of him. He thought about the amount of time it took the National Transportation Safety Board investigators to pore over an airline crash site. It was weeks, not days. He didn't have days to find the satellite phone. The remains of IM86 didn't care about his plight. It was coming like an out-of-control herd of stampeding buffalo.

He moved through the canyon of lush greenery created by the Starhopper's tumble through the jungle. He'd walk a few yards, examine the debris left behind, and then move on. The rising sun aided his ability to view his surroundings, although it caused the headache he was suffering to intensify.

The light enabled him to move more efficiently, no longer concerned with the infinite number of strangler banyans and vines that crept up the tree trunks and banyans, wrapping themselves tightly around them as they climbed to the top of the jungle canopy that was easily a hundred feet off the ground. To Gunner, every vine began to look like an anaconda, causing him to become more apprehensive.

He felt like he'd stepped into some surreal documentary being shown on the National Geographic network. He waited for an army of pygmies to emerge out of nowhere, holding spears and shrunken heads. Or a lone shaman might stand off in the wistful fog that hung over the jungle, decked out in tribal clothing, ready to douse Gunner with some type of mind-altering jungle medicine that would transport him back in time to Berkley, California, in 1966.

Gunner continued to tromp through the path created by the wreckage. He looked left and right, up into the trees and under larger pieces of the Starhopper.

He was becoming fatigued. He was fearful of dehydration despite being in a rainforest. Large trees, some of which were fifteen feet in circumference, rose high into the air. They produced a roof that partially blocked the sunlight. Beneath the canopy, along the jungle floor, it was darker and more humid. The understory of the jungle, where the reptiles and insects resided, was also full of fungi and microorganisms created by decomposing plant foliage and dead animal carcasses.

As a result, a pond of water, no matter how small, might appear to be drinkable. In reality, it could cause the human body to become consumed with bacteria, resulting in dysentery. Dysentery was an infection of the intestinal tract that resulted in severe diarrhea, nausea, and dehydration. In third-world countries, this bacterial infection was considered the number one cause of death.

Gunner came across several large bromeliads growing out of the side of a smallish kapok tree. The beautiful pink flowering plant, the jungle's version of a spineless cactus, was a plant with its own water tank. Their long-curved leaves overlapped at the base, forming a tight little bowl, creating a natural source of water for the plant and small animals.

After confirming there were no small frogs or tadpoles nestled in the leaves, Gunner slowly cupped his hands and extracted the water. He sniffed it, out of habit, and then touched it to his lips to check its taste. The moisture immediately rejuvenated his spirits.

He knew he was taking a risk, but he had to drink. During his attack on the asteroid, he didn't bother to drink water. He'd had his hands full. In fact, he couldn't recall the last time he'd taken a drink of anything, which meant his body had gone at least forty-eight hours without fluids. He was dangerously close to dehydration.

With a renewed sense of purpose, Gunner set out again, moving deeper into the jungle as the debris field began to narrow. He found the dead body of the Russian cosmonaut Semenova, the temptress who'd tried to poison him at the lunar outpost. Her body was hung over a gnarled, knotty tree branch about twenty feet off the jungle floor, swaying slightly despite the lack of a breeze.

Gunner walked forward to get a better look and almost tripped over her leg, which had been severed. He instantly recoiled, startled by the bloody mess that had become a meal for some type of small animal that had scratched away her uniform and took several bites of her flesh.

His stomach began to convulse. He'd seen dead bodies before, many by his own doing, but this was the second time in a matter of hours he'd witnessed one being eaten by critters. He instantly begged the universe for a knife, a machete, anything he could use as a weapon.

The search for his duffle bag was now surpassed by the need for protection. He had visions of a jaguar, the tropical rainforest's most efficient killing machine, biting his throat or directly through the temporal bones of his skull, piercing his brain before devouring him slowly, at its pleasure. Or the most recent visual of the anaconda, which could swallow him whole.

Gunner backtracked several dozen yards, looking for a piece of the Starhopper that he'd noticed earlier. It was a part of the under supports that had held the nuclear missiles on the spacecraft. He picked up the three-foot-long piece of twisted steel and swung it back and forth like a sword. Then he held it high, triumphantly, as if it were a genuine light saber from a *Star Wars* movie.

"Repurposing," he said aloud. "I like it."

In his lighthearted moment, the boy observing him from a distance went unnoticed.

CHAPTER 9

Unknown Tropical Jungle

Gunner forced his unwilling body to move again. The sun was directly overhead and he began to consider that his duffle bag was lost in the thicket forever. As he made his way through the last of the wreckage, he periodically stopped to check the cuts and scratches on his body. All were superficial, but still needed to be cleaned to avoid infection.

The rough landing into the jungle and the subsequent peeling back of the layers from the Starhopper's structure had exposed him to the plunge through the underbrush. It was his head that concerned him the most. He'd received minor concussions throughout his career and had been warned repeatedly they would eventually cause him permanent brain damage.

The minutes dragged on, eventually turning into hours as the setting sun raised a new issue of concern for Gunner—shelter. In extreme conditions, a person could die within hours without adequate shelter. While he didn't expect to be exposed to extreme heat or cold, and remarkably, it hadn't rained on him yet, a protective shelter was a necessity because of the dangerous wildlife that inhabited the jungle.

He'd already witnessed what had happened to the two Russians. The bodies of the third Russian and the other two American astronauts weren't seen. He immediately assumed they'd become food for the jungle's creatures.

Just as the debris field ended, Gunner declared the search for his duffle bag officially over. He'd have to go it alone without the crutch the satellite phone would've afforded him. The next part of his journey would be the most dangerous. He'd have to rely upon his training, knowledge of the planet he'd garnered from his education in Earth sciences, and instinct to make human contact.

It was impossible to gauge which way he should go. He forced himself to recall the final moments of the Starhopper's reentry into Earth's atmosphere.

He had been on a trajectory for Vandenberg Air Force Base in California, but due to the increased amount of meteor activity, Artie, the spacecraft's onboard artificial intelligence, suggested he try a different path.

The Gulf of Mexico was his first option, but again, the plan changed as Artie warned him of the destroyed satellites in his path. He modified his course, looking to the turquoise blue waters of the Caribbean Sea as his best option.

Everything appeared promising until the Starhopper was caught with a glancing blow of a passing meteorite, sending it careening past its intended landing zone.

"That's it!" Gunner exclaimed as his memory provided him an explanation of his whereabouts. "South America. Maybe Central America. Doesn't matter! I can walk home from here!" He let out a hearty laugh that caused a sudden silence among the local frog population.

Gunner looked through the heavy canopy to observe the position of the sun, which was lower on the horizon and just beyond the start of the debris field. Random streaks of light passed over him, now with greater frequency as the meteorites began to grow in number. He turned around and looked to the location of the crew module where he'd left Chief Rawlings. Using the hunk of metal in his right hand, he traced a line through the sky until it pointed toward the sun.

"The Caribbean Sea is that way," he began and then turned slightly toward his left. "Central America is that way. Water or land? What's it gonna be, boy?"

Gunner was in a jovial mood. He was now able to formulate a plan, albeit an uncertain one. But it was something.

For a brief moment, he contemplated staying where he was. Waiting to see if a rescue team arrived was the logical choice to make. Then he considered how long he'd been there already. Fifteen hours? Maybe longer?

If NASA had tracked the Starhopper's reentry, they would've dispatched choppers from any number of military installations in the region to the scene before the sun rose.

Gunner quickly surmised that the Starhopper's reentry was mistaken for all of the other crap descending through Earth's atmosphere at the time. He was on his own.

He closed his eyes to concentrate as the chorus of clown frogs whipped themselves back into a frenzy. The jungle was coming to life, and Gunner was beginning to become more comfortable in his surroundings. He was no longer consumed with what had happened to bring him to this point. He now had a purpose, a treacherous one, but doable.

Heather flashed into his mind. He recalled a vacation they'd taken to Hawaii. A rare moment when the two could steal away together without concerns for NASA or the Air Force. They wanted to view the islands from the highest point in Kauai. They could've taken the easy route, hopping aboard a tour helicopter with a bunch of other travelers. Or they could truly take in the breathtaking views afforded by the hiking trails along the coast to the top of the island. They chose the hike, and it was one of the most memorable days of their life together.

Gunner paused and his mind raced through that day. How they laughed with one another. The times they stopped to eat, or just talk. The moment where Heather grabbed him by the hand and pulled him off the trail, where they made love. And then their arrival at the summit, where they dropped their backpacks, laughed and swung around and around in each other's arms.

He took a deep breath and exhaled as a huge smile came over his face. Gunner looked to the sky and opened his eyes. He muttered the words, "I love you."

Then he realized something. In the past, his memories of Heather would make him sad. Then he'd become mad. Not this time. This time, his recollection of that day in Hawaii provided him a sense of warmth and joy. He wanted to remember her, their life and love together. He didn't want to be consumed by her death anymore.

He now had closure. He'd learned what had happened to his beloved Heather, at least in part. But that was good enough. He was able to move forward with his life, focusing on the good times together and not the end of them.

"Let's hoof it, babe." He said the exact words she'd used on that day in Kauai.

With that, Gunner set about beating a trail through the jungle. The thicket was full of bamboo, one of the hardest woods in the world. It provided him an ample resource of fresh water, which he consumed throughout the trek through the jungle. However, it also became burdensome to push through at times.

He rested only during the time it took to drink a few sips of water and confirm that he was still traveling toward the setting sun. In late April, from the position where the spacecraft wrecked, this would keep him on a generally northwest direction toward Panama in Central America.

He'd never been assigned a mission in that part of the world. He'd spent a considerable amount of time in Venezuela and Brazil. Never in Colombia, where he now assumed, or at least hoped, that he crashed. If he was farther south, like in the Amazon Rainforest of Brazil, he was in for quite a journey.

When it was available, Gunner would rub mud on his hands and neck to fend off mosquitoes. They were known to spread diseases such as malaria, dengue, and yellow fever. Predators were abundant throughout the jungle, from the tiniest parasites in water, to large reptiles like the anaconda he'd encountered, and crocodiles.

Gunner picked up the pace as he could barely make out a clearing up ahead. The undergrowth grew sparser, and he pushed his way through the new bamboo canes of spring that shot out of the ground. The big buttress roots of a majestic kapok tree created the clearing. Tall ribbons of wood spread in all directions for thirty feet under the hundred-foot-tall tree used by indigenous people for dugout canoes, furniture, and carvings.

He took a moment to observe his surroundings, remaining wary of predators. Satisfied he was alone, he eased into the clearing with his metal weapon raised to his side like a club. Gunner was pleased that it had a sharp, jagged end that could both stab and slice any threat.

Slowly, he walked around the root system, amazed at its appearance. He instantly saw the tree as a means of shelter. Using large *Monstera* leaves stacked on top of each other, he could shield himself from the rains that were to come.

He reached the back side of the tree and spotted a trail. It wasn't cleared, but it was well worn. At first, he assumed that it was a path made by native animals. Perhaps the tapirs used this route to root around for food at the base of the kapok.

Then he thought about the hogs he'd hunted in Florida. They had a routine in which they moved around Tate's Hell Forest between feeding grounds and water sources. The tapir resembled a hog, albeit with a funny snout. If this kapok provided a source of food, perhaps the trail led to water.

He considered the old adage instilled upon kids when they were in the scouts—when lost in the woods, follow the water downstream. Gunner imagined the same rule applied in a tropical jungle.

He abandoned his best option for shelter and briskly walked down the path. It was getting late in the day, but he was full of energy, and now he was on a mission to find his way out.

He pressed forward, ducking below limbs, gingerly walking around snakes, and swatting mosquitoes that grew in numbers.

The trail began to widen, and the sound of rushing water lifted his spirits. He was close to a stream or maybe even a river. Being mindful of his footing, he picked up the pace, lifting the piece of steel so that it acted as a shield against the numerous spiderwebs that crisscrossed the path.

The sound of the water grew louder, and Gunner's pulse raced. Adrenaline fueled him now. So did hope. Hope that was quickly dashed when he reached a ravine that dropped thirty feet to a river below.

The roar of a nearby waterfall was deafening now that he'd cleared the thick foliage of the jungle. Gunner was genuinely confused as to his whereabouts. He'd assumed that the crash site was not that far from the coast of the Caribbean Sea. It must've been on a plateau, high above the sea level. In the mountains.

He studied the landscape and traced the river's route through the jungle. It continuously dropped with one small waterfall after another. It was a sight to behold and worthy of a hundred photos to be shared on Instagram. However, Gunner now wondered where he was. The downstream flow of the river would take him in the complete opposite direction from where he presumed Central America was situated in relation to the wreckage.

And the trail. The trail led him to the edge of the ravine. This made no sense whatsoever. The tapirs wouldn't be able to make their way down the treacherous sides without falling to their death.

"Did I miss another trail?" he asked aloud.

He turned around and retraced his steps. He'd become excited at the prospect of finding water and had hurried toward it. Maybe he missed something?

He carefully observed the ground, and then he saw the opening. It was low to the ground, easily missed by a six-foot-tall human. Gunner lifted the branches and made his way under the palm trees until a small clearing emerged. It was well worn, with the tall grasses smashed down to the ground.

He smelled the odor of animal feces emanating from beyond the clearing. Was he in a den of some sort? The tapirs? Or something else?

He rushed through the clearing and continued following the path that ran parallel to the river, upstream toward the waterfall. After several minutes, he emerged at the edge of the ravine once again, but near the source of the falls.

He walked gingerly along the edge until he could see a small lake, its water as calm as glass except for the occasional ripple caused by a fish. The lake was fifty yards wide, easily swimmable by Gunner, who held advanced scuba diving certifications.

However, the waters of the jungle were fraught with danger, from electric eels to piranhas to the black caiman, a massive predatory alligator that fed on anything that unknowingly ventured into its territory.

Frustrated, Gunner sat on a nearby rock to rest and make a decision. He swatted at a giant yellow-leg centipede measuring eight inches that made its way along the muddy ground toward his ankles. Gunner had met up with one of these before in Venezuela. It had injected its deadly venom into an iguana, causing the creature to succumb to paralysis.

He called upon Heather for advice. "Downstream, the choice of a Boy Scout, but opposite to where I was headed. Or upstream, toward Central America, but higher into the mountains."

Gunner awaited a response, but none came.

Until a flash of color in the otherwise green underbelly of the jungle's canopy caught his eye. He turned his head and covered his eyes to block the sunlight that glistened off the small lake. He squinted, forcing his eyes to focus on the movement.

He could barely make it out, but the shape and color was unmistakable. It was rectangular and blue—Air Force blue. Somebody was carrying his duffle bag on the other side of the river.

CHAPTER 10

Unknown Tropical Jungle

Gunner resisted the urge to call out to the person carrying his bag. He was concerned they would dash into the jungle out of fear, never to be seen again. Clearly, whoever it was knew their way around the jungle, and he didn't. It wouldn't take long for them to escape and Gunner to get caught in a quagmire of vines, bamboo, and primal threats.

He trudged along the lake, swatting away mosquitoes as he slogged through the muck. Dusk was coming, the impenetrable darkness beginning to creep on all sides of the jungle canopy overlooking the water.

Gunner kept his eye on his duffle bag and the young boy who was carrying it. The kid ambled along the water's edge, pausing from time to time to toss a stone into the lake, or to readjust the duffle slung over his shoulder. The dark-haired, tanned boy appeared to be eight to ten years old. He was wearing blue jeans and a simple black tee shirt with a white soccer ball imprinted on the back.

The lanky, Hispanic youngster with jet-black hair began to climb up some large rocks that lined the lake as another waterfall appeared before him. Gunner had to duck into the woods on occasion as the young man looked behind him, seemingly aware that he was being stalked.

Gunner pushed through the underbrush, one eye on the kid, the other eye on his footing so that he didn't stumble over something, or some creature, that might kill him in an instant.

Higher up the hill, the second waterfall grew louder. Soon, Gunner was standing above a stream that poured over the side. He surveilled the other side of the lake, but the boy, and his duffle bag, was gone.

Panicked, he raced back to the edge of the waterfall and looked downstream, thinking the kid might have doubled back. When he didn't see any movement, he took off up the hill again to the area overlooking the lake. He saw no sign of the boy.

Gunner had to take a chance. "Hey! Kid! Over here! Can you hear me!"

He paused to listen, walking slowly along the top of the bank, cognizant of his footing, but focused on the other side of the stream.

"Come on, kid! *Oye, amigo! Aqui!*"

Still no response. Gunner felt the darkness growing around him. He was running out of time. He began to run up the hill, focusing his attention on the other side of the stream.

"*Amigo! Aqui! Por favor, amigo!*"

He stumbled and fell, sliding down the bank toward the stream, which was now thirty feet below him, the rocky bottom growing larger in his field of vision. Gunner grabbed the roots of a tree to arrest his fall, and pulled himself up to a resting spot.

He considered climbing down, but the drop-off was steep and the dirt wall was moist from erosion. The jagged boulders below left him no margin of error.

"There has to be another way," he mumbled. "Come on, kid. How'd you get—?"

Gunner abruptly stopped. In the darkening sky, he could make out a suspension bridge a hundred yards ahead of him. It couldn't be seen from the top of the bank, but halfway down, it was within view.

"Bingo!"

Gunner looked to the top of the bank and began his climb, carefully tugging on tree roots to ensure they were secure, and that they weren't a snake. The anaconda, and every other snake on the planet, would be in the forefront of Gunner's consciousness for some time. He hated snakes.

He reached the top, took a moment to wipe the mud off his khakis, and walked as quickly as the jungle would allow until he reached the suspension bridge across the ravine.

At first glance, the structure appeared to be safe. He'd walked across these rope bridges before. Most of the ones he'd traversed were made with wooden planks as a floor, and steel wire to create the supports. Some even had a safety netting underneath.

This rope bridge was very primitive. There were four ropes tied off to twin black palm trees overlooking the ravine. The base was made of tree branches tied to the two bottom ropes, and the two top ropes provided handrails, sort of.

There was no safety netting. The floor made of tree branches was designed in a haphazard fashion with the branches nowhere close to being evenly spaced. Some were even broken.

Gunner sighed and rolled his eyes. He silently cursed the jungle gods for putting him in this position. He weighed the risks. If he slipped and fell, he'd land in the dark stream, probably full of piranhas or crocodiles or snakes. *Death.*

He shook his head and gingerly stepped onto the bridge. While the span was still located over the ground, he jumped a little, testing its strength and resiliency to his weight. The rope bridge swayed and bounced, but it held firm.

Gunner stepped out a little farther, allowing himself a quick glance to the water below. He shook his head side to side in an effort to put the worst-case scenario out of his mind. Clearly, he wasn't afraid of heights. He'd proved that during the test flight of the F/A XX and aboard the Starhopper. He was not, however, fond of slippery things that resided in the murky waters of the jungle.

With a deep breath, Gunner went for it. He moved quickly across the bridge, avoiding the broken or weak-looking branches. He gripped the rope handrails with all of this strength, the course hemp fiber of the rope scratching his hands and wrists.

Gunner chuckled to himself, allowing his mind to wander from the predicament he was in. The marijuana plant had many uses apart from being the drug of choice for many with *medical ailments.* Making hemp rope from the fibers in the stalk of the plant was one of them. Gunner imagined that marijuana was grown in abundance in this part of the world, but nowhere near the number one cash crop in all of Western South America—the coca plant.

He reached the other end of the rope bridge and scurried onto the ground as if the thing were collapsing behind him. It was much darker, making the task of finding the kid with his duffle bag more difficult. But at least he had a lead.

And now he had a well-worn trail, one that had been built and made by humans and not the creatures of the jungle.

As Gunner progressed through the jungle, pleased to be walking on hardened soil as opposed to the mushy floor of decaying plants he'd experienced earlier, he thought about the new threat he'd face. The most vicious killer on the entire planet.

Man.

He caught a glimpse of light in the distance and his heart raced. He was going to get out of the jungle. Home. To Dog Island. His place with Heather.

And to Pop and Howard, both of whom had stood by him throughout his period of grieving. To Cam, his best friend since she wore pigtails and he grew the first few hairs on his chest. And Bear, the lovable beast of a man who'd lay down his life for Gunner.

He took a deep breath and picked up the pace. The single light turned in to several flickering flames partially obscured by the jungle foliage. His eyes darted ahead and then side to side, scanning for threats, as he'd been trained.

However, he didn't look down.

He knew he was in trouble the moment his foot planted and it felt like it had landed on a cloud. The previously hardened path became a hole covered by palm fronds, and very deep.

The lights that had appeared suddenly disappeared. The darkening sky turned to black. Gunner's excitement, the drive that had led him at a frenetic pace through the jungle to safety, landed him flat on his back, unconscious, in a twenty-foot-deep cavern.

Alone, but not alone.

CHAPTER 11

NORAD
Cheyenne Mountain, Colorado

President Watson hadn't slept since Wednesday night. Throughout law school, during his days of handling complex trials as a judge, and even during the rigors of the presidential campaign, he managed to get three to four hours of sleep. Since the early hours of Wednesday morning, sleep had eluded him.

The White House physician, who traveled with the president at all times, had issued him a stern warning an hour ago—*you're not physically capable of working without rest, and as a result, you're putting a tremendous strain on your heart.*

He'd been cautioned about stress and his weight before. The advice given had been taken by the president, who had dramatically changed his appearance by losing nearly sixty pounds during the course of the campaign. While he still experienced tension headaches, he was pleased to learn during his initial physical upon taking the oath of office that he was as healthy now as he had been twenty years ago.

This was still not good enough for his doting White House physician, who nagged him about what he ate and his lack of sleep more than his loving wife did. Truthfully, as he got older, he needed less sleep. It was not unusual for him to wake up at four in the morning before shuffling out of the master bedroom of the White House to the kitchen across the West Sitting Hall. Long before the staff entered the president's residence, he was scanning the cable news networks and reading online news sources on his iPad Pro.

President Watson was a workaholic who loved his country more than life itself. He was a devoted husband who never strayed, and a father who raised his two daughters to be respectable young women. He feared for their future, just as he did the future of America. Modern man had never faced a calamity like this one, and he hoped the news he'd received from Director Taylor and Dr. Zahn came true.

He addressed his wife, Patty, his college sweetheart who'd married him thirty-three years ago. "Honey, we may dodge a bullet, with a little luck. Well, at least a bomb. We, as a nation, can survive a bullet. Bombs can be far more devastating."

Patty rubbed his shoulders and ran her fingers through his thinning hair. "Mack, do you feel good enough to rest now. From what you've told me, the worst of it will happen tomorrow through Monday."

The president closed his eyes and nodded. Her shoulder rub served to relax him, allowing his mind to clear. "I don't want to be overly optimistic, but thanks to what the crew of the Starhopper achieved, far fewer people will die. Still, many lives will be lost."

"They haven't found them yet, have they?" his wife asked.

The president frowned and shook his head. "No, and truthfully, they didn't offer much hope. Patty, they're American heroes for the risks they took and the mission they accomplished. If not for their efforts, half of the six hundred million people living in North America would die in the next few days. They deserve our highest praise, but I'm afraid we'll never get the chance to give it to them."

He patted her hand and stood. He was known for pacing a room when he was thinking, and despite his upbeat mood, the wandering commenced as usual.

He felt older and was none too pleased to see how he'd aged since becoming president just a few months ago. He paused and looked in the mirror. He squinted, intentionally exaggerating the wrinkles around his eyes. Then he frowned, causing the tissue between his eyebrows to gather into a fold. Years of frowning had left deep wrinkles in the skin between his brows and on the bridge of his nose, as well as at the corners of his eyes.

Wrinkles are like pages in a story, he thought. In a novel, every word, paragraph, and chapter gave the reader an insight into the writer's mind as he tried to relate a story via written words. A person's wrinkles told a story, as well.

Did the face indicate a life full of worry? Or laughter? Was the person always sad? Did they work in the sun, causing damage to the skin? Was their skin flawless, despite their age, indicating that they nurtured their bodies?

He was deep in thought and feeling philosophical, so he poured out his emotions to his wife. "Patty, catastrophic events—like tornados, hurricanes, and now, this asteroid—don't discriminate. They don't pick and choose their innocent victims based upon class, race, gender, or sexual preference.

"The people who die, are seriously injured, or who lose all their belongings don't deserve it. Nor are they singled out for some reason like a past misdeed or a disbelief in God. They're simply in the wrong place at the wrong time.

"Natural disasters like volcanoes, earthquakes, and asteroids are very unpredictable. If they weren't, we could save most people. Heck, almost everyone, if they heed the warnings.

"This asteroid isn't going to pick and choose which city or community to strike. It doesn't care if a place has already suffered its share of pain like New York after 9/11 or Los Angeles after the 2019 earthquake. Calendars, schedules, frequencies mean nothing. Suffered enough already? Too bad, suffer again. There is no rhyme or reason. Only probabilities and hope.

"It's like playing roulette in the casinos back home in Las Vegas. Is it possible that the white ball could land on red twenty-three twice in a row? Yes, but the chances are slim. Could it happen three times in a row? Near impossible, but again, it could happen."

The president paused and ran his fingers through his hair.

His wife was genuinely concerned for her husband. "Honey, are you all right?"

President Watson nodded, although his face looked glum. "Yeah, well, I don't know. Maybe I'm just being too philosophical. Yet, something in my gut tells me that we're entering strange times—*an epoch*. You know, a period of time that's marked by important, history-altering events."

Patty joined her husband and wrapped her arms around his thinning waistline. "Do you think this asteroid is the beginning of something, um, biblical? Like *end times*?"

President Watson paused. "No, I won't go that far. I don't know, it just seems like this asteroid is only the beginning of some major challenges that we, and our country, will face. I just hope I'll be up to the task."

Patty turned him around and stood on her toes to kiss her husband. "We, as a family, will get through this, just as we have dealt with other problems in our past. You're a good man, Mack Watson, and the country, and the world, is lucky to have you navigating this ship through troubled waters. Please never doubt that."

He smiled and hugged his wife. Then he whispered, "Time will tell."

CHAPTER 12

NASA Mission Control
Johnson Space Center
Houston, Texas

Colonel Maxwell Robinson had no trouble sleeping, unlike the president. He kept abreast of the developments by staying in Mission Control Director Mark Foster's hip pocket, following him around every waking moment for news about the Starhopper's mission and the fate of its crew.

His efforts to keep Gunner Fox on the ground by planting the drugs in his room at Building 9 had been unsuccessful. Robinson was generally concerned that Gunner would come in contact with the three members of the Russian crew who were on board the ISS the day that Heather was killed.

Robinson knew what had happened, as did Foster. But the secret remained with them and a handful of Russian Cosmodrome personnel who were surely sworn to secrecy by one form of threat or another.

The two men understood why the colonel's superiors, on direct orders from the White House, ordered the incident details to be sealed. The clamor and uproar from the war hawks within the halls of Congress and the American people would be deafening. The second cold war could easily result in a hot war as America sought retribution—*an eye for an eye.*

So Robinson followed orders. He contained the truth and unwillingly entered into a conspiracy with Director Foster to maintain the cover-up. As he saw it, releasing the details of Heather's death would not bring her back, nor would it provide him, and others, the motive for what happened.

The Russians had refused to confirm the names of the people responsible for putting her outside the ISS in the first place, nor would they tell him whom she had been accompanied by. He never bought the Russians' explanation that a tragic accident had occurred resulting from her tether malfunctioning after being hit by space debris. Robinson understood the use of subterfuge. He was an expert at it himself.

Nonetheless, Washington didn't need an open, very public conflict with Moscow over her death. Robinson was charged with containing the truth, and he did. Now the final loose end to the saga, Gunner Fox, was AWOL.

When Mission Control lost communications with the spacecraft prior to the intercept point, Robinson became concerned there had been a malfunction. Make no mistake, he wanted Major Fox to succeed. He wanted every single nuclear missile on the Starhopper to find its mark to obliterate the asteroid.

He just didn't want Gunner Fox to return alive.

When communications were never reestablished, and the Starhopper failed to reemerge from the multiple nuclear blasts, Robinson quietly slipped back into his office and poured himself a glass of bourbon. And then another, providing himself a triumphant toast for killing two birds with one stone, as the saying goes.

Then Mark Foster interrupted his celebratory moment with the news. The buzz was killed and the sober reality revealed itself. An amateur astronomer, one of millions enjoying the spectacular light show provided by the meteors burning up in the atmosphere, was certain he'd seen the Starhopper fly over his home on the Yucatán Peninsula in the general direction of South America.

Fortunately, he was interviewed by the micromanaging Foster directly, who immediately reported the information to Robinson. As a result, that Friday afternoon had been extraordinarily busy. Ordering the unfortunate, accidental deaths of two people took planning.

The astronomer in Southeastern Mexico was easy. Robinson had a contact who was former Delta Force and worked in Cancun for the Drug Enforcement Agency, the DEA. Within hours of his phone call, and before he could crow to the media about his discovery, the young man died at the hands of a burglar looking for illicit drugs found hidden under his mattress.

The second victim would be more personal—Mark Foster.

Robinson had debated killing Foster after the incident involving Heather Fox. Foster was a loose end that was also a potentially loose cannon. However, he needed Foster alive to help run interference during the investigation. Fortunately for the Mission Control director, he'd kept his mouth shut and toed the line.

Now he was expendable.

If Major Fox wasn't dead from the spacecraft soaring into the Caribbean Sea, at least the only other person who threatened Robinson's legacy would be soon.

Foster had exhibited signs of becoming unstable. He'd taken full control of the Starhopper mission, and his overly emotional response to the loss of communications prior to the intercept of IM86 had been noticed by everyone within the Mission Control center at NASA.

Robinson had heard rumblings and whispers throughout the hallways of the Johnson Space Center over the last forty-eight hours.

Foster needs to get some rest.

Foster might slip back into the bottle.

He's taking this too hard.

Robinson knew that Foster would be all right, but his coworkers didn't. So the opportunity presented itself to eliminate another threat, another witness, to a cover-up that would land him in jail if the entire truth came out.

Tonight, NASA's mission control director of four years, Mark Foster, would commit suicide. He just didn't know it yet.

PART TWO

Saturday, April 28

CHAPTER 13

The earth shaking followed by clumps of dirt falling in his face shook Gunner back to consciousness. The thunderous explosion that reverberated through the ground was reminiscent of the mortar shells landing near him in Kandahar Province of Afghanistan when he was on an assignment at a NATO base there. Rocket and mortar attacks had been a way of life at Kandahar Air Field, where *duck and dive* was as much a part of one's daily routine as hitting the latrine when they woke up.

Disoriented, Gunner scrambled to his knees and tried to shake off the pain to his back resulting from the long fall into the man-made pit. He was sopping wet, as rainfall had filled four to six inches of the hole designed to trap intruders who wandered down the jungle trail unaware.

It was still dark outside, and Gunner tried to adjust his vision to take in any ambient light from the full moon or the glow of meteorites passing by.

BOOM! BOOM!

Two space rocks pummeled the Earth in rapid succession, causing more dirt and rocks to come crashing down on Gunner. He covered his head with both arms and frantically wiped his eyes to get out bits of wet dirt.

Gunner dropped to his knees to protect himself from the debris and to search for the steel piece of missile support he'd retrieved from the Starhopper wreckage. Relieved that it had made the trip to the bottom of the hole, Gunner stood once again and assessed his surroundings.

The hole appeared to be at least fifteen and maybe twenty feet deep. It had been dug out with shovels, the spade-like shape still appearing in the dim light. He felt around the sides of the pit, searching for tree roots or rocks jutting out to use for an upward climb.

Much to his chagrin, the walls were smooth, with only a few stubs of tree roots protruding out. He suspected others had experienced a similar fall and broken off the roots in an attempt to climb to the top.

Something stung his left ankle, so he reached down to swat at it. It was a two-inch-long leech. The parasitic worm was in the perfect habitat to flourish. And Gunner had provided it more than enough nourishment while he'd lain in the muddy water unconscious.

He flicked at it with his forefinger, but it had latched on. Gunner knew leeches were harmless, and the amount of blood he'd lost to it was insignificant. Once they were full, which didn't take long, they'd fall off and go on about their business.

His past experiences with leeches prepared him for the fact that his body had at least a dozen attached to it. He felt around under his shirt, on his neck and up his pants leg. This was like Thanksgiving for them, and he was powerless to remove them without a lighter, alcohol, or table salt.

Gunner turned his attention back to the pit. It was too wide for him to climb up by spreading his legs wide and using his thigh muscles to propel himself upward like a spider. His other option, thanks to the piece of steel, was to dig out a series of footholds and handgrips to climb up.

The sky was getting lighter, and fortunately, the asteroid remnants had taken a respite from crashing into the surrounding jungle, so he began to dig.

He had no difficulty creating holes in the walls of the pit, as the dirt was moist and soft. He quickly created the first set of holes and rose off the ground a few feet. Then, with a little more difficulty, as he had to hold on with his left hand while digging with his right, he made a little more progress.

Within fifteen minutes, the sky grew lighter as dawn approached, enhancing his visibility. Encouraged by his climb to the halfway point, he dug faster and more efficiently.

Three-quarters of the way to freedom.

Then the rain began to fall.

Gunner could feel his grip on the wall slipping. He halted his digging to hold on as moisture ran down the side of the pit.

First, his right leg lost its footing. The sudden slip and shifting of his weight surprised him. He desperately tried to regain his foothold. He stuck his toes back in place and shook his head violently to get the rain mixed with pieces of dirt out of his eyes and his longish hair. He released his grip to clear his vision and immediately grabbed the wall again.

That was when a large clump of dirt dropped on top of his head, causing him to look upward. A young boy was standing precariously on the edge of the pit, staring down at him. Gunner was startled by the kid's sudden appearance and lost his focus—and his grip on the wall. He slipped downward, his body bouncing off the side of the pit, causing it to twist until he landed hard on the piece of steel, which jabbed into his shoulder.

He groaned in pain as the metal sliced through his shirt and tore into his skin. Gunner rolled over to get the wound out of the stagnant, leech-filled water and immediately pulled his shirt off to wipe the murky soil off his arm.

He turned his attention back to the boy and asked for help. "Hey, kid. *Mi amigo. Por favor.* Help. Um, *ayuda?*"

Gunner had a decent vocabulary of Spanish words, but was not knowledgeable enough to comprehend the foreign language in a conversation. He also thought Hispanic people spoke really fast, so he didn't bother to try to understand.

The boy simply responded with a blank stare.

Gunner waved his arms back and forth, thinking the boy didn't see or hear him. "Hey, *niño!* Where are your parents? *Padres? Ayuda?*"

Still nothing.

The rain continued to fall, and Gunner reconsidered another attempt to dig his way out. He studied the walls and noticed the opposite side from his previous attempt was receiving very little in the way of additional moisture.

He started over, disregarding the boy, who stood peering over the edge of the pit. Gunner dug his first four holes and started upward. The light of day was growing brighter despite the rainfall.

He dug out the next set of grips and hoisted himself upward. He glanced toward the sky and noticed the young boy was gone. *Good,* he thought. *Maybe he went to get his daddy.*

Gunner kept digging, encouraged by his progress. The rain dissipated and the sun began to peek through the jungle's canopy.

He managed a smile and tore at the earth, fighting up the walls of the pit like the Marines clawing their way through the sand at Iwo Jima.

Almost there.

Gunner continued to where he could reach the wet grass at the edge of the pit, and then he heard it. The unmistakable metallic sound of a shell being racked into a shotgun. He froze and glanced upward. Four men had their guns trained on him, and Gunner let out a sigh.

The men began to step aside, and an older Hispanic man with a heavy accent began to laugh. "Well, well, *mi amigos.* We caught a DEA *cabrón.* Lock him up!"

The leader walked away laughing, and the end of a thick knotted rope flew over the edge of the hole and whacked Gunner in the head. He hesitated for a moment, wondering if he wouldn't be safer down in the hole with the leeches.

"*¡Ándale!*" one of the men yelled while pointing the barrel of his AK-47 rifle at the back of Gunner's head.

"Yeah, yeah," Gunner replied to the demand and pulled himself out of the hole, only to earn a buttstock to the back of the neck for his efforts, knocking him unconscious for the third time in twenty-four hours.

CHAPTER 14

Fort Mills
Near Delta, Alabama

"Have you heard anything on the ham radio channels, Pop?" asked Cam as she kicked the mud and pine straw off her wet boots. She and Bear were taking turns patrolling the perimeter of the cabin while the other rested or inventoried their supplies. Pop had readily volunteered to monitor the AM stations and the ham radio frequencies that Cam's father had jotted down in a spiral notebook years ago.

"No, Cam, not really," replied a dejected Pop. "Oh, I don't really mean that. Obviously, I'm looking for any kind of information regarding Gunner and the Starhopper. There's nothing on that at all. It's as if everyone forgot about them."

"I understand. It's always about *what have you done for me lately* with people nowadays. Gunner, somehow, prevented that asteroid from hitting our planet in one humongous piece, wiping us out all at once. I suppose that's been forgotten already."

Pop set the headset down and unplugged it, allowing the frequencies to be monitored over the speakers attached to the base unit. For the moment, the chatter consisted of a conversation between people complaining about FEMA.

"Here's what I've heard," he began. "The asteroid has basically been turned into a massive meteor storm that is impacting the entire planet, especially near the equator. Certainly, everything I've heard has to be taken with a grain of salt, but supposedly, the timing of the incoming meteor storm will begin to affect the lower forty-eight, Canada, and other countries around the world in the higher latitudes today and tomorrow."

Cam retrieved a handful of trail mix from the kitchen, which was combined with the living room area. She was staying hydrated with water from the property's well and munching the healthy snack throughout the day, hoping to preserve their stored foods for later. "I can see it in the skies. The instances of the fallout are more frequent and much brighter. It's a matter of time before the larger meteorites find their way through the atmosphere."

"Is it still raining?" asked Pop.

"Nah, not really. Just a little misty drizzle."

Pop stood to peer through the curtains to get a look for himself. "Cam, which way is west, you know, toward Birmingham or, specifically, Talladega?"

Cam pointed toward the windowless wall of the cabin where the stone fireplace was located. "Talladega is about thirty miles as the crow flies on the other side of Cheaha State Park. Why?"

"Supposedly, a fireball hit the roof of a Walmart just east of town. Several aboveground gasoline storage tanks were hit, creating a huge fire. The flames got whipped up by the wind, and the wildfire is moving toward the east."

A concerned look came over Cam's face. She'd never really paid attention to the geography of the surrounding area. She made her way to the kitchen cupboards and searched through the drawers for a well-worn, folded map of Alabama. She spread it out on the table to identify their location in relation to the small Alabama city known for its NASCAR Superspeedway.

"I don't know, Pop. I think we're okay. The fire would have a long way to travel through the gaps and ridges of the state park. Plus, even this little bit of rain will slow its progress."

Bear emerged from his slumber, rubbing his eyes like a little kid who'd been awakened before he was ready for the day. "What's going on?"

"Nothing, really," replied Cam. "Pop's been monitoring the radio and I've been patrolling. I've heard nothing from Ghost or Houston, and there's been no sightings of Gunner and—"

An enormous explosion drowned out Cam's sentence and caused the cabin to shake so bad that years of dust and debris, which had settled on the open rafters, came fluttering down on top of them.

"Holy shit!" shouted Bear as he rushed to the front door and flung it open to get a look. Cam immediately joined him, and they walked into the grassy area between the cabin's porch and the lake.

Howard, who'd remained calm throughout the ordeal, as he tended to avoid the drama generated by humans, still managed to let out a couple of barks and a long howl.

"Look!" shouted Cam, pointing eastward beyond the back of the cabin. A huge trail of black smoke poured skyward well off in the distance.

"That's a little close for comfort," said Bear.

"Should we get in the root cellar or something?" asked Pop.

Cam walked away from Bear and stood with her hands on her hips, staring at the plywood doors that led belowground next to the cabin. She turned to address Bear. "Seriously, do you think it would matter? I mean, how deep would we have to be to avoid these things? That hit like a nuke!"

Bear studied the smoke pouring into the sky. "Man, that was miles from here, but it shook us like it landed on our heads. I don't think a root cellar would help us at all."

"There has to be something we can do," implored Pop. He was rubbing his temples and appeared to be on the verge of tears.

Cam moved to comfort him. "I'd love to have a better answer for you, Pop, but there isn't one. It'll be just pure luck to avoid being hit. A nuclear bunker might give us a chance, but even if we found our way into a cave in the park, it might not be enough and ..." She paused as she got the feeling that providing Pop a dose of reality might not be the best idea.

"And what, Cam?" he pressed.

"Nothing, Pop. It's just there are no good options. We've got to ride it out and hope for the best."

Pop managed a smile and stood a little taller. "And pray. I will absolutely ask God for help, without hesitation."

CHAPTER 15

NORAD
Cheyenne Mountain, Colorado

The president had been awakened at three a.m. by Chief of Staff Fielding and asked to report to the battle cab. The first meteorites were beginning to find their way to U.S. soil, and he'd insisted upon being present to make any decisions necessary to help the American people. It was now daylight across the nation, and the meteor storm was making its presence known from coast to coast.

"Mr. President, there's no way to put into words how tragic this situation is," began Peter Gower, the deputy director of FEMA. "As we've discussed, we are now in the throes of the meteor storm created by the destruction of IM86. The entire Northern Hemisphere is beginning to experience the impact of meteorites crashing to Earth, which areas near the equator felt during the evening hours."

"What are the worst hit areas of the U.S. at this time?" he asked.

"The worst damage has been caused by tsunamis, sir," he replied. "The Virgin Islands were completely covered with water for a time, and this had a profound impact on Florida's east coast and the Keys. The Coast Guard station in Fort Lauderdale reported a six-foot wave hitting the Atlantic Seaboard before we lost contact with them."

The president winced. "Lost contact?"

"Yes, sir, the station's ground personnel were evacuated, and the vessels were redeployed to sea."

"Why would you do that?" the president asked.

"Sir, boats are generally safer from tsunami damage while in ocean waters of at least a hundred meters in depth rather than being docked or moored in a harbor. In open water, the energy of the tsunami is distributed along the length of the wave created. The waves may be hundreds of miles long and travel at the speed of an airplane, but for the ships at sea, they simply ride the wave as it passes."

"You said something about the Keys?"

"Sir, the reports are that the wave washed over the Keys from Homestead to Key West. Key West and the island of Cuba took the brunt of the energy, virtually washing the buildings and any inhabitants into the Gulf of Mexico."

"Dammit." The president lashed out, slamming his hand on the conference table. "We warned people early on. Why didn't they listen?"

Gower shook his head. "Many did, sir, but others chose to ride it out and take their chances. Plus, truthfully, the interstates out of Florida were clogged with traffic. Hotel rooms up and down both Interstates 75 and 95 were full. Reportedly, people were turning back out of frustration."

"Is there any discernible pattern? I mean, can this not be predicted at all?" the president asked.

"Not really, sir," replied Dr. Zahn from the Jet Propulsion Laboratory, who had rarely left the battle cab since his arrival. "Which meteorites survive the trip through our atmosphere and where they strike is completely random. As the planet spins on its axis and makes its way around the sun, the meteors' approach affects different parts of the planet. I will say this, as predicted by my analysis, Eurasia is facing a far greater number of impact events than we are. It's hard to be more accurate in my assessment without the use of our orbiting satellites."

An Air Force colonel entered the battle cab and handed Maggie Fielding several pages of a computer printout. She nodded to him and he quickly exited the battle cab.

"Mr. President, I'm afraid I have some grim news."

"What is it, Maggie?"

"Sir." She paused and gulped. "New York City was hit with several small meteorites in rapid succession. Part of the city has been obliterated, including areas of New Jersey across the Hudson River."

"My god," he mumbled, placing his right hand over his mouth.

"Mr. President, the top of the Statue of Liberty took a direct hit. It's been destroyed, sir."

A hush fell over the room as tears began to flow and heads were hung in despair. The three-hundred-foot symbol of American freedom, which had greeted immigrants for generations, had stood proudly on Liberty Island since it was constructed in 1875.

"This is tragic," said the president, trying to contain his emotions.

"Sir, there's more," said Fielding as she flipped through the three-page report.

Unable to find his voice, he waved his arm at her, instructing her to continue.

"Another tsunami has caused massive amounts of damage along the Gulf Coast. A wall of water stretching from Galveston to New Orleans to parts of Florida's Panhandle has caused flooding as much as fifty miles inland. Hundreds of thousands of coastal homes and residents have been caught up in the wave, sir."

The president looked to Gower from FEMA. "What do you have on this?"

The FEMA deputy director was standing in the corner of the battle cab, holding his laptop, which was plugged into Cheyenne Mountain's intranet servers. "My system is updating now, sir, but what I am seeing is consistent with Ms. Fielding's data. I might add that the three large meteorite strikes in the New York City area has caused a collapse of the power grid throughout the ConEd system. There are also reports of seismic activity."

"Earthquakes?" asked the president.

Dr. Zahn answered that question. "Yes, sir. As these meteorites punch a hole through our atmosphere, they're hitting the ground at enormous speeds and energy. The multiple impacts could generate a massive elastic strain on Earth's crust."

Gower interrupted. "Mexico City is in shambles, sir, based upon these reports."

"That's not surprising," continued Dr. Zahn. "The Cocos tectonic plate that forces its way beneath the continental edge of the North

American plate may have been, well, um, aggravated."

"Aggravated? By a meteorite?"

"Yes, sir. Granted, the earthquake may have been coincidental, but unlikely. These meteorites are impacting the planet with the force of nuclear explosions. It's possible to cause small earthquakes and, in this case, a shifting of the tectonic plates."

The president shook his head in disbelief. "Is FEMA prepared to respond?" the president asked the deputy administrator.

Gower set his laptop down and removed his glasses to address the question. "Sir, dealing with this catastrophe will take more than FEMA's resources. We'll need everyone in our military, state-level first responders, and volunteers to help those in need."

The president paced the floor as the members of his disaster-preparedness team awaited his directives. He alternated between looking through the large plate glasses at the frenzied operations center, and back to the NASA feeds that provided updates of meteorite strikes.

Finally, he stopped, took a deep breath, and exhaled. "Maggie, take some notes, please. There's nothing we can do to stop this catastrophe other than what our brave astronauts have done already. We can, however, undertake to protect those who are in need on the ground. We've told them how to stay safe and shelter in place, etcetera. Next, we have to be prepared to hit the ground running when this calamity is over."

"I'm ready, Mr. President," said Fielding.

President Watson turned to Dr. Zahn. "Based upon the limited data that you have, can you tell me when this damn thing ends and the rebuilding can begin?"

"Sir, other than a sporadic, wayward space rock that would be considered a straggler, I would safely say Monday afternoon."

"Two more days of this?" asked the president.

Zahn furrowed his brow and nodded. "Yes, sir, at least."

CHAPTER 16

Unknown Jungle Compound
South America

There were concussions and then *there were concussions.* Gunner knew
the difference between the kind that put you out of commission in a
nearly comatose state and those you got over after a week of rest
coupled with some Tylenol.

Post-concussion syndrome was very real, and Gunner knew to
protect his head after being injured. He also knew that, with his
history, experiencing a second concussion in a short time frame,
followed by a blow to the head before the symptoms of the first
trauma had subsided, could result in rapid and sometimes fatal brain
swelling.

The whack on the head he'd received as the Starhopper tumbled
to a resting point in the jungle had knocked him out for many hours.
The second blow he'd received when he fell into the pit could've
easily resulted in the rapid onset of brain swelling, which is
oftentimes fatal.

The final blow, the smack to the back of the head from the butt of
a rifle, was the likely cause of his mind's fogginess and fatigue.
Gunner struggled to recall his whereabouts. He tried in vain to
retrace the events that led to his being bound with his hands behind
his back and his eyes covered with a dark blindfold.

To get his bearings, he remained completely still, allowing his
mind to focus on the senses of smell and sound to give him a clue.
Lying sideways on a damp, hard-packed dirt floor, Gunner fought off
the head fog. He listened to the muffled voices and the faint sounds
of whimpering. He wasn't alone, and he didn't dare move, as he

needed time to avoid any interaction with his captors.

A slight, imperceptible breeze washed over him, carrying an odd combination of the smell of cheap perfume and the stench of urine. He scowled, trying to make sense of the odor, and immediately thought of a porta-potty at an outdoor concert.

Heavy footsteps were approaching, the sounds he imagined a jack-booted thug making as he made his rounds through an off-the-books Russian prison.

More voices. Hispanic.

It was coming back to him. South America, maybe Central America, but certainly not the jungles of Africa or Southeast Asia. *I'm sure as hell not home, Toto*, he thought, crudely twisting the words of Dorothy in *The Wizard of Oz*.

The sound of the heavy boots disappeared, and Gunner decided to take a chance. He moved his leg slightly to see if it drew a reaction from his captors.

Nothing.

He tried it again, this time stretching out to gauge the size of his cell. Nobody was there, or they were biding their time for him to clearly show evidence that he was awake.

Finally, he went for it. He took a chance and wiggled around until he found the wall of his cell. Using his feet, he pushed himself upward until he was sitting on the floor with his back against the cold, rough cinder block. Using his knees that were tucked up to his chest, Gunner leaned forward, moaned from the pain as his brain reminded him it was concussed, and tried to work the blindfold up to his forehead.

He was only marginally successful, and his field of vision was only downward. However, the small amount of light that came in through the slits of windows caused more pain to shoot into his skull.

Gunner shook his head vigorously from side to side, somehow thinking that would make it better. He was wrong. The pounding continued, forcing his eyes closed despite his best efforts to open them.

He worked on the blindfold again and was able to push it up

above his brows. Gradually, he allowed his eyes to adjust so that he could see his surroundings.

He was in a cell that was barely five feet square. A bucket of water with a ladle sat in one corner and another steel bucket, most likely a substitute for a toilet, sat in the other. One entire wall was made up of three-quarter-inch rebar welded together to form a gate and cage-like structure.

Gunner scooted over to the gate and spoke in a loud whisper. "Hey, can anybody hear me? Is there anybody else in here?"

No one answered.

He tried again, a little louder this time. "Hello. Can you hear me?"

Gunner had no time to defend himself as a muscular, heavy arm appeared from around the corner of his cell and rammed the sharp end of a cattle prod into his bare chest. The twin prongs of the high-voltage device seared into Gunner's skin, causing him to scream in pain.

His sweaty skin began to burn as a result of the intense heat generated by the device. The smell of his burning flesh reached Gunner's nostrils as he desperately pushed himself out of reach of the man administering the torture.

He spoke English with a heavy Hispanic accent. "Hallo, gringo! You are like the other DEA, weak. No?"

Gunner thought, *No, asshole.*

"Juan, step back from the cell," ordered a man in Spanish.

Gunner curled into a ball and stayed as far away from the cell bars as he could.

A tall, broad-shouldered Hispanic man wearing a dark suit, white starched shirt, and no tie towered over Gunner. "Do you want water, DEA man?"

Gunner stared back at his captor but didn't respond.

The man began to laugh. "Oh, maybe Juan is wrong. Maybe this DEA man is a tough guy, eh?"

Gunner could hear several other men laughing in the background.

"You want more juice, gringo?" asked the short, muscular man identified as Juan.

In the dark recesses of his jail cell, Gunner managed a wry smile, and then he raised his middle finger toward Juan.

"*Excelente!*" shouted the well-dressed man. "He is a tough guy. They are my favorite to break. Like a wild horse, my friend, you will break. Trust me. And when you do, I will simply kill you like the other DEA *cabrón* that come sniffing around."

Gunner scowled and bit his tongue. He had plenty to say, but it wouldn't serve any purpose yet. For now, he needed to study his captors. Learn their habits and their weaknesses. Identify what might trigger them to make a mistake.

He'd learned this the hard way, many years ago. He was a prisoner, again, and he knew what to do.

CHAPTER 17

Unknown Jungle Compound
South America

Gunner quickly recovered from the cattle prod puncture and set about loosening the wrist cuffs. The task of escaping the zip-tie wrist cuffs was made more difficult because his hands were bound behind his back. This was not insurmountable, as Gunner had practiced dealing with this form of restraint many times.

First, he crawled around so that he was kneeling in the center of the cell. Then he moved his hands under and forward of his butt so that his wrists were immediately behind his ankles. Having the wall as leverage made the next step easier.

He spun around and placed the balls of his feet against the wall so that his toes were extended upward. He inched forward as close to his feet as he could and worked his bound wrists under the soles of his shoes until they were clear of his toes.

Now, with his hands in front of him, he could use his strength to break the restraints. Had Gunner been conscious when the zip ties were applied, he could have made this final step easier. He knew to clinch his fists together with the palms facing down when the restraints were affixed to his wrists. By widening his bound wrists as much as possible, when he turned the wrists to face each other, enough slack was created for him to maneuver his arms later.

The restraints were very tight. His constant twisting and tugging against them to loosen the plastic had resulted in many bleeding cuts in his wrists. However, Gunner was determined, and the pain was slight compared to his still-throbbing headache.

He lifted his wrists to his mouth and used his teeth to position the lock so that it faced him with his palms together. Gunner took a deep breath. He was ready.

With his palms flat against one another, he brought his arms up and then quickly pulled them down toward his body, pulling them apart toward the end of the downward thrust. He continued this motion for several attempts, each time causing a weakness at the point where the restraints were locked. Then, with one final effort, he grunted and slammed it downward with all of his strength. The restraints snapped open and fell to the floor between Gunner's knees.

He exhaled for the first time and looked down to examine his wrists. He rubbed them and wiped the blood off on his khakis. He sighed and was about to find his way to his feet when he saw the same young boy he'd observed by the lake, and later peering at him from the edge of the pit, standing emotionless a few feet in front of his cell door.

Gunner's heart sank. He'd just broken free of his wrist cuffs and was prepared to break out of the jail cell; however the young boy who didn't help him before was now in the way of his freedom.

He sighed and then decided to befriend the boy in the hope that he wouldn't say anything about what he'd just witnessed. Rather than standing and towering over the kid, Gunner sat on the floor with his legs crossed in front of him, and pulled his arms behind his back to hide the fact he'd broken the cuffs.

"What's your name? Um, *nombre? Tu nombre?*"

The boy's eyes were dark, sad. Unresponsive. His jet-black hair was unkempt and fell over his forehead onto his eyebrows.

Gunner smiled, the universal signal of friendship, in most cases, anyway. He tried to exude body language that would allow the boy to feel comfortable in his presence. He needed an ally, and this kid might find a key to let him out or, at the very least, bring him his satellite phone.

"*Mi nombre es, um, Fox.*" Gunner leaned forward to get a better look at the boy. He smiled again. "*Mi Fox. Tu nombre?*"

No reaction.

Gunner could see the sadness in the boy's face. He had nothing to live for. No place to play. The soccer shirt he was wearing didn't necessarily mean he could play soccer anywhere. He, too, was a captive of the men who ran this compound, most likely a drug cartel outpost in the mountains of Colombia.

He decided to try a different tactic. While he wasn't in a humorous mood, he needed to do something to get the boy's attention. So he called on some of the things people do to make babies laugh, including funny faces. It required that he reveal his unbound hands, but the risk was worth it.

He started by puffing his cheeks out, bugging his eyes, and then he slapped both cheeks with the heels of his hands, causing the air to escape, thus creating a farting sound.

Nothing.

Gunner crossed his eyes and picked his nose with both hands at once. When this didn't work, he scratched the top of his head and underneath one of his armpits to emulate a monkey.

Finally, a smile came across the boy's face.

Gunner did it some more, inching closer to the door so that the boy could see him better. The boy managed a giggle. Gunner smiled and became more animated, emboldened by the progress he was making.

"*Alerta!*" shouted a woman's voice.

Gunner froze, but the boy continued to look at him in wonderment. Gunner was captivated by the kid's odd behavior and was therefore caught off guard when the cattle prod was shoved through the bars once again. This time, the amount of voltage used was much higher.

He screamed in pain and began to double over as he saw the boy being shoved to the floor by the guard. The guard maliciously threatened the boy with the cattle prod and then turned it on Gunner again, jabbing it into his tender ankles, where the last of the leeches had finally loosened their death grip on his flesh.

"Arrrgggh!"

Gunner was in agony. The open wound magnified the effects of the electricity making contact with his tender flesh.

Another jolt. This time, the muscular guard found Gunner's throat.

He pushed away from the gate and curled up in a ball to avoid being struck again by the torturer. He caught a glimpse of the boy getting to his feet and running past the guard, receiving a slap in the back of the head as he left.

The guard jabbed the cattle prod into the cell, trying to make contact with Gunner's body. He got ready, intending to grab the device on the next opportunity, but it never came.

A thunderous roar could be heard followed by an intense heat. Seconds later, he heard the explosion and felt the impact of a meteorite falling in their vicinity.

The guard fell to the floor and covered his head. Shrieks and screams, all female, filled the air. Gunner tried to process it all while looking for an opportunity to attack his captor.

He crawled on all fours and lunged for the cell door. He reached through the bars and grasped at the cattle prod, hoping to give the guard a good long dose of electricity.

Then a large black leather cowboy boot stomped on his left hand, causing him to recoil his arm.

"You are ready to die, DEA gringo, yes? You play with Juan like two lovers. You will not play with me!"

The well-dressed man seemed unfazed by the closeness of the meteorite that had just sailed by them. He ordered the guard, Juan, to get off the floor, and the man quickly scurried out. Then he turned to Gunner and spat on him. As he laughed, Gunner could see a single gold tooth glistening in his mouth.

The man abruptly turned and shouted at the women as he walked down the hallway. The clanking sound of metallic locks indicated they were left alone again.

He leaned back against the wall and rubbed the wounds created by the cattle prods. He tried to analyze everything that was happening to him, but the one thing that puzzled him most was the young boy.

Then a young-sounding woman spoke to Gunner. "*El niño es sordo y mudo.*"

"Wait, what? What does that mean?"

Several of the women shushed the young girl who spoke to Gunner.

"*Por favor*, tell me."

Then like a chorus of cicadas in the forest, they all joined in.

"Shush! *Tranquilo.*"

CHAPTER 18

Defense Threat Reduction Agency
Fort Belvoir, Virginia

Special Agent Theodora Cuccinelli possessed an extraordinary analytical mind that was coupled with an innate empathy for those in peril. Had she obtained a psychology degree, she could've easily become one of the FBI's top profilers. However, that was not her passion. She grew up in a time when every aspect of life revolved around the use of computers.

She was recruited by the bureau during her junior year at Cornell University in upstate New York. The Ivy League school might not have the notoriety of its counterparts—Harvard, Yale, and Princeton—but it was considered one of the top ten universities in the nation for its computer sciences program.

While in college, she'd created a paper banner that hung in her dorm room. It read *Data is My Friend.* Early on, she thought she might be destined for any number of computer-related careers, from multimedia programming to managing information systems to the field in the highest demand—cyber-security consulting.

The nature of war had shifted in the world from bombs and bullets to keystrokes and pen testing, the practice of looking for security vulnerabilities in a software or computer network in order to exploit them.

For a while, much to Cuccinelli's regret, she participated in challenges with her fellow students. Rumors were rampant that a professor at MIT had recruited some of his top graduate students to profit off their capabilities. Known around the dark web as the Zero Day Gamers, this group would routinely perform ransomware attacks on businesses and small municipal governments.

These hackers spent their free time conducting penetration tests of the servers of their targets until they were able to breach the system. Once in, they'd insert malware that could only be removed by them, but for a fee, of course. If the owners of the network refused to pay, their data would be lost and the hardware would be ruined. It was less expensive to pay the data kidnappers, so most did.

As the news of the Zero Day Gamers' exploits spread around college campuses, many students with advanced computer skills tried their hand at hacking for fun. It became a game, one where the goals and challenges were continuously made more difficult.

Teddy Cuccinelli had been drawn into the game. She meant no harm and certainly had no intention of inserting ransomware for profit. She, like so many brilliant young minds, was bored with her studies and had very little social life except with her fellow computer nerds.

So she joined in the fun and was good at it. There wasn't a private enterprise system that she couldn't breach. As her talents grew and her exploits became known, she began to draw the attention of the FBI Cyber Division.

She'd single-handedly breached the server network of Connecticut Electric, the state's largest utility. As was always the case, she spent a few hours one evening, solely out of curiosity, navigating through the company servers, viewing their personnel files and financial data.

To her, it was no big deal and just another opportunity to mark a notch on the wall of successful hacks.

To Connecticut Electric, and the FBI Cyber Division, who'd been closely monitoring their computer network due to a series of intrusion attempts in recent months, it was a big deal.

The next day, Cuccinelli had walked out of Collegetown Bagels with breakfast and began the short stroll down College Avenue to class when several black sedans with darkened windows descended upon her. Within seconds, she was thrown against the trunk of the car, handcuffed, and her bagels rolled down the sidewalk while she was whisked away.

A moment of transgression that might've easily ruined her life turned out to be an opportunity of a lifetime. Over the next several days, the FBI interrogation gradually turned into an interview. The lead investigators with the Cyber Division were so impressed with Cuccinelli, that they reached out to their recruiters to travel to the Albany office to talk with her.

Her career path took a drastic turn from playful hacker to FBI special agent dealing with cyber warfare. She was no longer Teddy Cuccinelli, computer nerd. She'd become—*the Jackal.*

While the FBI utilized the Jackal for her computer talents, they overlooked her empathetic side. A side that could've assisted the profilers who searched out the nation's serial killers and internet predators who used social media to attract their victims. It was the Jackal's empathy that kept her sitting at her desk day and night in search of Gunner Fox.

She'd developed feelings for Gunner, but not in a romantic way. She'd studied his psychological profile and background. What she saw was a unique love story between an American warrior and his idealistic wife, one that ended tragically as she pursued her dream of space travel.

She understood Gunner's angst, and after meeting him in person, she made a promise that he knew nothing about. Heather might be watching over him from Heaven. And Cam might be by his side on their missions together. But she would watch his back from the omnipresent cyber world, lending an assist whenever she could.

So she'd sat at her desk, staying vigilant. She studied camera footage from around North America, straining her eyes to differentiate meteorites from spaceships.

When NASA, in particular Houston's mission control, was less than cooperative in turning over their data on the mission, she hacked into their computers to have a look for herself. She studied the Starhopper's last known coordinates. She calculated time, speed, and distance. She created a working hypothesis of the best-case scenario because the worst-case scenario was too painful to consider.

She also took into account something of which she was certain.

Despite Major Gunner Fox's outward demeanor and tendency to take risks, he wasn't suicidal. He didn't want to die. He was a survivor and would consider it a failure to succumb to death because of his inner sadness. It was for that reason that she never left her desk.

Based on her calculations, the Jackal focused her efforts on a thousand-mile radius from the heart of the Caribbean Sea. She studied the highly classified data obtained from NASA regarding the destruction of satellites in low-Earth orbit. America's adversaries relished the opportunity to take advantage of its weaknesses, she surmised, and the loss of reconnaissance and military hardware in space would embolden them.

She plugged in her findings on the damage to the satellites and studied it in relation to the intercept point of IM86. If her calculations were correct, and assuming the Starhopper was able to navigate through the debris field, she determined that the Caribbean Sea, or thereabouts, would be the safest possible place to return to Earth.

To be sure, this conclusion took nearly twenty hours of nonstop research and calculations by the Jackal. It took Artie, the Starhopper's onboard artificial intelligence, less than two seconds to reach the same recommendation. The Jackal was far from being considered a slow learner. It was just that her brain wasn't as big as Artie's.

Nonetheless, she was on the right track, and with each passing hour, by process of elimination, she was able to focus her efforts on the most likely landing area for the Starhopper—somewhere between Nicaragua and the Amazon Jungle in Brazil.

Her eyes were growing weary and she'd just popped open her last can of Red Bull when Ghost entered her office.

"Have you slept?"

"No, sir. There'll be time for that later. I've got a general area stretching from Central America to the northern parts of South America. It took a while to make this determination, thanks to the stonewalling I got from NASA."

Ghost sat in the chair across from the Jackal and sipped his coffee. He leaned forward with a solemn look on his face.

She immediately picked up on his demeanor. "Sir, what is it?"

"I've just been told that Mark Foster, the Mission Control director, committed suicide sometime during the night. They said he'd been distraught over the whereabouts of the Starhopper and the state of affairs in general. He decided to opt out."

The Jackal furrowed her brow as a look of disbelief came over her face. "Sir, I had a phone conversation with him yesterday morning. Granted, it was somewhat frenzied, as everyone was searching for the spacecraft, but I wouldn't describe his mental state as distraught. To me, based upon our phone conversation anyway, I'd say he was determined, if anything."

Ghost shrugged. "Well, either way, the man is dead, and now Houston is continuing their search without him."

The Jackal slumped back in her chair and looked to the wall where she'd outlined all the people involved in the death of Heather Fox. The dotted lines connected to one central figure, Colonel Maxwell Robinson, but some led to the photograph of Director Foster. Her focus on the wall caught Ghost's attention, who began to study it as well.

"What are you thinking?"

"I don't know, sir. I mean, I want to remain focused on finding the Starhopper and Major Fox. But, well, something about this suicide raises alarm bells for me. Foster was connected to Mrs. Fox's death, and he was also connected to the Russian professor although he wasn't implicated in any wrongdoing. Moreover, he had a direct relationship to Colonel Robinson."

"Are you wearing your FBI hat at the moment?" asked Ghost.

"Sir, I never really take it off. I'm just saying that if my theory about Colonel Robinson's involvement in the cover-up of Heather Fox's death is correct, he'd stand to benefit by eliminating the only other American who was privy to what really happened—Mark Foster."

"But there's still someone who needs answers ..." Ghost said as his voice trailed off. A wave of sadness came over him as he considered Gunner's likely demise.

"He's still alive, sir. I know it. And when he finds out what Maxwell Robinson has kept hidden from him for all these years, he'll have a new sense of purpose, one that doesn't bode well for the colonel."

CHAPTER 19

Unknown Jungle Compound
South America

Gunner tried several times to converse with the women who were being held in the jail cells all around him, to no avail. Every attempt was greeted with a swift rebuke—shhhh. They were frightened, fearful of the same kind of treatment that he was receiving, and worse. He honored their wishes and left them alone. After a brief period of silence, except for the occasional sonic boom of a meteorite exploding in the region, Gunner drifted off to sleep.

He was awakened, not by an explosion or his sadistic captors, but by a feeling. A presence.

Gunner woke up with a jolt of sudden energy and retreated to the back corner of his cell, crashing his back into the metal bucket designated for his human waste. His eyes grew wide in an attempt to focus on the small figure who sat in front of the bars.

As he gathered his wits, he realized that the young boy had returned, and he was sitting with his legs crossed in front of him on the dirt floor. Yet again, an unemotional blank stare was on his face as he studied Gunner.

"Hey, kid," whispered Gunner, recalling that the boy had been struck by the guard. "Are you okay?"

The boy just stared at him. *What's with this kid?*

The young boy had changed into a lightweight hooded sweatshirt bearing a bright red soccer ball on the front with the insignia *Federacion Colombiana de Futbol.* Gunner leaned forward to get a better look.

"Colombia? Soccer? Is this Colombia?"

Still nothing.

Gunner inched forward and sat cross-legged in an effort to mimic the boy's posture, doing anything he could to make a connection with the kid.

The boy remained stoic for a moment and then pulled one of his hands out of the sweatshirt pocket sewn underneath the soccer logo.

He began to draw in the dirt with his index finger. He created a large circle and then added ears, two eyes, a nose, and a mouth. He stopped and sadly looked at Gunner's face, then broke eye contact and stared down at the face.

"A face? Is that your face?" asked Gunner, puzzled by what the boy was doing. And then, in an instant, he understood as the boy drew in the dirt again.

He scrubbed the dirt to remove the ears and mouth from the face drawing. He looked up to Gunner as a few tears streamed down his dust-covered cheek, leaving streaks of moisture. He pointed his fingers to his ears and mouth and slowly shook his head side to side.

Gunner closed his eyes and sighed. The boy was deaf and couldn't speak.

El niño es sordo y mudo.

Now he understood what the woman had been saying earlier. The young boy couldn't hear or speak, which explained why his interaction with Gunner was so strange.

Gunner desperately wanted to reach out to hug the child. Let him know that it was okay. That he wasn't defective. That he was simply *unique.*

But the bars separated them, as did their relationship. Gunner was the prisoner of the boy's family members, who treated him poorly from what Gunner had witnessed. In a way, the kid was a prisoner as well. He was imprisoned by silence and the inability to vocalize his feelings or thoughts. And he was imprisoned by being an outcast, a simple child who could be abused because he was different.

Gunner took a deep breath, sat a little taller, and smiled. He didn't know sign language other than how to ask someone if they signed.

He formed both hands into the form of the number "1" using his index fingers. Then he drew a couple of large circles in the air with the tip of each finger. He moved them up, back, forward, and down, alternating the circular movement as if he were pedaling a bicycle with his fingers. He studied the boy for a reaction.

The boy seemed to understand what Gunner was attempting to do, but his face became sullen and he shook his head side to side.

"I guess your scumball parents didn't bother to learn sign language, much less teach it to you. They are real pieces of work to let you wander around this jungle without the ability to hear or call out for help."

The boy tilted his head, trying to understand what Gunner was saying. It was possible he was learning to read lips, but the language barrier would hinder that process.

Gunner got the boy's attention and patted his chest. Then he began to draw in the dirt. He had to show the boy that he was friendly, so he drew his own face and put an oversized smile on it.

The boy returned the smile and drew a smile on his face-drawing also.

Gunner tapped his heart and then pointed to the boy, followed by a thumbs-up.

The kid emulated the gesture.

Yes! Progress!

Gunner took a chance, hoping to gain the confidence of the boy. He patted his chest again, and next to his face, he drew a crude rendering of a rocket ship flying toward a crescent moon. He looked at the boy, hoping for a reaction.

The boy's eyes grew wide and he pointed toward the outside of the building. He pointed at Gunner and made a motion with his hands clasped together as if they were flying toward the sky.

"Yes! Yes! That's me. That's my rocket ship!"

Gunner was a little too exuberant in his reaction, and a chorus of shushes emanated from the other cells.

"Sorry!" he quickly apologized and turned his attention back to the boy.

He erased his dirt-floor chalkboard with the palm of his hand and began to make another drawing. He created an image of his duffle bag with the handles on top. Then he wrote in oversized letters F-O-X.

"Fox," he said aloud. "My *nombre* is Fox."

The boy was puzzled, but one of the women overheard the conversation.

"*Zorro. Su nombre es Zorro.*" Fox translates to *zorro* in Spanish.

"*Gracias,*" said Gunner, although he wished she hadn't overheard him say that. He immediately speculated the ransom that would be demanded by his captors just doubled. Not that a demand for ransom would be a bad thing.

Go ahead, assholes, call Washington to demand money. You think the hellfire brought on your heads by the asteroid is bad, wait'll you get a load of Cam and Bear.

Gunner managed a smile and continued to communicate with the boy. He drew a picture of his satellite phone and pointed from the duffle bag to the phone to him. He touched the drawing of the phone again and then positioned his thumb and index finger to his mouth and ear. He smiled and nodded at the boy, feeling hopeful.

The boy scowled and then looked to his left down the hallway that led to the last cell where Gunner was held. Apparently, the guard on duty had abandoned his post, leaving the two to have this extended conversation.

He looked back to Gunner and slowly reached into his sweatshirt pocket. When he pulled out the satellite phone, Gunner's heart leapt out of his chest. His eyes grew wide and he lurched forward to reach through the cell door bars.

He instantly regretted the spontaneous move, as it frightened the boy, who had obviously become accustomed to physical abuse without warning. He pushed himself away from the cell with his feet and leaned against a wall, a sudden look of fear coming over his face.

Gunner tried to apologize, waving his arms in an attempt to erase his actions. He patted his heart again and pointed to the boy; then he knocked himself on the side of the head a couple of times and rolled his eyes around.

This drew a chuckle from the kid, and Gunner realized his silliness made it all better.

But not quite. When he tried to motion for the boy to come closer, he refused and remained several feet away.

The boy began to fiddle with the satellite phone, running his fingers over the buttons and sporadically flicking the antenna.

Gunner smiled and nodded his head. Once again, he held his index finger and thumb to his face to emulate the placing of a phone call. He nodded some more and pointed to the ground. He drew the moon again and the phone next to it. He pointed to the boy, then to the two drawings, and then made the hand gesture creating the telephone.

The boy nodded.

Gunner resisted the urge to reach for the phone again. Instead, he drew the location of the power button on the side of the device and drew an arrow in the dirt pointing to it.

The boy understood and pushed the button upward. The lights illuminated on the phone's keypad.

Yes! Gunner shouted inside. *Leave it on, kid! That's all it'll take.*

His face beamed as he thought of the signal from the satellite phone searching Earth's orbit, attempting to make contact with any remaining satellite that connected his location to the vast intelligence network of the United States.

But his hopes were immediately dashed as one of the guards stormed down the hall, smacked the kid with the back of his hand, and brusquely turned the satellite phone off.

CHAPTER 20

Defense Threat Reduction Agency
Fort Belvoir, Virginia

The Jackal was having difficulty staying awake, and the eyestrain from studying the computer monitors was taking its toll. Her eyes burned and itched constantly. She searched up and down the hallways of the DTRA, asking the few inhabitants of the building that morning for eye drops to alleviate the dryness. Her head ached, her back and neck were sore, and her ability to concentrate was waning.

In addition, the dozen Red Bull drinks she'd consumed in the last day and a half were simply making her jittery, but not necessarily alert. She needed to sleep, but she forced herself to remain attentive to her computer monitors, hoping for a signal or any type of sign that the Starhopper had made it back to Earth.

Ping!

The Jackal shook her head rapidly side to side, trying to awaken her brain. Had she dozed off? Was she dreaming? She searched for her clock icon on the bottom right side of her computer monitor.

Ping!

Again, and she was certain of it this time. She forced herself to sit upright, and in doing so, she knocked over the last of the Red Bulls sitting atop the desk next to her hand. She scrambled to move paperwork out of the way, and then, with the back of her hand, she slapped the can off her desk and sent it careening off the wall next to her. She'd deal with it later. A hollow promise.

She grasped her mouse and navigated to the screen that was dedicated to monitoring the satellite phone's activation. So many things had to work out in her and Gunner's favor for this moment to occur.

The satellites designated for interagency global communications needed to be intact despite the deluge of meteors approaching the planet. The satellite phone had to have made the trip into space to begin with, and then followed Gunner onto the Starhopper. And finally, it had to have made its way back to Earth.

She furiously made entries in the software program in attempt to narrow down the phone's location. There had been no attempt to communicate, but the simple process of turning the phone on for a moment had generated sufficient activity to approximate its whereabouts.

"Why couldn't it have been turned on longer!" the Jackal lamented aloud.

"What?" asked Ghost, who'd unexpectedly entered the room.

His voice startled her, but she quickly recovered. "Sir, I've got something. I'm reconfirming to make sure it wasn't a false signal."

"Talk to me."

"Sir, I've got a ping notification for Major Fox's satellite phone. I don't need to explain how lucky we—"

"Location," interrupted Ghost as he quickly walked around the desk to look over her shoulder.

"The phone was activated for only a moment, sir. Two pings would indicate less than thirty seconds before it was turned off."

She continued to navigate her mouse through a software program that displayed a map of North and South America. She continued to narrow down the size of the map, using the coordinates of the satellite reporting the contact in relation to Earth at the precise time it was received.

The Jackal leaned back in her chair and exhaled. "There. That's the best we can do for now. But it's something." She pointed to the monitor that revealed a map containing Brazil, Venezuela, Colombia, Panama, and Nicaragua.

"That's a lot of territory," mumbled Ghost.

"Yes, sir, it is. However, it confirms my earlier theory that the

Starhopper—if being piloted by AI, or with the assistance of AI—would seek this region of the Americas to land as opposed to the United States, where the meteor activity in the upper atmosphere was more significant."

Ghost began to wander the office, pausing momentarily to stare at the photograph of Colonel Robinson on the wall. "We don't have enough to go to NASA yet. Plus, protocol requires me to go through this ass clown."

"I agree, sir. We need more information; plus I need another ping contact to ensure this was not an anomaly."

Ghost continued to think. He closed the door and addressed the Jackal in a hushed voice. "I'll probably lose my job for what I'm about to say, and if you'd like to excuse yourself from duty due to the danger posed by the asteroid debris, I'll understand."

"Sir, I'm not going anywhere unless you order me to. And then I'd just go home and do it."

Ghost stood and laughed. "You're a spunky one, aren't you?"

"My dad always said I've got spunk. I didn't really like it back then. Kids don't want to be known as being spunky. They wanna be smart, beautiful, or athletic. Being spunky was the functional equivalent of being cute, which in my mind meant something less than beautiful."

Ghost smiled and shook his head. "Spunky."

"Yeah, I know. Anyway, sir, with all due respect, I'm all in. What do you want to do?"

Ghost took a deep breath and responded, "Find our people and tell no one. If they're in danger, I want trained professionals to get them home, not a bunch of scientists followed by an army of media and paparazzi."

The Jackal nodded and got back to work.

CHAPTER 21

Unknown Jungle Compound
South America

Gunner scrambled to cover up the crude drawings that he and the boy had made in the dirt while the brutal guard grabbed the kid by the hair and dragged him away from Gunner's cell door. This infuriated Gunner, who lashed out, making no attempt to hide the fact he was free of his wrist cuffs.

"Hey, asshole! Leave the kid alone. You wanna come down here? I've got something for ya!"

Gunner balled his fists, steeling for a fight. He waited for the man to return, grinding his teeth as the anger built up inside him.

Until he was hit with a blast from a high-pressure water hose. The water stung him, ripping into the skin of his chest and opening the wounds created by the cattle prod. He retreated to the corner of the cell and turned his back to the onslaught, allowing the skin to peel off in chunks as he attempted to protect his face and genitals.

Then the water stopped, but his cell door was quickly opened and he was shoved against the wall, causing his chin to bleed. Two men pulled his hands behind his back and cuffed him again. This time, however, he wasn't left in the cell. They dragged him into the hallway and pulled him towards the exit, periodically smacking his face against the concrete wall.

Gunner shook the water out of his eyes and took in his surroundings. There were wooden cell doors lining the hall, with small slits in the center to allow the passage of food trays. He glanced down at the openings as he was dragged along. Every one of them contained a set of morose, defeated eyes peering out.

"Movimiento!" one of the guards shouted as he pushed Gunner into a door frame, causing him to stumble. The other guard had a death grip on his wrist cuffs, and despite Gunner's best efforts, he wasn't able to wriggle away from his clutches.

Seconds later, he was in the bright sunshine in the middle of a compound. Pain seared through his head as the suddenly bright light aggravated his concussion symptoms. At first, he closed his eyes, giving them several seconds to adjust to the light. After a moment, he barely could open them to view the compound.

He stumbled and fell to the ground, earning him a kick to the groin. Doubled over in pain, Gunner studied the compound. He counted seven or eight structures of various sizes and shapes, all constructed in a circular fashion around a central courtyard. A concrete fountain, which no longer pumped water through the angel figurine that sat atop it, partially obscured his view of a gate that appeared to be ten feet tall and made of wood planks.

He was brusquely pulled up by the stronger of the two guards and shoved forward toward a building that resembled a barn. As they approached, the smell of farm animals filled his nostrils. Hay, feed, and manure reminded him of days he'd spent on his grandfather's farm in Tennessee as a boy.

The other guard, the one who'd pulled the boy away from the cell by his hair, did the same to Gunner. His neck snapped back, the sudden movement sending a jolt of pain down his spine. His body was seriously battered, and he wondered how much more he could take.

He was about to find out.

He was shoved into the barn, where several more guards, reeking of sweat and alcohol, awaited him. They grabbed him by the arms and shoved him onto a wooden chair in the center of the barn, punching him as they did. He was restrained by a larger rope tied around his torso several times. The hemp caused his wounds to burn, and the tightness restricted his breathing.

One last blow to his face was administered. Blood began to trickle out of Gunner's mouth, the metallic taste causing his empty stomach to turn. His eyes searched wildly inside the barn in an attempt to discern what was going to happen next. When a tall, dark silhouette appeared in the barn's opening, holding a wand or baton of some sort, he understood.

The man in the dark suit and cowboy boots approached Gunner slowly, creating an atmosphere of fear and drama. He was carrying a cattle prod similar to the one that had been used on Gunner in the cell, only larger.

His captor wasted no time getting to work. The man jabbed the cattle prod into Gunner's midsection and then pulled the trigger, sending countless volts of electricity into his body. Gunner shook violently and his bladder released, causing him to urinate on his chair and the hay beneath him.

The guards let out an uproar of laughter. They referred to him as pig, cow, and the universal word of ridicule in the Spanish-speaking world—*cabrón*, which literally meant male goat but could be applied to nearly any situation depending on the context.

"My name is Jorge Barrera Blanco. I tell you this because you will not leave here alive, Señor Gunner Fox!"

Blanco shifted his grip on the cattle prod, allowing a fat droplet of blood to fall off the tip of his preferred weapon and splash onto Gunner's thigh. As he spoke, the barn became suddenly silent, allowing the impact of the dripping blood to make an audible splat. Blanco glanced down at the crimson smattering of blood as it dripped down Gunner's leg, and smiled.

Gunner tried to control his breathing. The tightness of the rope coupled with the humid conditions in the barn was causing him to hyperventilate. He sat upright, allowing more room for his diaphragm to expand, filling his lungs with much-needed oxygen. He disregarded the stench of manure and focused on his breathing.

Blanco pressed the sharp tips of the cattle prod against Gunner's right cheek, puncturing the skin and drawing blood. "What are you doing here, DEA Agent Gunner Fox? Why are you alone? Are you lost? Are you here to rob me like so many other American scum have tried? What?"

Blanco screamed the last word and sent more volts of energy into Gunner's body, this time placing the cattle prod dangerously close to his heart.

Gunner couldn't help himself, and he screamed, "Arrgghh!"

This drew a sadistic smile from Blanco, who walked around Gunner, holding the cattle prod in the air triumphantly. "Yes, you will soon talk, *cabrón!*"

Blanco took the tip of the device and jabbed it into the ball of Gunner's throat, once again piercing the skin and drawing blood.

A thick glob of blood and saliva dripped from Gunner's mouth, down his chin and splattered on the seat between his legs. The fluids grabbed Blanco's attention, and he removed the cattle prod before forcing it between Gunner's legs. Gunner tried to clamp his legs together and squirm away, but two sets of powerful hands held him still.

"Answer my questions, mister DEA agent, and I will put away my toys. Tell me, how did you find me, and what are you doing on my property?"

Gunner's eyes spoke volumes. His hatred and desire to kill the man was unmistakable. He'd tortured men before, but not like this. There were ways to get answers without inflicting sadistic pain upon his fellow man.

Blanco leaned forward, pressing his weight against the handle of the cattle prod until it punctured the tender skin just above Gunner's crotch.

"You have not experienced pain, DEA man, until I pull this trigger again. You will beg me and God for mercy. *Comprende?*"

Gunner sneered and made a decision. He wasn't with the DEA, the sworn enemy of the drug cartels. He was a potential monetary asset, a kidnap victim whose life was valuable to his government. Certainly, the U.S. government had a policy against negotiating with hostage takers, but this was different.

"I'm not DEA," Gunner hissed. "I'm an astronaut."

His captors in the barn remained eerily silent until Blanco reared back and began to laugh. The chuckles and guffaws rose to a crescendo as if Gunner had uttered the most hilarious words this group of criminals had ever heard.

Blanco strutted around the barn, laughing until he momentarily lost his composure. *"Astronauta?"* He continued to laugh, especially when one of his portly guards began running through the barn in a circle, making a whooshing sound in a feeble attempt to emulate a rocket lifting off.

"Yes, I am an astronaut."

Blanco rushed toward Gunner and hit him over the head with the cattle prod. Then he twisted a dial and crammed the device into Gunner's side, twisting the tip as he administered the largest thrust of electricity yet.

"Arrrggghhh!" Gunner shouted.

"DEA liar!" Blanco shouted back, spit flying out of his mouth he was so angry.

Gunner tried to recover. "I'm not lying! Don't you people have internet? Look it up. My name is Gunner Fox, and my spaceship crashed across the river. Go see for yourself."

Blanco scowled and gritted his teeth. He jabbed Gunner in the chest again, sending more electricity into his weakened body.

"I will get the truth from you, DEA man, or I will feed you to the jaguars!"

Gunner was about to lose consciousness. He tried to gather his strength to resist the torture, but even the truth wasn't working. If he lied and falsely admitted he was with the Drug Enforcement Agency, he'd be killed instantly. The truth was his only salvation although he doubted it would set him free.

He decided on a different tactic, one that might serve to call the cavalry. "I have a satellite phone. It was in my bag the kid found by the wreckage."

Out of the shadows of the barn, a man approached Blanco. He was similarly dressed and was clean-shaven, unlike the rest of the crew. He looked more like an accountant than a member of a brutal drug cartel, but then, Gunner surmised, somebody had to count the money.

"This bag?" asked Blanco.

"Yes. The boy found it and I followed him here. I just want my phone, and I'll forget everything about this place, and you."

Blanco chuckled and turned to the accountant-looking assistant. He tossed Gunner's duffle bag to the side, and the man handed him the satellite phone.

Blanco held it high overhead and began to laugh.

"*Mis amigos*, DEA Agent Gunner Fox wants to make a phone call. Just like the jails the DEA put our people in. One phone call."

The men in the barn began to grumble and look angrily at Gunner. He suspected that any one of them would relish the opportunity to beat him to death simply because he was American and possibly with the DEA.

"Please, I'll prove it to you. Just—"

Blanco cut him off. "Ahh, do you want to call your mommy?" he asked sarcastically. "Or maybe your friends in Washington?"

He spit on Gunner and began to laugh. He powered on the satellite phone and began wildly punching the illuminated buttons.

"*Hola? Hola?* Is this the DEA? Gunner Fox says please send help!"

The men began to laugh, and Blanco threw the satellite phone across the room until it careened off the barnboard walls and landed in a pile of hay.

He turned back to Gunner and rammed the cattle prod into his throat. He set his jaw and scowled as he pulled the trigger, shaking Gunner with massive bursts of electricity until darkness swept over him.

CHAPTER 22

Defense Threat Reduction Agency
Fort Belvoir, Virginia

"Holy crap! Holy crap!" exclaimed the Jackal as she pushed away from her desk to jump out of her chair. Her chair rolled backwards, crashed against the wall, and began to spin in a circle, creating enough centrifugal force to make Sir Isaac Newton proud.

She flung her office door open and sprang into the hallway, looking rapidly in both directions. She began to run toward Ghost's office and then caught herself as a uniformed MP emerged from the break room with a cup of coffee. She slowed herself to a brisk walk and casually approached Ghost's office.

With the MP watching her, she lightly tapped on the door until she heard Ghost invite her in.

"Yes, Cuccinelli?" he asked.

"Sir, I've got 'em," she said excitedly. "I mean, I've got the precise position within a fifty-mile radius."

"Where?"

"Colombia, sir. Toward the Panamanian border."

"The Darién Gap?" he asked.

She grimaced and nodded. "Um, yessir."

Ghost sighed and hesitated for a moment. "Okay. Okay, I'm glad we've got something. I don't have to tell you that there aren't many places on the planet that are worse than where the crew of the Starhopper has touched down."

"Yessir, I'm aware. I have some work to do before I can conclusively determine a location. I need to access the DEA databases as well as the FBI missing persons files. They are full of

109

information gathered from local investigations throughout the area, both in Panama and Colombia."

Ghost was still somewhat subdued. He picked up a pen and began to tap it on his desk. He dropped it and then leaned forward in his chair, staring at his phone.

"Um, sir, this is good news. I mean, I can—"

Ghost raised his left hand and stopped the young FBI agent. "I'm sorry, please don't misunderstand. I applaud your efforts, and this is fantastic news. I just don't know what to do with it."

The Jackal stepped backward, glanced in the hallway to confirm it was empty, and then gently closed the door. She spoke in a hushed tone. "I assume you're referring to notifying NASA, the DOD, and the administration?"

Ghost nodded. "Who am I to make this decision?" he asked rhetorically before continuing. "You have gone beyond the call of duty to locate our people, and I now have an obligation to pass it up the chain of command."

The Jackal shrugged and smiled. "Sir, what chain of command would that be? I understand that there are people within the government that you take directives from, but are they necessarily your boss or commanding officer, since you're technically no longer in the military?"

"It's an odd position to be in," he began in reply. "Off the books works both ways. If I do something that doesn't sit well with the president or that blows up in my face, they can easily disavow the operation. Likewise, if I decide to handle a matter in a certain way without consulting with the people who assign these black ops to me, then they can't necessarily complain, can they?"

The Jackal understood and, despite her criminal justice training, decided to assist Ghost in circumventing the law and military protocols. She stood as tall as her five-foot-three-inch slightly built frame would allow.

"Sir, I know what *going rogue* means. I also am fully aware of the consequences. At this moment, nobody other than the two of us knows about the Starhopper's whereabouts. If you're concerned about their well-being and have genuine doubts as to whether another agency can bring them out of the Darién Gap, then you should trust your gut. And let me say, if you go down, I'll be honored to go down with you, sir."

Ghost leaned back in his chair, studied the Jackal and then clasped his hands behind his head. "I like your confidence, Cuccinelli."

"You mean my spunk, right, sir?"

Ghost chuckled. "Yeah, that too. I need to know something. You're gonna access both FBI and DEA files that are unrelated to any active operation we're involved in. Aren't you concerned about getting caught?"

The Jackal laughed. "Sir, puhleeze. I'm the Jackal. The last time I was caught was the day before I was recruited into the bureau. Don't worry about me, sir. I'll gather all the intel that's available. I'll leave the extraction team up to you."

Ghost leaned forward and smiled. "That's easy. Let's get to it."

CHAPTER 23

Fort Mills
Near Delta, Alabama

Darkness had set in, and the group anxiously awaited the transport from Maxwell Air Force Base outside Montgomery, Alabama. The initial celebration and exuberance was soon tamped down by a dose of reality. The fact that Gunner's satellite phone had made it back to Earth was cause for hope. The fact that nobody had used it to call for help was a matter of great concern.

Pop tried to reach logical conclusions. For one, he argued, only a human being was capable of turning the device on and off. Perhaps a trained or overly curious ape could do it, but there were no apes in South and Central America. Pop relayed at length the details of a National Geographic special he'd watched that differentiated between so-called New World monkeys found in the Americas and Old World monkeys in Africa and Asia.

The consensus among the three refugees to Fort Mills was that the satellite phone had been accessed by a human that either didn't understand how to use it or, because of some injury, was unable to.

It was the latter theory that caused Pop to become concerned for the safety of his son. Cam and Bear gave him the obligatory pep talk, attempting to reassure him that Gunner was a survivor.

They withheld their knowledge of the Darién Gap. It was considered the most dangerous jungle in the world for many reasons, the least of which had to do with the animals that inhabited the region.

"I hear the chopper," announced Bear as he returned inside from the front porch. The rain had finally stopped and an unusual chill had set upon the Southeastern United States. Meteorites were now battering the central part of the U.S., and Ghost had warned them that traveling by chopper to Fort Belvoir was risky. They could be dodging bullets that came at them faster than any projectile imaginable.

The threat didn't deter them from doing what it took to rescue their friend. *Ride or die, they stuck together.* The mantra they'd adopted hadn't changed as a result of the circumstances.

"Okay, Pop, we've got to head through the woods to meet the chopper," began Cam. "Listen, you know we're gonna do everything we can to bring our boy home, right?"

Pop began to well up in tears. He nodded his head but couldn't manage to speak.

Bear tried to help. "That's right, Pop. We've got this. We'll find Gunner and be back before you know it. Now, are you good with the weapons I fixed up for you?"

"I am. I plan on keeping the generator off except during the daytime. I've got the curtains pulled, and I'll only burn a single candle."

Cam hugged him. "We don't want you to be paranoid, just aware there are people out there who may need food and shelter. Sadly, you have to be skeptical of everyone."

He smiled and hugged her back. "That's why I'm glad we hid things away and packed some provisions in the plane. If I have to bug out due to the fire over the ridge, or some bad dudes showing up on the doorstep, I'll at least have the basics with me."

"All right," continued Cam. "If you have to leave, you're gonna try Dog Island first, right?"

"Yes, but only if I'm forced out of here. We're right in the middle of this storm, and the tsunami threat will be with us until Monday night or so."

"Good. Your second option is Maxwell Air Force Base. Ghost has already cleared your aircraft and N-number with flight control. Remember, don't use Ghost's name. Simply identify who you are, give them your plane's registration number, and everything should be fine." The registration number of an aircraft was commonly referred to as an N-number or tail number.

Bear handed him the satellite phone they used to stay in contact with Ghost. "We wrote down the frequencies for you to monitor on the ham radio, and you can watch for our call on the satphone."

Cam added, "But, Pop, just 'cause we don't call doesn't mean there's trouble, or, um, you know."

Pop smiled. "I understand. I've lived with you three going off to do what it is you do for years. I've never doubted that you'd come home in one piece. Battered and bruised at times, but home nonetheless."

"Exactly," said Bear. He nodded toward the door, indicating to Cam that they needed to get going. The three exchanged hugs again and Pop led them outside. As they hoisted their gear and jogged down the driveway, Pop hollered to them, "Godspeed, Patriots!"

PART THREE

Sunday, April 29

CHAPTER 24

Eight Years Prior
Fox Residence
DeFuniak Springs, Florida

Heather Fox helped her husband ease into the claw-foot tub in their master bathroom. She fought back the tears as she examined his body, which was covered in bruises, cuts, and skin ripped open to reveal pink flesh underneath. He slowly lowered himself into the warm bath supplemented by Epsom salts. She'd warned him that the bath salts would cause his wounds to sting, but he insisted, saying that it was the pain from the unseen wounds underneath his skin that bothered him the most. Heather wasn't sure if he was referring to a physical pain or mental anguish.

Once he closed his eyes and began to relax, she knelt down behind him and gently washed his body with Gerber's baby washcloths she used to wash her face at night. They were much softer than the more common cotton kind. Gunner's skin was raw enough without a coarse washcloth to aggravate it.

Heather chose to stay quiet, stifling her desire to quiz him on the details of what had been done to him. His arrival at their home was completely unexpected, as he'd told her that he'd likely be gone for weeks. She'd suspected something was wrong the night before when she saw several dark-colored vehicles bearing blue and white government tags drive slowly past their house.

Gunner had always cautioned her against rushing to judgment or worrying unnecessarily. If something had truly gone awry on one of his missions, she'd hear from Cam or his superior officer first.

He exhaled and pushed himself a little higher in the tub. The bleeding on his chest had stopped, and he was able to flex his arms and legs to work out the soreness in his muscles. It had been a long trek home, one that tested his mettle as much as the torture he'd been put through.

Gunner broke the silence. He reached his arm out of the water and squeezed Heather's hand, who continuously nurtured his body by gently washing it.

"Honey, let's talk about this one time, and then never again, okay?"

Heather reluctantly nodded and stood up. She wandered to the bathroom window overlooking Lake DeFuniak, which was across Circle Drive from their century-old home. According to local folklore, the perfectly round lake had been created by a meteorite. This made for a good story to tell tourists, although most likely it was a sinkhole that remained filled by an underground stream flowing from twin lakes to the west of the town.

She sighed and allowed the tears to flow. She kept her back to him so that he couldn't see them, but Gunner knew his wife too well.

"Honey, I'm sorry," he apologized unnecessarily.

Heather looked upward and tucked her hands inside the long sleeves of her sweater. Her sniffles gave away her tears, so she wiped her face and turned to look at him. "There's nothing to apologize for. I just wish I could wrap my head around why this was necessary."

Gunner squeezed out the wet cloth and turned on the faucet, allowing cool water to soak it. He wiped his face and scrubbed at some dried blood matted in his hair. "It's part of my job. If a mission doesn't go as planned, I've got to always be prepared for anything. Heather, I mean anything."

She frowned. "Look at you, Gunner. What they did to you was barbaric. It's torture!"

"Honey, it could be worse. I have to be prepared for the day when the enemy takes me hostage. That's what this was all about."

She stood defiantly now with her hands firmly planted on her hips. She shook her head in disagreement. "Well, they oughta change the name from SERE school to torture school, because that's all it is. A bunch of sick bastards who get their jollies by torturing good men like you because they're too weak to go through it themselves."

Gunner had explained the purpose of SERE school to her when he was notified by his commanding officer that he was assigned to the location in Washington state. Founded in the aftermath of the Korean War, the military began to train U.S. service members to withstand enemy interrogation. SERE—an acronym for survival, evasion, resistance, and escape—developed over time into a program that was especially useful for Special Forces personnel like Gunner.

The trainees were taught to adhere to the Code of Conduct, six articles that were ingrained into their psyche so that they would not break under interrogation. Then they were submitted to all of the advanced interrogation techniques utilized by the enemy through the years, including the controversial method of waterboarding.

The first steps in the SERE school involved psychological methods of breaking the prisoner down. Loud music, sleep deprivation, and withholding food and water were just the beginning of the torture.

Solitary confinement was next. Gunner had been forced into a small box with only a few holes allowing him to breathe. His captors then administered the *box treatment*—jumping jacks, running in place, and incessant pounding on top of the box.

Then came the interrogation. Round after round of questions. With each refusal, a slap to the face was earned by the prisoner. After subsequent rounds, which Gunner resisted, the torture became more brutal.

During those few days, he'd been beaten, starved, stripped naked, hosed down, and electrocuted in the chilled environment of the concrete cell. He was nearly hypothermic, shivering so bad at times that he couldn't speak.

"Honey, the thing is, I think I outlasted everyone else who'd been assigned to SERE school with me. When I escaped, all of the other cells appeared empty, and it wasn't because they were receiving a beatdown. They'd been scrubbed clean. I was the last one."

"Well, congrats, airman," she said sarcastically. "Can we expect a ribbon or a pay raise?"

Gunner sighed and reached for her hand. She resisted him for a moment, standing with her arms folded in front of her in an attempt to close off her feelings. Finally, she succumbed and pulled a chair up next to the tub.

They held hands for a moment, and then Gunner explained, "I know this may not be what you want to hear, but what I've been through may save my life someday."

A few more tears rolled down Heather's cheeks, but she wiped them away and smiled. "I understand. I just wish—"

A pounding on their front door cut off her sentence.

"What the hell?" asked Heather.

Gunner exhaled and began to push himself out of the tub. He pointed toward the towel that was draped over the sink. "I need to get dressed," he began. "Those are probably the MPs."

"Police? Why?"

Gunner chuckled. "Well, interestingly enough, I broke the rules."

"What rules? Look what they did to you. What kind of rules allowed for that?" Heather was incredulous.

"We were told up front that we weren't allowed to escape," said Gunner as he wiped himself dry and made his way to the closet.

The pounding on the door grew louder, causing Heather to look outside, where she saw two base police vehicles from Eglin idling in the driveway. She spun around to address Gunner's explanation. "I thought it was SERE school, and one of the E's stands for *escape*."

"That's true. But I was required to remain there until it was over."

"Fox, open up!" a voice bellowed from their front porch, followed by more pounding.

Gunner quickly finished dressing and then turned to kiss his wife. "Honey, they might arrest me, but it'll be okay."

"That's bullshit!" she exclaimed as the tears began to flow again. "Can't you just tell them that you escaped for the sake of your health? I mean, look what they put you through."

Gunner chuckled and gave his wife one final hug before he

surrendered. As he walked toward the stairwell, he turned.

"No, I'm gonna tell them the truth. I escaped for their sake. If I didn't leave, I would've killed them all."

CHAPTER 25

Present Day
Defense Threat Reduction Agency
Fort Belvoir, Virginia

The two pilots of the recently upgraded AgustaWestland AW149 helicopter had their hands full during the trip from Delta, Alabama, to Fort Belvoir. Primarily built for use by the Egyptian Air Force, the U.S. Air Force operated several dozen for transportation of personnel on short trips of seven hundred miles or less. As a chopper pilot, Bear was impressed by the chopper's handling, and thankful.

"Here comes another one!" he shouted into the internal communications system, causing Cam to pull the headset away from her ears. The pilots had already muted his set so he didn't distract them as they flew at ten thousand feet above the ground.

Meteorites could be seen breaking through the atmosphere and exploding to Earth in the cloudless dark skies. Approaching midnight, air travel was usually light anyway, but the FAA had grounded all commercial traffic two days ago, and military traffic was authorized on an emergency basis only.

While the pilots, and their passengers, could see the meteorites streaking through the sky, it was impossible to react to them. Plus, the approaching space rocks that burned up in the atmosphere caused several false alarms as they traveled. All they could do was race to Fort Belvoir and hope luck was on their side.

Cam remained calm and mostly quiet during the trip. She needed the hours of relative solitude, other than Bear's occasional excited utterances, to transition from caretaker of Pop and Fort Mills to warrior.

Over the years, she'd hardened inside. Her childhood was not unlike what many girls went through, but was complicated somewhat because she enjoyed the company of boys. Initially, it presented many challenges. Over time, as she grew into a young woman, this upbringing served her well.

A smile came across her face as she recalled an event when she and Gunner were twelve years old. Cam had developed physically before most of the other girls her age in the sixth grade. During the prior summer, her female figure began to form and she became more attractive, not the tomboy the kids enjoyed playing pickup football games with.

As the new school year began, she was initially teased playfully about her breasts, but eventually the teasing went too far. Her chest was the constant brunt of unwanted attention by the predominantly twelve-year-old boys who were entering the age of puberty. Many would grab at her in an attempt to touch them, and eventually they became overly aggressive.

When Cam grew up, the era of *boys will be boys* was over for the most part. That wasn't necessarily the case when you lived in military housing. Going to someone of authority in school was frowned upon as snitching and was an indication you were weak.

Getting your military parent involved was an even worse idea. Oftentimes, in a stressful job like defending their country, service personnel might overreact to their daughter or son being the brunt of bullying. An emotional, physical confrontation between military parents, or their spouses, might result in the end of a promising career.

Cam did her best to repel the unwanted advances, but one day, the situation got out of hand.

She'd just finished her physical education class, the last of the day for her, and was headed back to the locker rooms underneath the school's gymnasium. Several older boys, eighth graders, were waiting near the bleachers as Cam approached.

Before she knew it, they'd encircled her and began to taunt her about her appearance. Cam tried to cover up her body, embarrassed by the way they spoke to her. When she tried to push her way past to get to the safety of the girls' locker room, they blocked her path.

That was when the incident got physical. As she'd endured before, the boys began to grab at her tee shirt. One wrenched her breast so hard Cam screamed in pain. The other boys began to laugh and became emboldened by the perceived sign of weakness.

She was knocked to the ground, and two boys dropped to their knees and began pawing at her. Cam, who was much smaller than the older boys, tried to break free of their grasps, but couldn't. As she flailed about, she caught a glimpse of rapid movement out of the corner of her eye.

It was Gunner.

He'd heard the screams and the boys' taunts. Later, he acknowledged he didn't know it was Cam being assaulted. He just saw that a pack of wolves was attacking their helpless prey.

She grinned, remembering how referring to her as helpless prey earned her best friend a slug to the arm. She was not helpless, she insisted. Only *temporarily inconvenienced.*

In any event, the beatdown administered to the four eighth graders served to put the male population of their school on notice. Cameron Mills was off-limits, and if you thought otherwise, ask Gunner Fox.

From that day forward, Gunner had become her protector, the big brother she never had. The two became inseparable until her father was reassigned and they parted ways during high school. The two kids had matured enough to handle the separation and continued to keep in touch via social media. But the bond they'd formed that day and their mantra, *ride or die,* would stick with them for life.

Now it was Cam's turn to return the favor. She knew Gunner was still alive. They had a connection, kind of like identical twins. When one experienced joy, so did the other. When one was hurting, they did it together regardless of distance or circumstances.

Cam could feel that Gunner was in pain. Not emotionally, but certainly physically.

She pressed her face against the window of the helicopter and watched another small meteorite zip past in the distance, generating a massive ball of fire as it hit the ground.

She smiled, thinking of the pain that Gunner was enduring. Not in a sadistic sort of way but, rather, relishing the fact that her best friend was alive.

Twenty minutes later, the chopper made a hurried, rough landing, the pilots every bit as anxious to get on the ground as Cam and Bear were. It was just after midnight and Fort Belvoir appeared to be largely deserted at this hour except for several office lights along the west wing of the DTRA building. Offices, Cam recalled, that belonged to Ghost, the Jackal, and their support staff.

"Thank you, gentlemen," said Bear as the door was opened and he hopped out of the helicopter. "Glad to have my feet on the ground. Apreesh!" The odd word was Bear's unique way of saying *I appreciate it.*

Cam provided the brave pilots a thumbs-up and they responded by saluting the major. At times like these, Cam didn't think in terms of rank and protocol. Her mind was elsewhere. A remote location in Latin America where the Starhopper and its crew awaited rescue.

"Come on, Bear. Let's get briefed and then wheels up to get our boy home."

"I'm with ya," the big man bellowed. "Hey, I wonder if they'll assign us a bird like the tilt-rotor we took into Russia. That ride was sweet and I hated ditching it in Alaska."

Cam shook her head in disbelief. *Is that all boys think about is their toys and, well* ... she laughed off the rest of her thought.

Personally, while she was fond of boys, she didn't think about the toys very often, although she often referred to herself as a *gun-whore.* It was a vulgar slang reference, to be sure, but a female who prided herself on having a large variety of shoes or handbags often referred to herself as a *bag-whore* or a *shoe-whore.* So, in Cam's mind, someone like herself who enjoyed having a wide variety of weapons at her disposal was, in fact, a gun-whore.

The security door to the DTRA building swung open and Ghost, together with two security personnel, waved them over. Bear and Cam double-timed it inside the building just as another flash of light streaked across the sky.

CHAPTER 26

Defense Threat Reduction Agency
Fort Belvoir, Virginia

Ghost ushered the duo through security and hurried them down the hallway to the Jackal's office. After some pleasantries were exchanged, Cam and Bear were briefed on how the Jackal had searched for the Starhopper. Then she explained how she'd narrowed down the location of the satellite phone to the Darién Gap. A large television monitor had been wheeled into her office on an aluminum easel that she accessed via Bluetooth. An image of the region was displayed for the group to study as she and Ghost led the briefing.

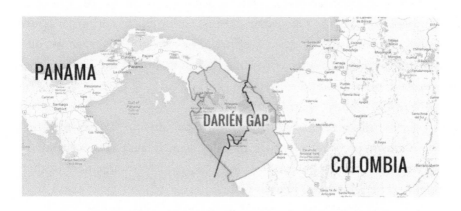

Ghost gave the team a general overview. "Panama's location connecting Central and South America has made it a key transit point for the transportation of drugs and human trafficking out of Colombia, with the ultimate destination being the States.

"The Panamanian government is well known for negotiating areas of refuge for drug cartels and other criminal organizations, especially in what is widely known as the most dangerous jungle in the world— the Darién Gap."

The Jackal added to Ghost's statement from a law enforcement perspective. "Panama has an extremely weak judicial system and high levels of corruption that have allowed transnational cartels and money launderers to stake a claim in the region. Between the Colombian guerilla groups and the Mexican drug cartels, this stretch of Panama is completely lawless."

Ghost continued. "What makes the Darién Gap the most dangerous jungle in the world is more than the wide variety of animals, reptiles, and insects that are deadly, but this conglomeration of brutal criminal enterprises we've described. Basically, Panama has ceded the territory to them in exchange for staying away from the Panama Canal Zone, which, as you know, is critical to the free flow of goods through the Americas."

Cam pointed to the map. "This is a big area to cover, and from what I can see, half of it is in Panama and the lower half is in Colombia."

Ghost interrupted her. "That's why the politics of this are complicated. Despite the circumstances, Colombia would insist upon being involved in any rescue effort. They would never allow our military on their soil unaccompanied, even to rescue the heroes who saved the planet from destruction."

"Freakin' idiots," mumbled Bear.

"I can't disagree, Lieutenant," Ghost continued. "Then, from the Panamanian perspective, their unholy alliance with these criminals prevents them from sanctioning any U.S. military involvement in that region, especially in the Darién Gap."

"Let me guess," started Bear. "We're on our own, right?"

"Obvi," replied Cam as she gave her partner a playful shove. She turned to Ghost. "Sir, if you've confirmed that the radio is active and there are no verbal transmissions, can we assume we're dealing with a hostage situation?"

Ghost gestured to the Jackal and stepped aside. She changed the screen and provided an overview of the jungle. "We believe Gunner and the Starhopper crew are somewhere in this vicinity near the Atrato River. With our satellites falling like dominoes, I've been unable to identify a precise location, but I can say with a degree of certainty they are in the region of the jungle referred to as Peye on the map."

"Aptly named, I might add," said Ghost.

"Why's that?" asked Bear.

"In Colombia, the word *peye* is most commonly used as an adjective that denotes something bad. They mean it."

Cam sighed and stood. She walked toward the monitor and turned to the Jackal. "You have to have some idea within this radius, don't you?"

"I do. I accessed the DEA database to find the GPS coordinates of known drug cartel hideouts and residences of their kingpins. Unlike the Mexican cartels, who pride themselves on having large ranches and elaborate homes, the Colombians tend to live simply, using the jungle's foliage and tree canopies to avoid detection from our prying eyes. That said, there are several in the Peye region."

"We'll do a flyby and get a closer look," suggested Bear.

"Not a good idea, Lieutenant," cautioned Ghost. "A flyby is suggested, but not a closer look as you said. Your bird will be equipped with sufficient long-range optics to determine where the Starhopper crashed, and then you can triangulate that position with the known cartel locations within the surrounding jungle. If you fly in low, you could be seen. If our people are held hostage, they'll die, and then you'll find yourself in one helluva firefight. This mission requires surprise, not muscle."

"Roger that, sir," said Cam, who was taking the lead on this mission. She turned to the Jackal. "I assume you can give us the benefit of all this intel for the flight south."

"Already set, Major," said Ghost, who continued, "Together with your flight plan, a landing zone identified, and an extraction plan."

"How are we getting there?" asked Bear. "It's too far for a chopper, and I doubt a pilot will wanna ferry us through the meteorites crashing to Earth."

"Well, as luck would have it, elements of the USS *Harry S. Truman* Carrier Strike Group 8 were redeployed to the Caribbean Sea as part of the Defense Department's goal to guard our southern flank from any ill-advised Russian hostilities. We've got your gear ready and we'll get you to the *Truman* CSG. From there, you'll be on your own. As is always the case, you're disavowed with no support and no love from Washington."

"Are we going in by water or land, sir?" asked Bear.

"They'll probably have an HH-60H Seahawk bearing Panamanian Coast Guard flags. This will let you avoid scrutiny by either government. Plus, everything is in disarray down there. One more rescue chopper in the air won't garner any attention."

Cam was antsy, anxious to leave, but she had another question. "Sir, if we're disavowed, what do we do after we find Gunner and our astronauts?"

Ghost quickly replied, "Bring them back to the *Truman* and I'll deal with the consequences of the operation."

Bear spoke up. "What about those three Russian assholes who killed Heather?"

The room fell silent, as those responsible for her murder were on all of their minds.

Ghost turned to Cam. "Major, this is your op once you leave this office. I trust you'll use your best judgment and discretion based upon conditions on the ground."

"Roger that, sir. Let's go, Bear."

Nothing else had to be said.

CHAPTER 27

NORAD
Cheyenne Mountain, Colorado

President Mack Watson paced the battle cab deep inside NORAD. The White House physician had forced him, with the assistance of the First Lady, Patty, to return to his bedroom for some rest. That had lasted about thirty minutes before he surreptitiously evaded the two gatekeepers outside his door and made his way back to the center of activity at NORAD.

The nation was under attack, not from a foreign enemy, but from something natural or, in many respects, supernatural. In a way, it was poetic justice that the brunt of the meteorite activity was directed toward Russia.

Moscow had kept their knowledge of IM86 secreted away, allowing their greed to get in the way of what was best for humanity. Based upon NASA's data and the intelligence reports, the Russians were incapable of accomplishing the complicated diversion techniques to steer the asteroid away from destroying the planet.

It was all about firsts and one-upmanship for Putin. He was constantly thwarted from reconstituting the former Soviet Union through a combination of U.S. foreign policy and covert countermeasures. His level of jealousy for all things related to America resulted in a rash decision to keep the details of this planet-killing asteroid hidden from the rest of the world.

As a result, the late-developing mission had caused the bulk of the debris field to wreak havoc on Eurasia, which stretched from Eastern Europe to North Korea. Power outages, destroyed buildings, and loss of life were being reported across Mother Russia.

President Watson, however, was unconcerned at the moment with what was happening beyond the borders of the country he loved. He was singularly focused on helping Americans through this catastrophe, one that was unparalleled in modern history.

The largest reported meteorite, with a width of three hundred yards, had struck in a desolate part of Southwestern Nevada near Boundary Peak. Located in the White Mountains at the border of California and Nevada, it rose thirteen thousand feet above sea level, the highest point in the state.

Or it was, anyway. The impact of the large meteorite struck the peak with the force of a thousand atomic bombs, obliterating it and nearby Montgomery Peak. The rocky debris from the blast created a mushroom cloud reminiscent of a nuclear detonation. As the rock and dirt lifted skyward, creating the stem of the mushroom, a cap formed at the top, spreading out laterally. The vaporized rock was fused into small molten spherules, soaring into the atmosphere as a giant plume of white-hot marbles.

At the top of the mushroom cloud, these spherules cooled, solidified and began a rapid descent back to Earth in a two-hundred-mile radius of the impact crater that was once Boundary Peak.

As the spherules rained down upon the Western United States, friction with the atmosphere heated them up once again, creating a pulse of hot, infrared radiation, much like the way a heating coil in an oven emits heat. The spherules traveled at near the speed of light as they returned to Earth.

People were caught unaware from San Francisco to Portland, and from Las Vegas to Salt Lake City. All at once, in this entire region, the incredible heat pulse generated by the spherules cooked anything that was alive. Only those located in adequate shelters were spared unless they were standing too close to glass windows.

The brightly lit hotels and casinos were pulverized as windows were shattered and millions of light bulbs were splattered with the debris. Those who didn't die from the intense heat were killed or badly injured by the flying glass.

Throughout the Sierra Nevada and the famed Yosemite National Park, wildfires burned out of control, threatening to wipe out all plant material as far south as the Sequoia National Forest.

The destruction caused by the impact at Boundary Peak would be seen as the worst of the remnants of IM86. The death toll would be the largest of any across the planet, and the cost of rebuilding was beyond estimation. However, the concerns were even more dire for President Watson.

An environmental disaster threatened the entire country. One that environmental engineers had warned Washington about for many years.

One hundred miles to the southeast of the impact crater at Boundary Peak was Yucca Mountain. By comparison, at an elevation of sixty-seven hundred square feet, the mountain was dwarfed by the larger peaks of the Sierra Nevada. But its stature was not its claim to fame.

Forty years prior to the arrival of IM86, Yucca Mountain became a high-level nuclear waste repository, one of the largest in the world. An estimated eighty thousand metric tons of long-term storage of nuclear waste had built up over the years, despite warnings of scientists that the former volcanic mountain had characteristics rendering it unsuitable to store the highly irradiated nuclear material.

The seismic fault lines that ran on both sides of the mountain were said to make the repository unstable. While there was little chance of future volcanic activity in the long-dormant volcano, the possibility of earthquakes was always a concern for geologists.

The United States Geological Survey, the USGS, had contacted NORAD about unusual seismic activity following the impact at Boundary Peak. Traditional areas of heightened monitoring like the Hayward Fault, east of San Francisco, and the Sierra Nevada Fault that ran along the eastern edge of the Sierra Nevada mountain block at the California-Nevada border, were showing signs of stress.

Sandwiched in between these two major fault lines was the Long Valley Caldera, one of the most underrated, potentially destructive volcanic systems in the Americas.

The location of the massive impact at Boundary Peak might not have been quite as devastating in terms of damage or loss of life as it could've been had it hit a major population center like Los Angeles or New York City, but the effect it had upon the fragile geologic conditions of the region would be felt for years to come.

"Mr. President!" shouted Maggie Fielding as she entered the room, followed closely by the chairman of the Joint Chiefs. "Sir, we received intelligence indicating increased Russian submarine activity along the Atlantic Seaboard. We have reports of electronic interference with our military communication and navigation systems."

The president turned to his top military advisor. "What measures are you taking in response?"

"Sir, we're repositioning all of our naval assets to the Eastern Seaboard. We've ordered Carrier Strike Group 8 to be redeployed from the Caribbean Sea, and NATO has been advised that we're recalling the Second Fleet from the North Atlantic as well."

"Are these subs only?" asked the president.

"So far, sir, although they've turned their Kirov-class battlecruisers and several Gorshkov frigates in our direction. They're moving slowly, but that could change."

The president turned his attention back to his chief of staff. "Have we reached out to Moscow through diplomatic channels?"

He began pacing the floor again as beads of sweat appeared on his forehead. He made his way to the small kitchen bar and nervously opened a bottle of water. His mind raced as he tried to consider which was the bigger threat to America, the remains of the asteroid or the Russians.

"They're making attempts now, sir, but thus far, our ambassador is getting the runaround," replied Fielding.

President Watson finished the water and closed his eyes. Anger built up inside him and he unconsciously crushed the plastic bottle until it was the size of a paper wad. He spun around and looked into the eyes of his advisors.

"Dammit to hell, what's wrong with Putin? I'm sick of this shit! And screw diplomatic channels. I want to talk to that bastard myself!"

CHAPTER 28

Unknown Jungle Compound
Colombia, South America

Gunner lay shivering on the wet, muddy floor. Wave after wave of chills had overcome his body throughout the night as he was repeatedly doused with cold water, coupled with several jolts of electricity courtesy of his captor's cattle prod.

He was becoming dehydrated and resorted to lapping up water that pooled in the dirt. He'd consume anything to help quench his thirst, even his own urine, if he produced any.

Surprisingly, the interrogations had ceased after the session in the barn the day before. Gunner was puzzled by this because, generally, the purpose of torture was to elicit information. Perhaps the barbarous leader of the cartel believed Gunner's claim of being an astronaut. Maybe they'd finally had the boy lead them to the wreckage where he'd found Gunner's duffle bag. They might have searched his name on Google and confirmed he was telling the truth.

Or maybe they just wanted to continue their merciless and inhuman game of inflicting pain upon the American gringo.

Gunner had dealt with drug cartels before. For the most part, their criminal dealings focused on maintaining their territory, evading arrest, and making money. To be sure, stories of kidnappings, torture, and human trafficking accompanied any broad-range discussion of cartel activities.

He tried to keep in touch with his surroundings and especially sounds making their way into the holding cells. During his trip into the center of the compound, and even during his torture session in the barn, Gunner had stayed alert, cataloging what he'd observed.

One of the things he noticed as the night wore on, in between the constant attacks by the high-pressure water hose, was the fact that the frequency of meteorite activity had subsided considerably. And with the respite in the asteroid's attack, the drug business apparently picked up in the cartel's compound.

Convoys of trucks, their diesel engines creating a steady rumble, came and went throughout the night. At times, the guards entered the holding cells and dragged some of the women out, never to return. Hours later, they were replaced with other captives, who were admonished the same as Gunner with a stern rebuke when they attempted to speak to their fellow prisoners.

Gunner believed that he was deep in the mountainous region of the jungle based upon the overgrown foliage and the fact that he hadn't stumbled across any coca fields nearby. The large stream he'd encountered most likely flowed into a nearby river, which ultimately found its way into the Caribbean Sea or, depending on the crash site's location, the Pacific Ocean.

His failure to encounter locals cultivating the coca plants didn't surprise him, and the cartels rarely grew their own product. Their job was strictly packaging and distribution. All the coca was grown in either Bolivia, Peru, or Colombia, where, he assumed, he was being held, based upon the young boy's clothing.

In reality, cartels had become like supermarket chains. They bought coca and marijuana from local farmers, processed the drugs themselves, and then transported the drugs to America, the world's largest marketplace for illegal substances.

Human trafficking had become a byproduct of Latin America's intense desire to make a better life for themselves in the United States, regardless of their method or cost of entry. Young girls gave themselves up into a form of sex slavery as payment for their families to be transported into the land of opportunity. Others voluntarily became mules, carrying drugs through Mexico and across the border with the aid of the Mexican drug cartels.

It was a sickening business overall, and it stemmed from cartel compounds like the one where Gunner was being held. The drug trade was so lucrative that the prospects of being crushed by an incoming meteorite didn't concern these criminals one iota. Business was business, and America would always be open to consumption of their product, notwithstanding a temporary disruption courtesy of IM86.

Gunner was not asleep, nor was he fully awake. His mind was forcing itself to stay alert so that his body wouldn't suffer the wrath of his sadistic captors without warning. However, as he'd been trained to do, he was ever-vigilant, waiting for an opening to escape.

The women in the holding cells began to chatter amongst themselves in Spanish, an indication that the guards had left them alone. Gunner took this opportunity to ask questions.

"Does anybody speak English?"

They ignored him.

"Please, I just want to know where I am. Can you tell me anything?"

One of the women with a heavy accent responded, "Colombia, senor. North of the Atrato River in the Darién Gap."

Gunner rolled his eyes and shook his head. He looked upward to the heavens and whispered, "You couldn't have dropped me off anywhere else?"

He knew about the Darién Gap. It was like a war zone for the drug cartels, who fought each other for territory and control of the land route from South America toward the U.S. Each compound had its drug-production operation, but they also had a small army of hired guns designed to protect themselves from their rivals. The DEA or local law enforcement was the least of their concerns.

Gunner's cell was humid from the natural climate of the jungle, but also from the water that had mixed with the dirt floor. His body was cramped and sore in so many places that no one injury stood out amongst the others.

Out of nowhere, the young boy appeared in front of his cell. His face passed through the sunlight of the small window to the outside. Gunner had tracked the sun in his prior days of captivity and knew it was morning.

"Hey, kid," Gunner said and waved his hand toward the boy.

The boy didn't respond or smile. He rarely did. But in a gesture reminiscent of the young boy handing Mean Joe Greene, the famous Pittsburg Steeler football player, a Coke in a famous commercial from the seventies, the boy extended a bottle of water toward the cell door.

At first, Gunner hesitated. He had to consider that the boy was ordered to bring the water and it might contain some type of poison. Then he laughed at himself. Poison was the tool of assassins like the Russian cosmonauts. These people preferred the more direct approach—beating someone to death or simply shooting them in the head.

He took the water and gulped it heartily. He stashed the empty bottle behind his urine bucket. It wasn't much of a weapon, but it might be some use to him later. When you had nothing to work with, a plastic water bottle became a prized treasure.

The boy kept looking nervously down the hallway toward the exit of the cartel's prison. Gunner, with nothing left to lose, took a chance. He grabbed the lock and pointed to the keyhole. He used his index finger to make the motion of a skeleton key unlocking the mechanism.

He made eye contact with the boy, raised his eyebrows, and nodded hopefully. The boy reached his finger toward the keyhole and inserted it with a twisting motion.

Gunner got excited. "Yes! Yes! Key." He copied the boy's motion and then pointed at him. "You. Get the key." He pointed toward the door with one hand and twisted his finger in an unlocking motion with the other.

The boy's shoulders slumped and then he shrugged.

Gunner sighed. *The kid understands and wants to help*, he thought, *but he doesn't know how.*

He tried to cheer the boy up. He waved his hands, pointed to his face, and generated an overbroad smile. He even did a little dance in his cell, followed by another big smile.

The boy responded with a smile and even shook his body like he was emulating the waddle of a duck. Then, for the first time, he laughed.

Gunner was overwhelmed with emotion. The hardened warrior, the man America called upon to do their dirty work, from assassinations to the destruction of asteroids, shed emotional tears of joy.

He hung his head, dropped to his knees, and held his left arm through the bars. The boy stepped forward, took Gunner's hand, and squeezed.

In that moment, the physical contact, one that didn't involve a beating, changed Gunner's demeanor. It was as if he'd been provided a miracle cure for his wounds. He'd been given a new purpose, an inner strength that he hadn't felt in a long time.

He had a will to live like nothing he'd ever sensed before.

After a minute, the boy, still smiling, released Gunner's hand and stood for a moment. Gunner clasped his hands together and mouthed the words *thank you*. The boy formed his hands to signal okay, and then he gave Gunner a thumbs-up.

The breakthrough did more for Gunner than any hospital IV or pain medication could do. Only one other thing could make him feel rejuvenated like this, and that would've been Heather's touch.

He closed his eyes and pictured her with him sitting at the water's edge on Dog Island. He could see her, on her knees across from him, reaching out to hold his hands as they stared lovingly in each other's eyes. His mind convinced him that it was real.

Then he opened his eyes and saw the steel bars of his jail cell. The boy was gone, and so was his vision of Heather. However, the inner strength he'd received from the encounter was swelling inside him.

"I've had enough of this shit," he muttered to himself.

CHAPTER 29

The USS *Harry S. Truman*
Caribbean Sea

Cam and Bear, with the aid of two ensigns assigned to assist them, rushed through the enormous infrastructure within the bowels of the U.S. Navy's eighth Nimitz-class aircraft carrier. They'd only arrived hours before, and within fifteen minutes of disembarking the jet that delivered them to the USS *Harry S. Truman*, they were advised of CSG8's redeployment to the Atlantic Seaboard.

First, the lieutenant who greeted them upon arrival took them to a Valor AV-280 similar to the tilt-rotor aircraft they'd used during their incursion into the Far Eastern Federal District of Russia to surveil the Cosmodrome.

"I understood that we'd be assigned a Sikorsky," began Bear. "Something like the Guard's HH-60H."

"Sorry, Lieutenant, not this time. This particular Valor has been modified and won't suit our new mission's purpose. You'll have to make do."

"Fine by me," he said with a smile and a wink directed to Cam.

Bear was thrilled at the prospect of being behind the controls of the agile aircraft with advanced landing capabilities. Like Russia, he'd have to drop the plane with a precise vertical descent, one that didn't get the rotors caught up in the jungle's tree canopy.

Cam liked the aircraft because of its stealth technology and the radar capabilities. Without the aid of satellites and the invaluable eyes in the skies they provide, she and Bear would have to make their own determinations as to how to approach the drug cartel's compound where Gunner was most likely held.

141

They followed the two ensigns from one section of the aircraft carrier to another, picking up everything from weapons to surveillance electronics. A trauma medical kit was a must, together with a duffle bag of clothing in a variety of sizes.

The AV-280 was capable of carrying a lot of gear since this particular aircraft had been modified to reduce the passenger seating capacity from fourteen troops to six. When the lieutenant advised Cam and Bear of this fact, Cam whispered, "Good. That's four American astronauts, one Frenchman, and Gunner. Sorry Russkis. Here's a map. You guys can take a hike."

Bear roared in laughter at her statement, drawing a hateful look from the lieutenant, who was in a frenzy, as the entire crew of the *Truman* were at battle stations already.

They stopped for a final briefing by the lieutenant, who gave them the GPS coordinates of a *lily pad* in Costa Rica, a U.S. intelligence installation, the existence of which was formerly denied by the Costa Rican government. Located throughout Latin America, these dark sites provided temporary shelter for operatives who worked throughout the region. For Cam and Bear, it would be a logical place to refuel before they took the long trip across the Gulf of Mexico and back to Maxwell Air Force Base.

Cam and Bear were escorted to the AV-280, loaded the last of their gear, and observed the frenzied activity on the deck of the *Truman*.

"We're getting ready for war," commented Cam. "This has nothing to do with the asteroid, directly anyway. The Russians must be making a move on us, and we're beefing up our Atlantic defenses."

Bear helped Cam into the aircraft and closed the door behind her. "Why would they risk it? They're probably taking a lot of hits of their own."

"You know, Bear, I don't think Putin really cares anything about his people. He's an egomaniac. After all of these years, he wants to be seen as the freakin' king of the world. I think he'd risk it all to hit at us while we're in disarray or in the process of helping our own."

Bear chuckled. "Well, he'd better pack a lunch, 'cause I saw the look of determination on those sailors' faces. You don't kick us while we're down. Big mistake."

"I agree. Trust me, I wish we could join the fight somehow. That'll have to wait for another day. We've got a two-hour flight to the mouth of the Atrato River. Let's get started and I'll start to map out the GPS coordinates of the compound. We're gonna have to hike a considerable distance to avoid detection, and also, we need to stash this bird where the locals can't find it."

"Just like Russia," added Bear as he strapped himself in and began his preflight checks. "Man, I love this thing. When I get a pay raise, I'm gonna buy one, even if it's used."

Cam rolled her eyes and shook her head. "Why I put my life in your hands is beyond me," she said sarcastically.

"Yeah, yeah. Well, for now, I'm all you've got. Let's ride."

Bear got clearance from the air traffic control tower aboard the *Truman* and expertly took off, flying south-southwest across the Caribbean Sea toward the Darién Gap.

Two hours later, they flew over the coastal town of Villa Hermosa, and then Bear followed the Atrato River inland as it snaked its way through the jungle. Cam recorded video the entire route, and when they reached the approximate area where the satellite phone was emitting the signal, she had Bear circle several times so she could have the cameras get a good look.

"I wish it was night," she began as frustration set in. "The trees and all the other crap growing around them blocks the view of the lens. If it was dark, at least we could take advantage of infrared."

"I could fly lower," offered Bear. "It would make a big difference with the altitude change."

Cam hesitated. She was concerned that any aircraft in the midst of the meteor storm would attract attention and result in the death of the Starhopper crew, including Gunner.

"Do another sweep, but this time move in closer to the Panamanian border."

"Roger," said Bear.

He made a wide, sweeping turn, allowing Cam to get a visual through the small window on her side of the aircraft. Suddenly, she pushed upward in her seat and craned her neck to get a longer look during the pass over.

"What?" asked Bear.

"Back there. A break in the clouds. I saw something. It was like the jungle had been mowed down with a really big bulldozer."

"Maybe it was a meteorite?" opined Bear.

"I don't know, Bear, it didn't seem burned," she replied and then thought for a moment. She decided to take a chance. "Bear, circle back and take the same path as before. Lower your altitude. I wanna take another look."

The plane, while stealth to radar, could be heard if it flew too low. On this day, luck was on their side, as the roar of diesel trucks coming and going in the drug cartel compound obscured the sound of the plane's rotors.

It was both luck and dedication to finding Gunner that enabled Cam's sharp eye to find the debris field created by the Starhopper as it crashed back to Earth. Now, they pinned their hopes on finding a place to land and, hopefully, locating the crew.

CHAPTER 30

The Darién Gap
Near the Colombia-Panama Border

The AV-280 aircraft hovered low over the thick canopy of jungle as it descended toward a barely visible clearing created by a small meteorite that had leveled the surrounding foliage. The black charred spot, created by the intense heat of the space rock, generated a fire that had eventually been extinguished by the jungle's natural suppressant—rainfall.

Bear and Cam exited the Valor, immediately noticing the oppressive heat and humidity in the surrounding atmosphere. The air was thick, choking the fluids out of anything it came into contact with.

Living near the Gulf of Mexico for most of their lives, the two operatives certainly understood humid conditions, but the Gulf breezes generally provided some relief. Here, the wind was virtually nonexistent, and the thickness of the surrounding jungle stifled any air movement.

Bear was sweating profusely. The large-framed man, whose body fat was low, still had a propensity to sweat.

Cam was mostly unaffected by the unusual environment although she was somewhat nervous with anticipation. During the flyover, she'd had a better view of the debris field than Bear, who was focused on finding a place to land the tilt-rotor aircraft. She concentrated on searching for signs of life.

The two collected their gear from the aircraft. Both had chest rigs with protective plates inserted. They were outfitted as if they were conducting a hostage rescue. They carried flash-bang grenades, smoke, and a variety of explosive devices to be used to breach the compound.

In addition to their regular tactical gear, each was equipped with night-vision goggles, knives, sidearms, and a fully automatic M4 carbine. They wanted a compact and light weapon because they anticipated close-quarters combat in the event of a hostage situation.

Cam inhaled, closed her eyes, and soaked in the last few seconds of respite before they made the perilous trek through the jungle toward the last known location of Gunner's satellite phone.

The landing area they chose placed the Starhopper wreckage in between them and the drug cartel compound, but also within the radius of the signal's location identified by the Jackal.

"Are you ready, Cam?"

"Yeah. We're two miles north of the crash site. We'll start there and make our way toward the signal."

They stood next to one another and compared their GPS devices. There certainly were no roads in the vicinity, and they didn't expect a path to be available, which meant Bear would have to make it for them. Cam would be responsible for monitoring the jungle for threats, both human and animal, while Bear would use two sharp machetes to cut a path through the jungle thicket.

On any given day, the two of them could've walked two miles down the street in less than thirty minutes at a brisk pace. In the jungle, a mile an hour was an accomplishment.

The Darién Gap was a thick, unruly wilderness that was nearly impenetrable. Known for its biodiversity, the dense vegetation produced a perfect cover for smugglers of drugs and humans alike. Throughout the jungle, roads could suddenly appear out of the tree canopy and just as quickly disappear. Donkey trails were abundant, used by migrants carrying their worldly possessions toward the United States, not to use once they entered, but to trade for protection or transportation along the route.

As Cam intently studied the jungle surroundings, she realized how it was impossible to discern east from west without the aid of GPS. The jungle canopy was so overgrown that the sun was mostly blocked out, creating near nighttime conditions. Without a guide, or advanced technology, she surmised, one could spend days on end walking in circles like a dog chasing its tail.

"Stop!" Cam shouted as she swung around. The crunching sound of an animal approaching from behind them caught her attention. She swung around and dropped to a knee.

She didn't hesitate as she fired several rounds toward a fast-approaching jaguar. The animal was riddled with bullets just as it began its leap toward her. Howler monkeys roared in disapproval, and birds roosting in the trees above them flew off in fear.

Bear ran past Cam, hopped over the clearly dead animal, and raced back down the trail with his weapon trained on the path they'd just made. He looked around and then relaxed.

"Jaguars live and hunt alone," he said reassuringly as he returned to Cam's side. She stood quietly over the dead animal. The jaguar's powerful jaws were open, revealing the sharp teeth capable of killing its prey with one crushing bite.

Bear knelt down and touched the dead jaguar's torso.

A tear came to Cam's eye as she studied the beautiful animal. "That sucks," she said solemnly. "I didn't have a choice."

Bear stood and hugged his friend. "Cam, it would've torn us apart. I'm glad you heard it. I was thrashing away and completely—"

Cam interrupted him. "Bear, what does it say about me that I can shoot a hostile, the enemy, without remorse or hesitation, but killing an animal makes me sick to my stomach."

Bear hesitated, unsure how to respond. "Well, here's the way I look at it. This jaguar was doing what its instincts told it to do. Hunt, kill, eat. People are different. They kill because they want to, not because they have to. When we deal with the bad guys, it's either kill or be killed. So, as I look at it, killing them first is self-defense."

Cam sighed and rubbed the jaguar's fur one last time before slapping Bear on the back. "Let's get going."

They continued their trek through the jungle and eventually found their way to the crash site. Bear took a moment to rehydrate and wipe the sweat off his face. Cam remained vigilant, searching the site and the surrounding thicket for any form of movement.

"I don't wanna say it out loud," began Bear as he joined her side.

"Then don't," Cam shot back. Deep down, she couldn't imagine how anyone could survive the wreckage. "Come on. Stay frosty."

The landscape on both sides of the clearing created by the crash of the Starhopper was overwhelming to Cam.

Bear noticed as well. "These trees look like skyscrapers." He carefully pulled at a piece of the parachute that had been deployed just before the crash, and looked underneath. "Well, they don't do much about blocking out the sun's heat. But have you noticed something?"

"What's that?"

"Since we left the *Truman*, I haven't observed any more meteorites. Maybe their predictions are correct about the debris field moving farther north into the upper latitudes."

"Good." Cam's camouflaged pants got caught in a tangle of thorny plants and she pulled her leg away, causing a ripping sound.

They made their way up the debris field, climbing over the corpses of fallen trees that were strewn about until nature eventually swallowed them up over time.

The heat and strenuous trek through the jungle had taken its toll on them both, but they pushed on through the wreckage. They came upon the decomposing body of Semenova, which dangled from a tree branch. Small animals and birds had begun to pick at it, leaving it riddled with open holes. The stench of the corpse immediately caused them to cover their faces.

"That's not a NASA uniform," observed Bear.

"One of the Russians, female, I think," added Cam.

They continued, finding larger pieces of the Starhopper and pausing to inspect them all. More body parts were found, including the remains of two other American astronauts. Each time, Bear and Cam mustered the fortitude to inspect them, looking for any signs that they might belong to Gunner.

As they approached the end of the wreckage and the nose of the Starhopper, their hopes were raised. First Cam and then Bear began to jog toward the crew module when they saw the front row of seats intact. They jumped up to the platform, where they discovered the large amounts of blood created by the intense battle in space, coupled with the anaconda's devouring of Commander Sokolov.

"Jeez, Cam. What the hell happened here?"

"I don't know. Look, the seats are intact, but there's blood everywhere." She walked toward the pilot's seat to get a closer look. "Holy shit!"

"What?" asked Bear, who refrained from joining in her excitement. He hustled toward her, stumbled, and the two almost crashed into one another.

Cam picked up the seat harness and showed Bear. "These have been cut through. Bear, somebody survived this!"

Bear swung around and began to scan the debris field from a different perspective. With the aid of being elevated five feet off the ground, he could see more of the remains of the Starhopper.

He slapped Cam's arm and pointed toward a large section of the outer shell of the spacecraft. "Do you see that? Does that look like a body?"

Fear and apprehension washed over Cam's body. Someone had survived, but there was a body that was wrapped and preserved forty feet away.

She exhaled and wiped her face with both hands. "We've gotta go see."

She eased herself off the crew module and waited for Bear to join her. Together, they trudged through the low-lying tallgrasses in the direction of the body. After Bear killed a snake in their path, the two worked together to retrieve the body off the metal and set it on the jungle floor.

Blood had soaked through the parachute material, which only added to the grim reality that Gunner might be dead. The two shouldered their weapons and slowly unwrapped the shroud of material.

Once again, the heat and humidity of the jungle had caused the body to decompose rapidly. The stench was overwhelming, but the two persevered. Finally, the rotting corpse was rolled over so that it could be seen in its entirety.

"Oh my god!" shouted Cam, who stood and walked away. "It's not him. Bear, Gunner's alive. I knew it!"

"It's Chief Rawlings," said Bear, tapping the astronaut's name stitched on his uniform. He quickly covered the body back up with the parachute material, replaced it atop the spaceship's wreckage, and joined Cam back on the ground. "Only Gunner would've taken the time to do this. Besides, I think we've accounted for all of the astronauts except for one Russian and Gunner. Dude, our boy's alive!"

"Yes. Yes, he is," said Cam with a sigh of relief.

CHAPTER 31

Drug Cartel Compound
The Darién Gap
Colombia, South America

Gunner's captors were busy going about their business and for hours had left him alone. He noticed that the meteorite activity had stopped, and the constant flow of vehicles traveling through the compound was an indication that the cartel had more important things to do than stick him with a cattle prod.

He took advantage of the hiatus from his torture to rest his body and clear his mind. Despite his weakened state, he was certain he'd be able to fight if the opportunity presented itself. He considered taking his friendship with the boy to another level.

He'd already asked the boy to find a key to open the cell door, assuming the kid understood his attempt via primitive communications. The next logical step was to ask for a gun, but he was afraid that would lead to severe punishment for the boy if he was caught. Besides, the guards who checked on him from time to time never appeared to carry a weapon within the compound's prison. The cattle prod was their means of subduing the prisoners.

Gunner stood as he heard the heavy metallic locks turn, and a rush of moist but fresh air entered the cells. The sound of women whimpering indicated a new contingent of captives had arrived and were being introduced to their temporary home.

One by one, they were thrown into their cells, accompanied by a jolt of electricity being administered via the cattle prods. The intense surge of energy was designed to beat them down physically and emotionally, thus creating a subdued prisoner.

Gunner counted three new captives, and after the guards verbally beat them down, they laughed and left. As was always the case, the women began to chatter away, asking questions of the other prisoners. They were, of course, greeted with the customary *shushes*.

All of them complied except one. She began to speak rapidly in Spanish and refused to stop.

Gunner liked her feistiness, so he took a chance and called out to her, "Hey, can you hear me? Do you speak English?"

The woman became quiet, and after a moment, she replied, "Yeah. My name is Caroline. What's yours?"

Her Spanish accent was not as heavy as the other women. "Wait, are you an American?"

"Sort of. I was born in Mexico but went to California with my family. What's your name?"

"Gunner."

"Gunther?"

He laughed. "No, that was my grandfather's name. I'm Gunner. Listen, can you answer any questions for me?"

"Shhh!"

The other women scolded Gunner and Caroline, but the two ignored them. Gunner felt like the guards were busy assisting with the constant flow of vehicles in and out of the cartel's hideout and obviously weren't monitoring the jail cells.

"Yeah, I've been here before."

"As a prisoner?"

"Um, no. Not exactly. I used to, well, I got caught up in some bad stuff, you know. I was brought here, to the cells, but then, well, I talked myself into another room, if you know what I mean."

"I understand," said Gunner. "You don't need to say more. Your English is great, by the way." He was trying to establish a rapport with the woman.

"I started school in San Diego when I was six. I'm more American than I am Mexican."

"How did you end up in Colombia?"

"It's a long, ugly story. Anyway, these guys are brutal. I'm surprised you're still alive. You must DEA or FBI. That's valuable trade bait for Jorge Blanco."

"I'm not either one of those, but he must think I am. Either way, I'm still alive, barely. Tell me, what else do you know about the compound?"

"Not all of them live here. They have hideouts all over the jungle, especially down by the Atrato River. If they have to escape, they take speedboats toward the sea and the ocean."

"What about security?"

"They all have guns, and some patrol the fences. Nobody tries to break in here. They get killed before they step foot on the grounds."

"Does Blanco have a weakness?"

"No."

"Anything?"

"No. I was his girl, and we had a kid. My son can't hear or speak, so he turned me into a mule as punishment."

Gunner didn't mention that he knew about the kid. He decided not to offer up any information in case she had been planted in the cells to befriend him.

"Sorry," he mumbled. "Um, why did you come back?" His question seemed innocent enough, assuming he had no knowledge of the boy.

"I want to take my son to America. I thought I could reason with Jorge. I was wrong."

So far, she hadn't told him anything that he couldn't assume for himself. Gunner decided to press on. "How close is the town? Any place that might have a phone or police?"

"There is no place like that here. Mister, you might as well be in outer space."

Gunner rolled his eyes. *No, thanks. Been there, done that.*

CHAPTER 32

The Darién Gap
Colombia, South America

Cam and Bear didn't take the same approach to the drug cartel's compound as Gunner did. They relied upon their GPS devices and the promise of more favorable terrain by moving toward the west initially and then northward toward the coordinates of the satellite phone's signal.

The stream and series of lakes encountered flowed toward the Atrato River. As day turned toward night, a thick fog filled the valley where the water carved its way through the jungle. Cam reached the water's edge and looked up the mountain and down toward a lake, which widened the stream considerably.

A slight breeze blew toward them, moving the misty fog to give the stream the appearance that it was breathing. In the fog, the trees of the dense forest became more like silhouettes against the late afternoon sky.

"It's too wide to cross," observed Cam. "I can't imagine what lives in this stream."

"Oh, I can imagine," said Bear, who was not fond of the ocean, lakes, or streams, especially those in a remote jungle. He pulled his binoculars out of a pouch in his chest rig and looked downstream. "Hey, Cam. I see a canoe on the other side of that lake. Maybe there are some houses nearby?"

"Lead the way, but watch your step. This time of day, things start to come out of their hidey holes, if you know what I mean."

"Roger that."

They traveled along the bank for a few hundred yards when Bear suddenly stopped and raised his fist in the air. They both instantly dropped to a crouch and readied their rifles.

The sound of something rustling in front of them had caught Bear's attention, and he immediately thought of the jaguar. With his rifle trained on the location where the sound came from, he walked carefully, heel to toe, in an effort to mask his approach.

Suddenly, a dog wandered out of the underbrush. The appearance of the mangy hound startled Bear, but he held his fire. The dog stopped to sniff the ground in search of food and then sat down. His hind leg furiously scratched at his matted fur to dislodge some annoying fleas.

Then the dog froze. He turned his attention to the direction that Bear and Cam were traveling, downstream toward the canoe. He sniffed the air. His ears flattened and his tail dropped between his legs. With a slight whimper, he began to hustle along the stream's bank, obviously disturbed by the scent he'd picked up.

"I've got a bad feeling about this," whispered Bear.

"Yeah, me too. Let's follow him. If something's spooked him, he's looking for safety."

Bear rose from his crouch and began to jog down the path. Cam was close behind, her head on a swivel, looking for danger.

As they approached the end of the dirt trail, they reached a clearing that contained a small settlement made up of bamboo walls and adobe-like brick foundations. The roofs were made up primarily of layer upon layer of palm fronds.

Bear reached the clearing first and found cover for the two of them to observe the locals. They both used their binoculars to scan the area. Cam was the first to spot the villagers' cash crop.

In South America, farmers of the coca plant chose ground that sloped slightly toward water so the substantial amount of rainfall received in the jungle didn't drown the plants. Once the field was cleared, it was ready for cultivation. Seeds were gathered from mature plants in December through March. They were placed in water to separate the bad seeds. The good seeds were initially placed in growing pots or shaded areas of the field to protect the new plants from the sun.

Within twenty to thirty days, the coca plants germinated and then were replanted in the field to a depth of about ten to twelve inches depending on the rainfall in the area.

Now, in late April, the seedlings were being transplanted. Neat rows had been tilled and the workers were carefully dropping the seedlings into holes spaced three feet apart. This particular field would generate fully mature plants in twelve to twenty-four months after being cared for by this group of villagers. Then they'd be harvested and sold to the drug cartels for further processing and shipment to America.

"Do you see any armed guards?" asked Cam.

"No. Only broken-down old people and a handful of kids. Kinda weird. They're either younger than teens or older than Pop."

"The others have different jobs, like transporting or manufacturing product," added Cam. "Look along the water, there are more canoes."

"I see 'em. How do you wanna play it?"

Cam stood and shrugged. "I know a little conversational Spanish. I'll just ask permission."

She walked ahead of Bear and into the clearing. She kept her weapon at low ready as she approached three elderly women who were cooking in cast-iron pots over an open flame. One made eye contact with Cam, but the others never looked up.

Cam lowered her weapon farther as Bear continued to scan the clearing. She spoke with the woman, who turned to look toward the canoes. Without hesitation, she called out to one of the boys who was assisting an old man weaving a bamboo basket.

Minutes later, the boy was paddling at the back of the canoe and Bear was at the front, trying to find his rhythm. At first, the effort was comical as Bear's muscular arms overpowered the canoe, counteracting the smooth, consistent strokes of the village boy. After several strokes of the paddle, Bear figured it out, and crossing the lake became easier.

Cam thanked the young man by giving him a peanut-butter-flavored OhYeah! energy bar on the other side. In return, he pointed toward a trail that had been cut through the jungle. It appeared to meander in the general direction of their destination, so Cam led the way through the jungle. Unlike the first part of their travels to rescue Gunner, they made much better time, which suited the two of them just fine. Because it was now pitch black in the jungle of the Darién Gap.

As night fell, their surroundings became murky as if they were wearing a mask that prevented their ability to breathe. They both paused to drink some water. Bear hadn't taken time to eat, so he munched on part of an ER bar, which contained over four hundred calories each.

Periodically, the trail widened and the skies could be seen. Cam looked in amazement at the silver stars that burst over the violet background of space. Without any air or light pollution, the sky could be viewed in its perfect, unfiltered state. It was beautiful, and now there was only the occasional meteor burning up in the atmosphere to provide any kind of movement.

The storm was subsiding and their only challenge was to find and rescue Gunner.

CHAPTER 33

Drug Cartel Compound
The Darién Gap
Colombia, South America

Cam and Bear arrived at the compound just as a merciless storm passed over the Darién Gap. The rain came in waves, followed by winds that caused the tree canopy to open and close, at times allowing the rain to pelt them with stinging drops.

Cam had never experienced weather quite like it. Certainly, Florida's Gulf Coast had seen its share of hurricanes during her time there, but she'd never endured a tropical storm that sent rain down with this kind of intensity. It was stifling and made it difficult to breathe.

On the other hand, the inclement weather gave them the opportunity to study the defenses of the drug cartel's compound. Despite the din of the rainfall, they were able to make their way around the perimeter of the chain-link fence topped with razor wire that surrounded the buildings. They stopped occasionally, discussed possible access points, and speculated about the use of certain buildings.

Like two lions stalking their prey, they were formulating a plan of attack. One that would quickly locate Gunner and free him from imprisonment without getting all of them killed in the process.

A lone guard walked the inside of the fence, his flashlight beam flaring and darting around the jungle thicket. He ambled past their position, never bothering to look up from under the hood of his green parka.

The tropical storm certainly assisted them, as did the darkness.

While they would've enjoyed the benefit of seeing the entire compound in the daylight to better assess their rescue options, the distraction the weather provided was invaluable.

The two retreated into the jungle and made their way toward a block and stucco building with barely discernible slits allowed as windows. The lack of light and the prisonlike appearance of the smallest building on the compound led them to believe that was where Gunner might be held. Assuming he was alive, of course.

Cam didn't like to think in those terms, but everything they did in the next three hours would have to keep an exit strategy in mind. She had no idea how many gunmen they'd be up against, not that it mattered. The three of them had faced much greater odds on other occasions. However, during those missions, they had the benefit of extensive briefings and preplanned methods of attack. In addition, during the operation itself, they had headset communications and eyes in the sky thanks to drone technology.

This was different. They were going in blind, against an unknown enemy, and they were looking for a hostage who might or might not be there. Yet there was no doubt—they were going in.

"Dammit!" complained Bear in a barely audible whisper. The jungle canopy had created a canvas of sorts, one that held rainwater until the weight overcame the broad palm fronds. It was as if the duo were standing under a bucket full of water, and someone pulled a rope to tilt the contents over their heads.

"Zip it, you big baby." Cam chastised Bear for his outburst, albeit a quiet one. She tapped him on the leg and pointed toward the building that likely contained the prison cells. "Let's maneuver ourselves to the other side of that building so we can get eyes on the front door. I wanna see if there are any guards on the inside, or if a schedule is in place for checking on whoever's locked up."

They walked around the perimeter, following behind the patrolling guard, who was easily visible by the beam of his flashlight. At one point, Bear abruptly stopped and grabbed Cam's arm.

"They've got an underground sensor system," he whispered. He pointed at a wire that ran along one of the chain-link fence's posts up to a white box. "See the antenna on top of the box? That's the battery box. It also contains a transmitter. Now look at the wire. It runs down the post and into the ground."

"Swell," muttered Cam. "Is there any way to determine how close it was installed to the bottom of the fence?"

"Step on it," said Bear with a smile she couldn't see.

"No shit. C'mon, Bear. Whadya think?"

"Well, common sense tells me two feet or less, especially in the jungle, which is full of four-legged monsters. The fence can only be breached by climbing it or crawling under it. This would require someone to get within a couple of feet of the base where the chain link hits the ground."

Cam looked up and down the fencing and asked, "Can we cut the fence? You'll have to stretch, right?"

"No problem. I grabbed a pair of lineman's pliers while we were on the *Truman*. Large bolt cutters would've been better, of course, but they were too bulky to tote through the jungle." Bear reached to his left hip and pulled the pliers out of his utility belt. He ran his thumb across the beveled cutting edge.

Cam paused for a moment as another flashlight's beam danced across the center of the compound, moving from left to right toward the prison building. "It looks like another one of the guards might be making the rounds. Let's get into position."

The two of them quietly got into position to observe the entry to the prison building. Cam and Bear adjusted their night-vision goggles in order to have a better look.

"They're preoccupied. Go ahead and cut us an opening. As soon as he exits the building, I'll cut him and get the keys."

"Exit?" asked Bear.

"The same way we came in. We won't have long, and they'll have the benefit of knowing their way around the jungle. But it's all I've got."

Bear shrugged. "No prob." He quietly started cutting the fence.

CHAPTER 34

Drug Cartel Compound
The Darién Gap
Colombia, South America

Gunner had no way of keeping track of time, but it seemed the guard came around every three hours. Based upon his recollection of geography, Colombia was likely in the eastern or central time zone. That meant about fourteen hours of daylight this time of year.

With a break from the beatings, he was both mentally and physically ready to make his move. The guard's routine brought him into the prison building at dusk and dawn, as well as three times during the night. Gunner assumed that was around nine, midnight, and three in the morning.

In his mind, midnight gave him his best opportunity to make his move, as it would then allow him at least five or six hours of darkness to hide and escape back toward the crash site, where he'd find the stream and follow it like a good Boy Scout would've done.

Plus, he was very much aware of the torrential rains that evening. The tin roof over his head was full of nail holes that allowed rain to soak the muddy ground of his cell. The gusts of wind threatened to lift these corrugated panels off the trusses, and for a moment, Gunner wondered if there was a way for him to scale the block walls to make his escape.

So he lay in wait, running various scenarios through his mind. The guards' approach to their rounds was always the same at night. A single man, unarmed except for a flashlight and the cattle prod. They never brought food or water. They didn't converse with any of the prisoners. And the only contact they made was the occasional jab at one of their captives if they attempted to reach for him or got mouthy.

Patiently, he paced the floor of his six-by-six cell, periodically grabbing the bars to stretch his arms and shoulders. He was like a prizefighter waiting for the bell to ring so that he could pound on his opponent. Gunner's adrenaline was surging, and his heart began to race. For better or worse, he sensed this was his opportunity. He could never know what the next day might bring, and the tropical storm certainly gave him the possible distraction to act.

His body jerked to attention when he heard the sound of the lock opening at the building's entrance. The sound of the rain grew louder as the door swung open, and the cooler air entered the building. The door was quickly shut and Gunner closed his eyes to focus his senses on the guard's movements. He tried to visualize the man's actions, his attempts to peer inside the cells of the women. Maybe fantasizing about taking them sexually as he passed by.

Then something unexpected happened. A change in the routine that caught Gunner off guard. The new arrival, the girl who identified herself as Caroline, began to speak to the guard in Spanish. Gunner recognized her voice despite the language barrier.

He also recognized her tone. Heather had spoken to him like that at times. It had a sexy, alluring, inviting resonance to it, one that was irresistible to men.

He placed his ear to the bars, waiting to hear the guard's next move. Would he be tricked into opening her door? Was she trying to escape? Was she simply trying to exchange sex for a meal or a blanket? Or was she selling Gunner out?

Gunner waited, straining to understand the words being used. They both spoke of Blanco, his name being bantered back and forth as if it were a ping-pong ball.

"*Por favor, Juan.*" She was begging now. She obviously knew the man. She got her answer.

"No, Carolino," he said, using the Hispanic form of the name Caroline.

Gunner steadied his nerves, focusing on the man's steps toward him. He prepared himself.

The guard appeared at Gunner's jail cell and didn't bother to look at his prisoner. Gunner needed to get the man's attention.

"*Estúpido*," began Gunner with a hearty laugh. Then he asked, exaggerating the roll of his *r*'s to inflame the man, "*El marica?*" Gunner slapped at the bars as he used his minimal command of the Spanish language to call the husky man a douchebag and a sissy.

As Gunner hoped, it angered the guard, who swung around toward his cell and rammed the cattle prod through the bars. The two sharp prongs jabbed into Gunner's chest, just above his left nipple. The electricity scorched his skin to the point where it smelled of burned flesh.

But this time, Gunner didn't cower away. Instead, he surprised the guard by grabbing the cattle prod with both hands and pulling it into the cell, bringing with it the man's right arm, which was wrapped through the device's leather strap.

With his arm stuck through the bars up to the elbow, Gunner brought his right arm down with a forceful blow that struck the guard's forearm, instantly snapping the radial bone and the ulna simultaneously.

The next few seconds were surreal, Gunner would recall later. The man's eyes and mouth were wide open, yet he couldn't utter a sound. The pain of the broken arm was so great that his screams of agony weren't released.

Gunner, however, didn't hesitate. With the man's right arm dangling through the bars, held together by tendons and meaty flesh, Gunner grabbed the man's hair and rammed his face against the steel posts, instantly breaking his nose and cutting a long gash in his forehead.

The man let out a primal scream of pain, one that far surpassed anything Gunner had allowed during his torture sessions. Juan, his torturer, was helpless now, and his captive took advantage.

Gunner grabbed him by the shirt and held him against the bars of the cell. He reached for his belt and grabbed the keys to the locks.

While he held the guard tight with his powerful grip, he opened the cell and freed himself.

Gunner took a deep breath. The next step would be dangerous, and he needed to calm down the uproar in the cells as the women excitedly shouted to one another.

"Shush!" he yelled, using their own admonition to calm them. "Caroline, tell them to be quiet."

In Spanish, the girl from San Diego got their attention, and within seconds, the cell block quietened. In the meantime, the guard was recovering from the pain. He was about to call out for help, but Gunner stopped him.

Using the cattle prod.

"Arrrggghhh!" the man screamed in agony. Gunner had rammed the device into his cheek, drawing blood, and replaced it with electricity.

He jerked the twin prongs out and stuck the man in the Adam's apple, puncturing the tender part of the neck. It immediately began to swell as the electricity caused the man to shake violently. After Gunner removed the prongs, the man clutched his throat and began to choke. The swelling blocked his airway and he was suffocating.

Gunner didn't care. He tore the man's shirt off and ripped the sleeves from its stitching. He tied it around the man's mouth and nose to complicate his breathing further. Then he bound his hands behind his back to subdue him. Finally, he shoved his body into the cell and slammed the door behind him.

Gunner looked like a demented lunatic as he stood over the man who was choking to death. Another gust of wind struck the side of the building, and more torrents of rain pummeled the roof. He was now ready for the next steps.

But first, he had to break the bad news to the ladies in captivity.

They were all reaching for him through the tiny slits in their solid doors, pleading in their native tongues to release them from their cells. Gunner couldn't, yet. They'd either get in his way or, worse, simply run into the compound and be slaughtered by gunfire.

"Caroline? Where are you?"

"Here. Here I am." She stuck her hand through the slot and wiggled her fingers.

Gunner quickly approached her door and knelt down so he could see her. Sad, sunken eyes stared back at him.

"Listen to me. You've got to trust me, and you have to convince the others to trust me also. Okay?"

"No. No! You can't leave us here. They'll kill us."

"I'm not gonna leave you, but I can't release you yet. If I do, they will all die, and I can't live with that. Please trust me. I've got this, okay. I will be back for you."

"No, we'll be quiet. I'll tell them not to say a word."

Gunner grimaced and shook his head. He couldn't risk it. He began to hear shouting coming from the compound. He was out of time.

"Trust me, Caroline. Tell them. I'll be back for you all."

Gunner squeezed her hand and raced toward the exit door, dropping the keys on the ground under a folding chair. He flung the door open and burst out into the rain-soaked compound, pausing briefly to take in the fresh air. He was greeted by a welcoming committee that was anything but welcoming.

PART FOUR

Monday, April 30

CHAPTER 35

Drug Cartel Compound
The Darién Gap
Colombia, South America

Cam followed the guard across the compound with the benefit of her night vision. Similar to the way drug dealers operate in the shadows of America's streets, the cartels lived in a world of darkness at night in order to avoid detection. The faint, flickering glow of candles could barely be seen through gaps in curtains on the residential buildings. The flashlights of guards patrolling the fence and compound were generally pointed downward to illuminate the path to their next destination.

The stocky man entered the prison building and closed the door behind him. While Bear carefully cut the chain-link fence, stretching his muscular arms to avoid triggering the ground sensors that ran along the outside of the compound, Cam backtracked through the jungle to get closer to where she assumed the cartel's prisoners were held.

The lack of windows and the driving rain prevented her from hearing any conversations. She cupped her ear in an attempt to focus, shielding her hearing from distractions. Frustrated, and with the patrolling guard due to come back around soon, Cam began to make her way back to Bear's position, when she heard a man scream in pain.

She swung her weapon around toward the prison building, where she observed a flickering light emanating from holes in the roof and gaps in the block walls. Only, this light was different from the soft glow of a candle burning. It was bright white, almost electrifying in nature. With each flash, a man's screams of agony grew louder.

"Gunner," she muttered as she raced back toward Bear.

Just as she reached him, he addressed her first. "I heard it too. I'm almost there."

He continued to cut away at the fence, link by link, working diligently to create an opening large enough to fit his six-foot-four frame through it.

The man screamed again, only louder this time.

"They're torturing him, Bear!" exclaimed Cam, forgetting her need to stay quiet. Her desire to protect Gunner from suffering temporarily got the best of her. Fortunately, the raindrops pelting the buildings and their tin roofs drowned out her voice.

"Almost," said Bear.

"I've got movement in the compound," observed Cam. "Two men are coming out of the barn building, and two more are making their way from the front gate."

"Weapons?" asked Bear.

"Affirmative. Long guns. AKs maybe. They don't appear to be in a hurry, but they're all headed to the prison building."

The screams and flashes of brilliant light stopped. Cam removed her night-vision goggles and used the scope on her M4 to follow the activity.

"Okay, I think we can breach the fence now," announced Bear.

"Dammit, Bear. I think we've lost the element of surprise. I count one guard already in the building and another four headed that way."

Bear put away the pliers and raised his rifle's scope to make his own assessment. "We need a distraction, but not one big enough to raise the roof, if you know what I mean."

"What are you gonna do?"

"Smoke and mirrors. I'll be right back."

Bear took off to his right and disappeared into the undergrowth of the jungle. Cam tried to follow him through her scope, but he was lost in the thicket within seconds. She quickly turned her attention back to the prison.

"Come on, Bear, do whatever it is you have—" she began to complain when she heard shouting.

"*Fuego! Fuego! Aquí!*"

A voice warning the others of a fire could be heard screaming from the back of a warehouse building. She swung her rifle around to find the source. Smoke was billowing up from behind the building, creating odd wisps and tendrils as it found its way skyward.

"Good job, Bear," she said to herself with a smile.

She turned her attention back to the prison building. The diversion worked. The four guards descending upon the makeshift jail stopped and began jogging toward the warehouse. Most likely, Cam assumed, the coca plants were stored there for processing. A fire would be devastating to the cartel's operation.

Bear came lumbering through the jungle and dropped to one knee by her side. He was fighting to catch his breath in the moist environment.

"That gives us an opening," he said in between breaths. "I'll hold the fence open for you."

"*Fuego! ¡Ándale,*" shouted the men heading toward the warehouse. Urgency was demanded.

Bear spread the opening for Cam to slide through, and she turned to assist him. Within seconds both of them were inside the compound and had dropped to a crouch to avoid detection.

Cam let out a sigh. "Well, shit. Now we woke the whole damn place up."

Bear added, "Yeah, I've got at least a dozen men coming out of the building on the far end that looks like barracks."

"And two of the original guards are turning back toward the prison."

"Wait. Cam, look! Is that Gunner?"

CHAPTER 36

Drug Cartel Compound
The Darién Gap
Colombia, South America

Gunner knew he had to act fast, but he'd hoped for a little bit of a head start. Once he'd emerged from captivity, his goal was to make his way to the front gate, overpower the night-shift sentries, and escape into the jungle. He'd noticed the razor wire strung across the top of the perimeter fencing when he was being dragged to the barn for a torture session. There appeared to be only one exit—through the twin wooden gates.

Through the rainstorm, he'd seen flashlights bobbing along the ground. Cartel security guards were coming from two directions, descending upon the prison building. Gunner instantly regretted not snapping the man's neck, which would have permanently quietened his agonized screams.

So he stood with his back against the grayish, white block wall, naked except for his no-longer-white briefs. At least his captors had allowed him to retain some semblance of dignity. He imagined that would've been taken from him next.

The blowing gusts of wind and the rain had lowered the temperature, which didn't bother him. In fact, it was just the opposite. He was invigorated by it, and the taste of freedom. Almost, anyway.

"Fuego! Fuego! Aquí!" Gunner's head snapped away from the approaching guards and toward the sound of the man's voice, which was muffled by the downpour.

The guards suddenly turned and began jogging toward the smoldering building. Smoke was pouring over the top of the roof until the tropical storm winds sent it flowing in all directions.

The entry gates were directly across the compound. Attempting to cross in the open with the renewed activity would be suicide. While he was grateful for the combined distractions of the powerful rainstorm coupled with the smoke emerging from the other side of the compound, he was concerned this would empty the residential barracks.

Gunner darted toward the left, away from the back fence and the smoking building. He decided to take a circuitous route to the front entry, using the buildings on both sides of the barn as cover.

He couldn't waste a second, sprinting from the prison building to a kitchen and pantry storage area, where he'd observed men drinking the day he was tortured in the barn. He dropped to a crouch and eased his way along the front of the building until he reached a wooden door. He slowly slid the iron latch upward and pushed the door open.

Then he waited before entering. The compound's mess hall was a temporary stop for Gunner, one in which he hoped to find a gun, or at least a knife. Hell, he'd settle for a meat hammer or a rolling pin. He had enough anger built up within him that he'd pound anybody to death who got in his way, as long as he could dodge their bullets.

He slipped inside the building and attempted to scan his surroundings. With the falling rain, there was no light, making visibility near impossible. He felt his way through the dining area, bumping into wooden tables and chairs.

More shouting emanated from the compound. "*Fuego! ¡Ándale,*" fire, hurry.

Gunner couldn't argue with the hurry part. He fumbled his way through the kitchen and began to feel around for the utensil drawer. Working blind, he reached into a wooden cabinet and found what he was looking for, the hard way.

His finger was pricked by the sharp end of a butcher knife. His hand recoiled as if it were bitten by a snake, and then, oddly, Gunner let out a laugh. He'd experienced worse pain in the last forty-eight hours.

He grasped the knife by the handle and then gingerly explored the wooden hutch for anything else of use. He knocked over a tapered candle holder, which gave him hope that he might be able to find a lighter.

Gunner closed his eyes, the pitch-black conditions making them useless to him anyway. He focused on his sense of feel and used his intuition to continue searching. Then he found them. A carton of old-school paper matches.

He set the knife down and struck one of the matches. The soft light illuminated the kitchen, providing him more than enough to explore. Gunner set one of the tapered candles upright and lit it. He walked through the kitchen, holding it low to the ground so it wouldn't be detected from the outside.

There was more shouting, but the words were indiscernible. They were, however, certainly closer to where he was hiding. It was just a matter of time before they searched the prison, wondering where the night-shift guard had disappeared to.

Unable to find any more suitable weapons, Gunner then considered that he needed a second distraction. There was an open window protected by two wood shutters on the far side of the pantry storage area. Next to the window sat two cans of kerosene and several lamps.

He chuckled. "I've got some *fuego* for ya."

With the aid of the low light, Gunner moved quickly. He poured kerosene over most of the wood furniture in the dining area and then accumulated the partially filled lamps in the center of the building.

He emptied a large bottle of habanero pepper hot sauce and filled it with kerosene. Then he soaked a torn piece of dishtowel with kerosene and stuffed it into the top of the bottle. His Molotov cocktail, Colombian style, was ready.

Gunner made his way to the rear window. Along the way, he poured more kerosene on the floor to create a trail. He also spread the matchbooks evenly along the way so they'd add additional flames as the fire hit them. His eyes began to burn as the kerosene vapors filled the enclosed building.

"Perfect," he muttered. Like many flammable liquids, it wasn't the liquid part of the kerosene that burns, but rather, the vapors that were associated with the substance. Once the vapors mixed with oxygen, all they needed was an ignition source to wreak havoc.

Gunner opened the wooden shutters and was greeted with a gust of moisture-filled air. He didn't waste any time as he hopped on the ledge, a butcher knife in one hand and a burning Molotov cocktail in the other.

Feeling good despite the challenge ahead, Gunner couldn't help but channel the Terminator when he said, "*Hasta la vista,* baby!"

He tossed the flaming kerosene-infused bottle inside and paused to watch the floor burst into flames. Regretfully, he hung around a split second too long.

CHAPTER 37

Drug Cartel Compound
The Darién Gap
Colombia, South America

Cam and Bear shouldered their rifles, opting instead to use their silenced sidearms. They ran along the fence, allowing the backdrop of the jungle thicket to help shield them from detection. Between their camouflaged clothing, gear, and face paint, the two operatives could hide from their adversaries on a sunny day. The tropical storm added to their cover.

Cam kept her weapon trained on the three men who were hustling toward the prison building. Her speed and agility were unparalleled as she made her way across the forty-foot clearing between the perimeter fence and the block structure unnoticed.

Bear agreed to hold his position until she waved him forward. He donned his night-vision goggles again to surveil the compound. It appeared chaotic around the warehouse where he'd set off the smoke flares. The men frantically searched for the source of the fire. Bear knew it was a matter of time before they found the canisters of smoke that he'd triggered.

He returned his attention to Cam, who was waving him on. He ran at a low crouch to join her when he heard the distinctive spits of her silencer. Bear swung his weapon toward the center of the compound, but he couldn't locate any identifiable targets.

She fired three more rounds just as he arrived. Bear flattened his back against the wall and caught his breath. He vowed to drop some pounds when they got back to the States.

"Three kills," advised Cam. "They were coming from the main building to our left."

Bear nodded and pointed toward the warehouse. "We don't have much time. We need to clear this building and find Gunner."

"I'm goin' in. You watch my six."

"But, Cam—" Bear began to protest, but she was gone. He was uncomfortable with any member of their team entering a building alone, but he also understood that somebody needed to watch for the approach of hostiles. Once the guards determined the smoke grenades were a ruse, they'd immediately assume a hostage rescue was taking place.

Bear holstered his sidearm and readied his rifle. He methodically grabbed for the half dozen pouches filled with thirty-round magazines. Then he slipped inside the building's entryway to give himself some cover from both the attackers and the rain. He could also hear Cam as she cleared the prison building, in the event she needed assistance.

At first, Cam moved silently through the long dark hallway. Her deerlike steps couldn't be heard by Bear. Then she began to call out, "Gunner. Gunner! Are you in here?"

A woman responded, "He's gone. Will you let us out?" Bear could not detect an accent. *An American!*

"When was he here? Was he alone?" asked Cam.

Bear quickly reviewed his surroundings. Satisfied that no one was approaching, he backpedaled a few steps into the building so he could eavesdrop.

"I think he was alone. They tortured him. Please let us out."

"I will, but when did Gunner leave?"

"Just a little while ago. He overpowered the guard and left us. He said he'd come back. Are you with the DEA, too?"

"Huh?" replied Cam. She ignored the question and finished her search of the cells.

Bear saw several men headed toward the prison building. He retreated farther into the building to warn Cam.

"Hey, we've got company!" he whispered.

"Gimme a minute." In the dim light, Bear could see Cam at the end of the hallway, where she found the unconscious guard, bound and gagged. He was locked inside the cell, and a cattle prod was bent in half outside the door on the dirt floor. She picked it up and immediately considered what it had been used for. She swiftly pulled her silenced sidearm like a gunslinger and then unemotionally planted a round between the guard's eyes.

The men in the compound were shouting now.

"Cam, we've gotta go!" Bear was feeling a sense of urgency as he made his way to the exit door and began to identify his targets and the kill order.

Cam arrived behind Bear, patted him on the shoulder, and pointed to the left. "He probably headed in the direction of the main gate. If I were him, I'd take advantage of your distraction and use the buildings as cover."

"Cam, we're gonna have to shoot our way out of here. There are men pouring out of several buildings now."

"We still have a lot of options, including our grenades. We need to find Gunner, but also, we need to take the heat off this building. Those cells are full of women."

"Jeez," said Bear, who readied himself to race around the back of the prison building, when an explosion rocked the compound.

CHAPTER 38

Drug Cartel Compound
The Darién Gap
Colombia, South America

The blast created by the kerosene vapors forced air out of the small airtight building, propelling Gunner through the window opening until he hit the ground and tumbled into the adjacent concrete structure. The impact caused him to lose his grip on the knife and momentarily knocked the wind out of his already battered body.

Instinctively, he curled into a tuck and roll position to protect his head and face. An intense heat accompanied the fireball that shot out of the window he'd crawled through, scorching his hair and his already tender back.

But it was the concussive effect of the blast that brought him to the brink of unconsciousness. Only the sound of gunfire kept him alert, as it reminded the conscious part of his brain that he was in mortal danger.

He gathered himself and crawled around on all fours in search of the butcher knife. The muddy ground caused him to slip and slide, and he became frustrated. Gunner decided to give up the search in the interest of time and pushed his way up to his feet.

Just as he found his balance, he was smacked in the back with the butt of a rifle. Muffled by the torrential downpour and the flaming building behind him, Gunner never heard the man sprinting across the compound toward him. He barely caught a glimpse of movement in his periphery, just enough for him to turn his body to lessen the impact of the blow. With no time to react, he was knocked to the ground anyway.

The man immediately planted a boot on the back of Gunner's neck and mashed his face into the mud. Gunner's head had been battered and not nearly recovered. It exploded with throbbing pain, thumping, roaring, and tearing through his cranium as if his nerve endings were being squeezed by a powerful hand.

His eyes began to water as the pain spread down his spine and along his shoulders. He tried to blink away the excruciating pain, and he focused on his assailant. Gunner pulled his left arm back toward his body and caught the man's ankle hard enough to cause the attacker to lose his balance in the mud.

The boot relaxed on the back of his neck, giving Gunner the opening he needed to fight back. He squirmed out from under the boot, and the man wobbled somewhat. It resulted in the hapless guard's death.

Using his catlike reflexes, Gunner rolled over in the mud and raised his leg to kick the man in the groin. His bare foot landed solidly on his target, causing the guard to immediately double over in pain. This provided Gunner another target, the man's heavily bearded face.

The heel of Gunner's foot caught the man squarely in the nose. He could hear the sound of snapping bone and felt the man's warm blood splatter all over his uncovered legs. The guard's head snapped back and he fell to the ground, unsure which injury to grasp with his hands.

Gunner didn't hesitate to finish off his assailant. With expert hands, he landed a crushing blow to the underside of the man's jaw, followed by another to the back of his head just below the ear, killing him instantly.

He caught his breath and grabbed the man's AK-47 rifle. He jumped to his feet and swung the rifle around toward the center of the compound. Heavy gunfire was being exchanged, yet it was not directed at him.

He eased along the building, casting an eerie shadow as the flames found their way through the roof and fully engulfed the kitchen. Gunner wiped his eyes of sweat and mud, hoping to get a clearer understanding of what was creating the chaotic war zone that didn't involve his destruction of the cartel's mess hall.

The intense gun battle unfolded in front of him. The cartel's men were hidden behind vehicles, the block walls that contained a fountain, and their dead comrades. On the far side of the compound, he could detect the distinctive muzzle flash of an M4 carbine.

The cavalry had arrived.

CHAPTER 39

Drug Cartel Compound
The Darién Gap
Colombia, South America

Just as the gunfire between the cartel's guards and Bear started, it ceased moments later. Bear provided Cam cover fire so she could make her way to the next building around the perimeter leading to the front gate. The explosion rocked their surroundings, drawing an odd silence over the compound once again except for the crackling of burning wood emanating from the engulfed structure.

"Move!" shouted Cam, not only indicating to Bear that she'd survived the blast, but that she was in position to cover him.

"Moving!" he responded, hustling from the prison building toward a truck parked between the burning structure and the prison building.

"What the hell caused this?" asked Bear as he slid in behind the old farm truck.

"It's gotta be Gunner," replied Cam. "I wanna shout to him, but I don't want these assholes to know he's loose, or that we have anything to do with his escape."

Bear leaned around the truck and fired off a quick burst from his M4. A single stream of gunfire was sent in their direction. Bear fired back and then turned to Cam.

She talked under her breath. "We've gotta keep movin'. Gunner's smart enough to recognize return fire. He may not know it's us, but he'll take advantage of the gun battle to make his way to the gate."

"You're right," said Bear. "If he escapes before we can find him, he'll disappear into the jungle and we'll be screwed."

"Agreed," said Cam. She surveyed their surroundings and then pointed toward the fence. "Head around the back of the building. We'll use the distraction of the fire to our advantage. Keep tight along the fence until we reach the gate. Then shoot anything that moves."

"Roger that," said Bear. "Move."

"Moving." Cam darted across the opening and Bear laid down gunfire, emptying the last rounds in his first magazine. Expertly, he dropped the spent magazine to the ground and pressed another one into place.

"Move!" shouted Cam, and Bear scampered to catch up, relying on her protective fire to give him the few seconds he needed to clear the gap.

They rounded the burning building and darted across another span of thirty feet before they were behind the next structure. Suddenly, gunfire erupted again. Bullets rained down upon them, stitching the block wall to their side, splintering the stucco that hadn't already fallen off from age.

"This way," yelled Cam, who raced around the back of the building and appeared in the next opening. More bullets sailed past her, tearing up the muddy ground but missing their target.

Bear rounded the corner and eased up the side of the building next to her. A quick spurt from an automatic weapon could be heard coming from in front of the building. The guards returned fire, releasing a barrage of bullets that splintered the wooden trusses that held the tin roof in place.

Cam took a chance. She eased up to the corner of the building and called out, "Gunner! Is that you?"

"Cam?"

Cam's smile almost broke the skin of her face as it spread from ear to ear. "Yeah. Bear too. You okay?"

More gunfire was sent in their direction.

"Yeah, better now," he replied. "Listen, I think this AK is about spent. I'm pinned down behind this donkey's water trough. Well, dead donkey, anyway."

"Hold on," she said and then turned to Bear. "Hey, mister football player. How far can you toss one of your grenades?"

Bear raised his arm to flex his biceps. "C'mon, Major. What do you think?"

"Throw one toward the barn over there," she answered. "We need to distract them again, and it should cause a helluva fire."

Bear adjusted his gear and retrieved a grenade from his utility belt. Then the former Air Force Falcons football player heaved the grenade forty yards until it crashed into the broad side of the barn. The incendiary grenade's impact with the wood had the desired effect.

The explosion was slight, but the burst of fire was spectacular. The entire side of the barn was in flames, and the dry straw inside immediately caught fire.

Instinctively, the guards turned to fire wildly toward the distraction, giving Gunner time to race from behind his protective cover and join his friends at the back side of the block building.

Cam hugged him, and Gunner exchanged high fives with Bear. After the brief reunion, Cam got a better look at her friend.

"You've been foolin' around with the drug kingpin's missus? Caught with your pants down, were ya?"

Gunner laughed and, for the first time, took a look at himself. "Yep, guilty as charged. She was a handful, I'm tellin' ya. Liked it rough, too."

Several rounds ripped through the mud at their feet, reminding them of their predicament.

Bear pushed Cam and Gunner to the side so he could approach the corner of the building. He used his rifle's scope to determine the location of the guards.

He described what he saw. "They've fanned out, guys. I believe they've figured out where we are." He dropped to a knee and prepared to fire upon them.

"We've gotta do the same," said Gunner, who took charge of their escape. "There's only one way out of here that I know of, and that's the front gate."

Bear explained their point of entry. "We cut a hole in the fence, but it's on the other side of the compound from our position and we'll never get there."

Gunner reached for Cam's night-vision goggles. He studied the compound, refreshing his recollection from the times he was dragged through the middle of the clearing. He took them off and passed them back to Cam.

"On the other side of the barn is Blanco's residence. He's the head of the snake and the number one prick. He'll be guarded, but he's also arrogant enough to go toe-to-toe with us. If we can make it to there, we'll take him out, and the rest will either run off or throw their hands up. Most of them are locals who don't care about us or their employer, but probably fear his wrath if they don't fight."

Cam pulled her sidearm out of its holster and held it up next to her rifle. "Your choice. I'm good either way."

"I'll take the silenced nine," said Gunner, referring to her Beretta nine-millimeter pistol. "I don't want Blanco to know what's comin' his way."

"They're gonna have him guarded, right?" asked Bear.

"For sure," said Gunner, who took the handgun from Cam. "Navy issue?"

"Long story," said Cam.

Bear handed Gunner two grenades. "Here. Take these. Use one to kick off the festivities. I'll follow behind and let another one of these incendiary grenades blow up a truck or two."

Gunner looked skyward. The rain was lessening and the light of a new day was beginning to reveal itself. He took a deep breath. "Good, Bear. I'll use the other banger inside the house to back them down."

Cam chuckled as she slid past Bear toward the corner of the building. "Oh sure, you guys have all the fun while I get stuck behind shooting these fools."

Gunner laughed with her. "Yeah, tough duty. You're a stone-cold killer and we all know it. Have fun—don't miss."

"No prob, but hey, while you're in there, find some clothes, would ya?" said Cam as she readied her rifle to open fire. "Covered in mud and wearing your Underoos, you look like Tarzan."

"Zorro," Gunner shot back.

"Huh?" asked Bear.

"Zorro. The women in the jail said my name is *zorro* in Spanish."

"Okay, well, Zorro," she said sarcastically, "you and Tonto get movin'."

"That was the Lone Ranger, Cam," grumbled Bear. "Bernardo was Zorro's right-hand man."

Despite being in the middle of a deadly situation, Gunner paused to recall the classic fictional character. Bernardo was a deaf-mute. *Like the kid.*

Cam was ready and interrupted his thought. "Ride or die, boys!"

"Ride or die," said Gunner and Bear in unison.

She swung her weapon around the corner of the building and shouted, "Move!" Cam let out a few quick bursts of cover fire, signaling the guys to get started.

"Moving!" responded Gunner, who led the way to the next building amidst a hail of gunfire being thrown in both directions.

CHAPTER 40

Drug Cartel Compound
The Darién Gap
Colombia, South America

As he raced through the mud, Gunner saw shapes, ghostly aberrations moving through the compound, shrouded by the morning mist and the last drops of rain, which signaled the end of the violent tropical storm. In the distance, the sharp crack of thunder accompanied by lightning tore across the sky.

The menacing silhouettes that Gunner observed slipping from the structures indicated that the daylight allowed the drug cartel's guards the opportunity to position themselves for a fight. They were not necessarily trained military veterans. They were frightened and not willing to take the fight directly to their intruders.

However, they knew their compound and the buildings, which were constructed out of block with sturdiness in mind to withstand storms like the one they'd just endured. Gunner sensed their confidence, driven by numbers and familiarity with their surroundings. They moved swiftly and efficiently from point to point, fanning out their numbers to encircle the center of the compound while protecting the main house where Blanco lived.

Bear crouched by his side, as they now had a good view of the residence. It, like the other buildings, was nondescript except for a covered porch with tables and chairs for relaxing. It was the closest thing to a plantation house that a drug cartel kingpin could manage in the jungle. The Colombian cartels, far greater in number than their Mexican counterparts, lived in a constant state of flux.

The Bogota government had cooperated with the U. S. Drug Enforcement Agency to rid the country of its worst criminal element. As a result, the cartels had been pushed northward toward the Panamanian border in the Darién Gap. Here, they fought one another for territory. It was a lawless region of the world, and as a result, the cartels never got comfortable in one spot. While the Mexican drug cartels were known for their vast ranches and elaborate haciendas, the Colombians lived a more meager lifestyle despite their enormous profits.

"Ready?" asked Gunner, who wanted to begin their assault while the guards were still trying to position themselves.

"Yeah," whispered Bear in response. "See those two khaki-colored Jeeps parked together? I'll blow them first."

Gunner slapped his friend on the back. "I'll take the inside. You keep anybody else from joining the party."

"I've got ya," said Bear. He readied the grenade. "On your go."

Gunner readied his pistol and gave Bear the order. "Go!"

Bear heaved the grenade, which landed against the fender of one Jeep and then careened against the door of the other. The pinball-like action instantaneously detonated the grenade with a huge blast of energy that was supplemented by the igniting of the vehicles' gas tanks.

Both Jeeps jumped into the air, flipping on their sides in suspended animation for a brief moment before falling hard to the ground.

Gunner didn't pause to watch the carnage unfold. Both Bear and Cam opened fire on their available targets. The sounds of death filled the air as bodies were ripped open by automatic gun fire and the wounded moaned for help.

Gunner raced through the gap between the two buildings, his weapon trained on the front door. His bare feet sloshed through tiny puddles of water along the way. He was careful of his footing, reminding himself that speed could be attained; sudden stops would lead to disaster.

Two men emerged from the front door carrying automatic rifles.

They were confused at first as they focused their attention on the burning Jeeps. Gunner didn't waste any time dispatching the gunman closest to him. Two quick rounds from the Beretta, one to the torso, the other to the head, killed the man instantly.

The other guard turned toward Gunner and fired wildly over his head. He was rewarded with two hollow-point rounds that obliterated his right shoulder. He spun away like a rag doll, his finger continuing to pull the trigger, sending round after round into the porch roof. Part of his chest was missing, and he pirouetted to the ground, his gun sliding away into the mud.

Gunner rushed toward the porch. Another gunman emerged from inside the house just as Gunner arrived. He crash-tackled the unwary guard, knocking the rifle out of his hands through the sheer force of their bodies colliding. The pair spilled toward the ground, landing on top of the bodies of Gunner's two prior kills.

Gunner punched the man's chest, driving the breath out of his lungs. With a grunt, he brought the butt of his pistol down on the man's forehead, opening a gaping wound. It also knocked the man out.

All of the pain and weakness he'd endured from the days of torture were a distant memory. Gunner's inner soul was recalling what he excelled at—close-quarters combat.

And violence.

Through his training and firsthand experience, he'd developed a natural athleticism and an innate ability to sense openings in his adversary's guard. Gunner didn't care how the kill was made. It was always about self-preservation for him. Whether it was returning from a mission in a fighter jet, or a dark op with his team, he came home in one piece from these encounters, and his enemies didn't.

With water running through the holes caused by the errant gunshots, Gunner grabbed the man's rifle and pushed his way through the blood-covered mud so that his back was against the wall. He readied the automatic rifle in his left hand and the Beretta handgun in his right. One would be used for suppressive fire and the other for accurate kill shots.

He burst into the entryway of the residence and swung the rifle menacingly from side to side, ready to shoot any threat. Anger swelled within him when he saw a woman with two young children no more than six years old cowering in the corner of the room.

They appeared to be natives of Colombia or Panama. The woman was not one of Blanco's concubines but, rather, a caretaker for the home and the children. Her cowardly boss was most likely hiding within the house while the innocents were exposed to the gunfire.

They looked at Gunner with horror on their faces. He locked eyes with the family and then raised his pistol to his lips.

"Shush," he instructed. It was a directive understood around the world. *Be quiet.* All three nodded their heads and the woman hugged them tighter.

There were two hallways leading toward the rear of the house, and Gunner was about to pick one when another explosion shook the foundation of the block building.

CHAPTER 41

Drug Cartel Compound
The Darién Gap
Colombia, South America

The hail of gunfire outside the house almost drew Gunner to retreat so he could assist Cam and Bear. Shouts of instructions in Spanish filled the air, equally mixed with cries for help and wails of pain.

He took a few steps back toward the door and glanced into the compound. Apparently, Bear had located some fuel drums and dropped another incendiary grenade in their midst. Thick black smoke poured into the sky as a fire burned out of control. One of the guards rolled around on the wet ground in an attempt to put out the fire that had engulfed his clothing.

For an instant, Gunner considered the fact that Blanco had already escaped. However, the presence of the three armed men he'd killed indicated the sadistic cartel leader was still there. It wasn't likely the men had been assigned to protect the old woman and the two kids.

Daylight was upon them now, but the curtains of the residence had been pulled closed. Still, the low light gave Gunner the confidence he needed to search the house for his torturer. He slowly walked down the hallway toward a kitchen at the rear of the building.

He saw the shadow of a gunman, a rifle protruding from his shoulder, ready to shoot Gunner as he entered the room. He had other plans for his attacker.

He retrieved one of the flash-bang grenades from the waistband of his underwear and tossed it into the kitchen. He stepped back against the wall and held his hands over his ears as the stun grenade produced a blinding flash coupled with an intense blast.

"Arrggh!" screamed the man as he staggered haplessly around the corner. He'd dropped his weapon and bounced into the hallway, disoriented.

Gunner didn't hesitate as he fired a single well-placed shot into the man's head.

"Five," he whispered to himself. The Beretta's magazine held fifteen rounds, and it was important for him to maintain an ammo count.

Gunner rushed into the kitchen and scanned the room for threats. Satisfied that it was clear, he noticed the hallway on the other side of the house also entered the kitchen. He concluded it led to the bedrooms and then back into the front living area.

The barrel of the gun guided him into the dark part of the house. Gunner had one more flash-bang grenade left to be used to clear a bedroom, if necessary. He squinted, forcing his eyes to adjust to the dark space.

He heard a whimper emanating from one of the bedrooms. A fresh wave of adrenaline punched through his body as he thought of the brutality administered by Blanco. He now assumed the man was holding a hostage, a human shield, like the coward he truly was.

Gunner approached an open door, and he was surprised by a whooshing sound. A machete appeared out of the darkened hallway and knocked the rifle out of his left hand. A husky guard appeared from a curtain-covered closet that Gunner didn't see in the dark.

He lost his balance, and the machete-wielding man moved toward him, swinging wildly in an effort to rip the sharp blade into Gunner's body.

Gunner jumped backwards to evade the man's weapon, slipping slightly as he did. He fired two rounds toward the man, one of which found the steel blade of the machete. The force of the hollow-point bullet knocked the man's arm back, causing him to grunt.

Gunner gathered himself and took aim toward the man's hulking shadow. The next two rounds embedded in his thigh and stomach.

As he collapsed to his knees merely four feet from Gunner, a final round to the top of the head sent him crashing to the wood plank floor.

Ten, thought Gunner. He'd have to make these final rounds count, or he'd have his bare hands and little else to exact revenge on Jorge Blanco.

He heard whimpering again. Not cries for help. Not the muffled sounds of voices. Whimpering.

The kid!

Gunner realized that Blanco was using the deaf-mute boy as a shield against his attackers. He set his jaw and gripped his pistol a little tighter.

He approached the bedroom door, easing up to the frame to listen. It was a young boy whimpering, and it infuriated Gunner.

"Blanco!" he shouted. "Come out and leave the kid alone. It's just you and me, asshole. No guns. No knives. *Mano a mano.*"

"Die, DEA man!" Blanco shouted in return. He fired several rounds from a pistol through the doorway, splintering the wall across from Gunner.

He had to be careful because these flimsily built walls wouldn't provide him any ballistic protection. He lowered himself to a crouch, knowing that most untrained shooters had a tendency to shoot high, toward the head, the smallest and most difficult target on the human body.

His mind raced as he pulled the last stun grenade from his waistband. One of the biggest dangers to anyone coming in contact with the dangerous device was suffering from burns, temporary blindness, and permanent hearing loss. Burns and temporary blindness were fixable. Deafness was not.

The child, the only human he truly cared about in this scenario, had already suffered the loss of hearing. So Gunner performed some calculations. He considered the angle of Blanco's gunshots by studying where they'd embedded in the hallway wall. He was in the back right corner of the room, Gunner deduced.

Sorry, kid, he thought, hoping that the boy was cowering in fear with his eyes shut.

Gunner intentionally threw the grenade with a lot of force into the opposite corner of the room where Blanco was likely hiding. The pronounced impact against the wall insured its quick detonation.

The flash-bang grenade created a thunderous boom in the completely enclosed room. The walls shook and dust fell off the primitive ceiling that barely kept the rain out.

Gunner moved quickly to take advantage of his disoriented enemy. He circled around the door frame and moved in at a low crouch, focusing his senses on where Blanco was located.

He found the boy lying facedown on the floor next to the wall, but Blanco was not there. Gunner checked the boy's pulse. It was weak, but he was still alive, only knocked unconscious by the concussive effect of the blast.

How could Blanco disappear?

Gunner noticed a nightstand slightly askew. Then he saw a square hole cut in the wall and a panel knocked through on the other side.

He raced out of the room and toward the front of the house. Blanco was almost through the door when Gunner caught up to him.

The two men crashed into the open doorframe and spilled out onto the porch. Blanco was muscular, strong, and determined to live. He got the upper hand initially, laying punch after punch to Gunner's ribs and chest, which had been subjected to the cattle-prod torture repeatedly.

Gunner fought back with a staggering uppercut, ripping his fist through the air like a heat-seeking missile searching for Blanco's jaw.

The sound of fist crunching against bone revealed the result. The blow struck Blanco hard enough to smash his lower teeth off their gums, cutting into his tongue and sending his head snapping backward like a whip.

Blanco landed on his back next to one of the dead guards, his head hitting the ground with a thud. Gunner didn't hesitate. He pounced on his torturer, clamping his hand around the man's throat, fully intending to choke him to death.

The men stared at one another, a test of wills as Blanco gripped Gunner's wrist with both hands. He tried to bring his knees up to kick Gunner in the groin, but failed. The primal adrenaline running through Gunner's body caused the veins in his forearms to bulge through his skin.

Gunner looked demented. Deranged. Unhinged.

And, in that moment, he was.

He began to pound Blanco's head into the ground as he squeezed his thumb against his throat. He leaned over to apply all the pressure he could using his body weight. He smacked the back of Blanco's skull against the ground three more times.

Blood began to pour out of the man's ears as his eyelids began to flicker. His defensive grip on Gunner's wrists loosened and then fell away completely. Then a final gasp of air released from Jorge Blanco's lungs as he died.

Angry and frustrated, Gunner gave the man's head one more pounding against the ground before he pushed himself up. He waved for the older woman to come out of hiding and help him.

"*Por favor! Aquí!*" He reached for her arm, but she pulled away. "*El niño. Por favor.*"

Reluctantly, she rose from the floor and left with the other two children as they rushed down the hallway. With the threat extinguished inside the residence, Gunner made his way to the porch as he realized the gunfire had stopped.

Sunshine was peering through the jungle canopy, and the morning fog was beginning to clear. The heavy, moist air did little to alleviate the smell of burning gasoline, gunpowder, and death. Dozens of armed men lay around the compound. Most had been killed by Cam's and Bear's bullets. Others were still smoldering after being caught up in the carnage caused by the incendiary devices.

"Clear!" Bear's voice echoed through the compound.

"Clear!" responded Cam.

The two approached from opposite directions, carrying their weapons at low ready, but appearing relaxed.

Cam arrived at the residence first. She kicked Blanco's head. "Is this our kingpin?"

"Was," replied Gunner. "Jorge Blanco. One sick asshole."

Blanco's lifeless body was sprawled out in a pool of blood that belonged to him and his men. His eyes bulged, but nobody did him the honor of closing his lids.

"How're ya doin'?" asked Bear.

Gunner simply nodded. He turned to Cam. "Your Spanish is better than mine. Down the right hallway, there's an old lady with three kids. One of them is a deaf-mute who helped me. Would you—?"

Cam raised her hand. "Say no more. I'm on it. Under one condition."

"What?" asked Gunner.

"Dude, now will you get some damn clothes on?"

Gunner looked down at his muscular body, which was covered in a combination of dried and wet mud mixed with blood. He began to laugh. "Yeah, kinda scary lookin'."

Bear motioned for Gunner to follow him. "We'll rinse you off in the donkey's water trough and I'll find some shoes and pants your size."

"I've got a better idea," said Gunner as he turned his attention toward the barn. "Did the whole thing burn?"

"Nah, only this side. The rain doused the fire before it spread."

"Follow me," said Gunner as he jogged across the compound, studying the killed guards as he did. Bear trudged along, trying to keep pace.

Gunner arrived at the still-smoldering structure, and after confirming that it wasn't about to collapse, he made his way into the corner of the barn where the accountant had emerged the day Blanco tortured him with the cattle prod.

"I knew it! It's here." Gunner reached into a pile of loose hay and retrieved his blue duffle bag with his name screen-printed on the front. "I've got clothes. Now, show me to the donkey trough, and see if you can find me a pair of size elevens that aren't covered with blood or full of toe jam."

Bear shook his head and chuckled before he began his search. Gunner washed off and slipped on a pair of khakis and a white polo shirt. His mind flashed back to his first day of training in Building 9 at the Johnson Space Center. A lot had happened in the last two weeks.

"Gunner, do you know this young guy?" asked Cam, who'd emerged from Blanco's residence.

The boy who had befriended him ran across the compound and crashed into Gunner, almost toppling them both over into the water trough. Tears streamed down his face as he made eye contact with Gunner. Then the boy buried his face in Gunner's stomach.

Gunner ran his fingers through the kid's black hair. It was a kind, gentle gesture that the boy probably hadn't experienced since he was in the arms of his mother.

He dropped to a knee so they were face-to-face as he spoke, overemphasizing the words so the boy could read his lips. *"Tu madre. Sí?"*

A wave of sadness came over the boy's face and he began to cry. He shook his head slowly from side to side and withdrew within himself once again.

Gunner gently took the boy's wet cheeks in his hands and forced the distraught child to look at him again. He smiled, fighting back the tears. With his two thumbs, he wiped the moisture off the boy's face.

He patted the boy on the chest and then pointed at the prison building. He repeated the words. *"Tu madre. Sí! Sí!"* As he spoke, he smiled and nodded his head rapidly while pointing toward the building.

Like an excited puppy wanting to go see something, but unsure if it was okay, the boy raced toward the building, suddenly stopped, and turned toward Gunner in search of affirmation.

Gunner repeated, *"Tu madre. Sí! Sí!"*

The boy pointed toward the building. Gunner rose from his crouch and walked briskly to catch up to the boy. He wrapped his arm around his shoulder and the two walked side by side inside.

Moments later, shouts of happiness and celebration filled the air, letting everyone in the compound know of the joyful reunion between mother and son.

CHAPTER 42

Drug Cartel Compound
The Darién Gap
Colombia, South America

Gunner found the keys where he'd left them and released Caroline first so she could reunite with her son. As he opened the other cells, the women were fearful at first, but after realizing they were free, they ran out of the prison building and toward the front gate. The elderly woman who cared for the children convinced them they were safe, and eventually, most everyone gathered in the center of the compound.

Gunner introduced Cam and Bear to Caroline.

After exchanging some pleasantries, Caroline spoke in a hushed voice. "I need to help these women get home. Most of them are probably from Colombia or local villages."

Gunner glanced around the compound and counted half a dozen vehicles that were probably in operating condition. "We can try to top these cars off with fuel. Do you know your way around after you leave the compound?"

"Yes, but it's not that easy. The Darién Gap is full of bandits and other drug cartels. We'll need guns and money, or dope."

"Protection currency," offered Cam.

"Yes. None of these women would be able to fight their way through the roadblocks, but at least they'd have something to trade besides themselves."

Gunner wandered away with his hands on his hips, studying the buildings. He paused and studied the building that Bear had identified as the warehouse. "That's where they keep the drugs?"

"Yes," replied Bear. "Everything from coca plants to finished product. It's like an assembly line process in there."

Cam joined Gunner's side. "That gives them drugs and guns to barter. I say we burn up the rest of their product, as Bear calls it, when we leave."

"Agreed," said Gunner. "But something's off here."

"What?"

"Where's the money? This is a cash business. They had an accountant-looking guy who—"

Cam cut him off. "Yeah, Bear found him. He shot himself in the head."

"Another coward," mumbled Gunner. He continued to stare at the buildings. "C'mon, Cam, where's the drug money?" He turned to Caroline and continued. "Caroline, do you know where Blanco and his accountant kept their cash? Did they hide it in the jungle?"

She shrugged. "I doubt he'd leave it outside the fence. He never confided in me, you know. I was there for one purpose." She hung her head in shame.

Gunner had a hunch and he began walking toward the barn. It was a one-story structure with a loft full of hay. On the side that wasn't burnt, pens for animals were built together with a couple of toolsheds.

Cam and Bear followed him, leaving the women and children alone to talk among themselves.

"What are you thinking?" asked Bear.

"The first time they tortured me, the accountant guy showed up out of nowhere. I just thought he was creepy, you know, getting his jollies in the dark corner of the barn while they stuck it to the DEA guy."

"What's up with that, by the way?" asked Cam.

"They were convinced I was a narc," replied Gunner. "Trust me, being white, American, and DEA wasn't a good combo around here."

"Didn't you explain that you were an astronaut?" asked Bear.

Gunner chuckled. "Yeah, I tried the truth. They laughed

hysterically and then stuck me with the cattle prod some more."

The trio arrived at the barn and looked around. Gunner made his way to where he'd found his duffle bag earlier. At the time, he hadn't given the layout of the barn and the stacked hay bales a second thought.

Gunner looked up to the rafters and then walked around the pile of hay to study the walls.

"Well, I'll be damned," he muttered before slapping Bear on the back. "Help me out, would ya?"

Gunner climbed on the first row of hay bales and started grabbing the upper bales by the string, systematically moving the stack with Bear's assistance. Within a few minutes, he'd created an opening to the back wall of the barn.

Only, it wasn't a wall but, rather, a hidden storage room.

They worked faster now that Gunner might have solved the mystery. Cam casually strolled to the large opening of the barn that also served as the boundary between the charred remains and the undamaged side where they were removing the bales.

Gunner reached a door. "Bear, let me have your blade."

The metallic sound of the knife sliding out of the leg sheath could be heard. Bear gripped it by the steel blade and handed it to Gunner grip first.

Gunner went to work on the simple padlocked door. The drug cartel never imagined any of their adversaries getting this close. He easily jammed the knife into the door's latch and broke it free. After handing the knife back to Bear, he pulled the door open.

"Holy smokes!" exclaimed Bear. "This is the freakin' mother lode!"

"Literally," added Gunner, referring to the bags of gold stacked on the shelf.

Cam squeezed in between the two men like a little sister who wanted to see too.

The enclosed storage space was made of concrete block throughout. Walls, ceiling, and floor were white painted block. Inside, wooden shelves lined every inch of wall space except for a small desk at one end. A stack of ledgers and a calculator occupied the desktop.

But none of that was of interest to Gunner. It was the money and gold that astonished him. Bundles upon bundles of hundred-dollar bills, American, were shoved onto the shelves. In addition, ziplock bags of gold coins could be seen.

Cam entered first and walked around the room, staring at the amount of currency in absolute wonderment. Bear was next. He immediately grabbed a baggie of gold, commenting on how heavy it was considering it fit into the ziplock.

Gunner turned to see if they were still alone before entering. He tried to estimate how much cash and gold was in the small room. He studied the accountant's numbers, which were written on the stacks using masking tape. He marveled at the simplicity of their methods, and then his mind raced as his calculations entered the millions.

He touched Bear and Cam on the arms. "Guys, I think we've seen enough. Let's go outside and talk about this."

Each of them gave the drug cartel's ill-gotten gains a final touch and then reluctantly exited. Gunner pushed the door closed and led them to the outside of the barn.

"Okay, listen up, guys," he began. "I know what you're both thinking. But you gotta consider this. What we just found is blood money, earned by selling illegal drugs that landed on the streets of America. Do we really feel good about—?"

Cam spoke first. "Gunner, are you seriously considering leaving that behind? When did you get all moral and stuff?"

Bear was quick to weigh in. "Besides, what are you gonna do with it? Leave it here? Call the Colombian cops?"

Gunner raised his hands to calm his friends down. "No, nothing like that. I just wanted to make sure we're on the same page. This money can do a lot of good for a lot of people, including us. I don't judge and I don't give a damn if others judge me. I mean, do you think NASA or the DOD or even Ghost promised me a bonus for flying into space to kill an asteroid. Hell no."

"So what's the plan?" asked Cam.

"Well, we need to keep this quiet so we don't create a riot," began

Gunner in response. He nodded toward Caroline and the other hostages. "In case you haven't counted, they now have more guns than we do."

Cam looked over at the women, who were milling about, carrying AK-47s like they were walking sticks. "Do you think they'd take us on? Seriously?"

"No," replied Gunner, and then he hesitated. "No, I hope not anyway. I just don't want to have to kill any of them if they try."

Bear made a suggestion. "I counted a dozen baggies of gold. Let's give it to them. They can't readily spend the Benjamins anyway. Plus, who knows, the damn dollar has probably collapsed after the meteor storm."

"I agree with Bear," said Cam. "As they travel, it'll be easier for them to conceal gold while on the road."

Gunner nodded his agreement. He instructed Bear to retrieve the gold, and he'd explain to Caroline what they had in mind. Once they had the women and children settled in their vehicles, they'd send the caravan on their way.

Gunner approached the boy and scruffed the top of his head. A broad smile came over his face, although he hadn't really stopped smiling since he reunited with his mother.

He pulled her to the side and got right to the point. "Caroline, we found some gold coins that we'd like to give everyone. I don't know how much it's worth, but based on the weight, I'm gonna guess around a hundred thousand for each of you."

She didn't respond but, rather, immediately wrapped her arms around Gunner. She whispered the words *thank you* in his ear.

He continued. "I wish we could help all of you get home, but we can't. Are you sure you can handle this?"

"Yes. I know my way around, and there are people I can call upon for help. Once we make it to the river, our options are greater."

Gunner knelt down next to the young boy. "You know, I never got your name."

"Angel," said Caroline, pronouncing it in her native tongue as *an-hale*. "He's my Angel."

"Well, Angel, one day I hope your mother will tell you how much you have meant to me. I will never forget you, kid."

Gunner hugged the boy again and had difficulty letting him go, even as Cam told him everything was ready. Gunner finally released his embrace of Angel and then hugged Caroline a final time.

"Godspeed, Caroline."

"Same to you, Gunner Fox. I've never met a man like you. Thank you for saving us all."

Gunner looked to the ground, then to the sky, and nodded.

Bear opened the gates and waved to the women as they drove away from the compound in a variety of vehicles. Cam and Gunner joined his side, and within a minute, they were alone.

CHAPTER 43

Drug Cartel Compound
The Darién Gap
Colombia, South America

Bear closed the gates and joined Gunner in the center of the compound. Cam wanted to make one more sweep around the buildings to make sure there were no stowaways or stragglers.

"Bear, how did you get here?" Gunner asked.

"Over the river and through the woods, dude. You have no idea."

Gunner chuckled. "Yeah, actually I do. I mean what type of aircraft? I assume you flew in, right?"

"You bet. They assigned us another Valor AV-280, except this variant's better. It has more cargo space and double the fuel capacity."

"Where'd you come from?"

"We staged on the USS *Harry S. Truman* and CSG 8 in the Caribbean Sea. But they were buggin' out to the Atlantic. It seems the Russians decided to flex their muscles in the middle of the chaos."

Gunner shook his head and furrowed his brow. *Same shit, different day.*

Bear continued as Cam rejoined the group. "Anyway, we dropped it down about four clicks from here on the far side of the wreckage. The plan was to fly to an agency dark site in Costa Rica to refuel, and then haul our cookies back to the ranch."

Gunner strolled away and turned in a complete circle. "Can you drop the Valor here, in the middle of the compound?"

Bear began to point to the burned-out trucks and dead bodies. "Oh, I've got room, but the LZ is not so great," he replied, referring to the landing zone.

"We can clear it, but it'll take some time," suggested Cam.

Gunner had a thought. "Bear, can you make it to the Valor on your own?"

Bear took a moment to explain the difficult, roundabout way they'd used to find the compound. Gunner relayed his more direct approach, using the rope bridge that led directly to the crash site. The three of them studied their GPS devices and concluded that Bear would have to trek about three miles through the jungle, which was much closer than they realized.

"Sounds like a plan," said Bear. "I've got clear skies, six full magazines, and a healthy dose of paranoia to keep me alive as I cut through the jungle. No prob."

Gunner laughed and fist-bumped his friend. "I never thought otherwise. Be careful, and we'll have this place cleared and ready when you get back."

Bear and Cam exchanged high fives and he was off. For the next hour, Cam and Gunner moved the dead bodies into the warehouse. The two of them lined up the dead, face up, and then took photos of them on Blanco's cell phone. They planned on taking the phone and a box loaded with all of the books and records in it to the DEA, assuming they'd be able to use them in some manner.

Next, they searched all the buildings in the compound, looking for drugs or anything that might assist future drug cartels in the production of cocaine. They wanted to destroy it all on their way out. The drugs, equipment, and dead bodies were gathered in the warehouse building. Cans of gasoline and kerosene were at the ready to torch the entire place on exit.

Using a large farm truck, Gunner and Cam worked together to push the charred remains of the vehicles that were damaged during the battle with the cartel. When they were done, Bear's landing zone was more than wide enough to accommodate the tilt-rotor aircraft.

Finally, they gathered up everything from duffle bags to grain sacks to be used to load the bundles of money into the Valor.

Time passed quickly, and before long, the thumping sound of the tilt-rotors could be heard over the jungle canopy. Cam and Gunner stood in the middle of the compound, shielding their eyes from the bright afternoon sun.

They stared at the bags full of money in silence as Bear began his descent.

Then Cam turned to Gunner. "Heather would be proud of you, you know?"

He laughed. "Why, because now we're rich?"

"No, dumbass," said Cam jokingly. "You do realize that you saved the freakin' planet, right?"

Gunner shrugged. "Hell, I haven't even thought about that. Cam, when I was coming back from the asteroid, I was the only one alive. There was so much debris. I mean huge chunks of space rocks flying alongside the Starhopper. It looked pretty bad from my perspective."

"Well, we'll have to see what the final damage assessments are, but you saved a lot of lives up there."

Gunner frowned. "I took some, too. There's so much I have to tell you about the Russians."

"Same here," she replied. "Listen, we've got plenty of time for that. I'm talking about what you did for Earth. You did it, Gunner. I guess now we can call you a space cowboy."

"Shut up, Cam. I'll never go back into space."

"Never say never."

"Never. There, I said it again and I mean it. This pilot plans on keeping his feet right here on the ground, or at least in close proximity of it anyway."

The two separated to guide Bear to the cleared space in the compound. Gunner and Cam quickly loaded their gear and the bags of money on board the Valor. Together, they worked to start the fire inside the warehouse building.

Just as they lifted off, a series of small explosions occurred in which pockets of air were ignited by the flames. By the time the Valor reached the top of the jungle canopy, the entire compound appeared to be in the midst of an inferno.

"Okay, guys, let's head home," said Bear as he reached for the controls to convert the tilt-rotors to fly as an airplane.

"Not just yet, Bear," interrupted Gunner. "We've got one more stop to make."

CHAPTER 44

Fort Mills
Near Delta, Alabama

Pop considered himself to be a social creature. Unlike Gunner, who preferred to be locked away at his Dog Island beach house, Pop had to be on the go. When there were no visitors to ferry back and forth between Carrabelle and the island, he'd make the rounds on his golf cart, visiting with neighbors. Sometimes, he'd fuel up the Cessna 185 Skywagon and explore the Gulf Coast, meeting new people and entering into long conversations about nothing in particular.

At first, he was comfortable being left alone at Fort Mills with Howard. Cam and Bear were going to find his son. He found ways to stay busy, falling back on his old skills learned in the Air Force to catalog and organize all of their supplies.

He'd monitored all forms of radio communications at his disposal. The Bearcat radio scanner constantly monitored local first responders. The American Red Cross crank radio was set to a local AM station that provided updates from available news sources. But it was the ham radios that provided him a glimpse into the impact the remnants of the asteroid had on the nation and the world.

He'd fallen asleep on several occasions, slumped over on the desk where the ham radio base receiver was located. Once in a while, because he simply wanted to engage in human contact, Pop had initiated conversations with ham operators around the country.

Sometimes he was brutally chastised, unfairly so, for not having a license and the customary call sign. He'd determined that many operators were a little over the top in their efforts to protect their territory.

Others were more understanding, especially under the circumstances, where television outlets were unable to broadcast and news was only delivered through word of mouth.

Despite the challenges, he had a pretty good handle on the carnage being wrought around the world. He was relieved that the damage to the U.S. had been confined to three regions—North-Central California and Western Nevada, the Northeast, and the upper Midwest along the Canadian border. Cities around the Great Lakes were especially hard hit as large chunks of space rock caused tsunami conditions along the low-lying areas near the water.

It was his vigilance in monitoring radio chatter that allowed him to keep up with the wildfires burning in central Alabama. The earliest meteorites that struck east of Birmingham had taken their toll on the forests surrounding the remote community of Delta where the cabin was located.

At one point, as the Clay County Emergency Management Services asked for local residents to assist in monitoring the progress of the fire as it spread into Cheaha State Park, Pop took the Cessna for a ride.

For an hour, he flew from Interstate 20 to his north, and then south into the Talladega National Forest, observing the fire line and making notes of visible landmarks. He wasn't familiar with this area like he was the Florida Panhandle, but he'd grown adept at picking out distinctive features of terrain or man-made structures while he was soaring overhead.

He relayed the information to the local sheriff's office, and he was later credited with saving the lives of several families in the small community of Highland located to the southwest of Fort Mills.

The flight also helped him make a decision. As the meteor storm began to dissipate on Monday morning, word began to spread across the country that the lower forty-eight could breathe a sigh of relief.

To be sure, there were challenges and threats to everyone's safety, just not from above. The process of helping the injured, identifying the dead, and rebuilding the nation would begin on May 1.

Pop wanted to go home and so did Howard. The basset hound

never got comfortable in his new surroundings. He had difficulty sleeping, which was a real sign that he was distressed. That pup slept more than he was awake. He also missed Gunner, as did Pop.

His flight to inspect the status of the fire revealed that local firefighters had made a last stand, so to speak, at County Road 49 that ran north-south through the county. They'd used the best available fire-suppression tactics, including creating a fire line along the road.

A fire line was a substantial undertaking designed to create a break in a wildfire's fuel. Using heavy machinery like bulldozers and Bobcats, firefighters cut, scraped and dug at the earth in an attempt to widen an already existing barrier.

County Road 49 had become their last line of defense. Locals volunteered to assist in the effort, using hand tools and chain saws to clear the west side of the road.

On Pop's last pass, he saw that the fire had jumped the road and was now burning out of control to the immediate west of Fort Mills. The small lake and stream that separated the woods from his position wouldn't be sufficient to stop the flames, as they were continuously whipped up by wind.

So he began his calculations. He'd made the decision to return to Dog Island, and if it was gone due to a tsunami, then he'd try to make his way back to Maxwell as instructed. However, his hour-long flight had used up more of the aviation fuel than he'd planned. As a result, Dog Island was truly his only option.

The plane's empty weight was approximately two thousand pounds, and its maximum takeoff weight allowed for another thousand pounds of supplies, including the pilot and his sixty-pound passenger. Pop packed the most important supplies, including all of the radio communications equipment, weapons, ammo, and some food. He knew takeoff would be difficult, but he had confidence in his abilities to bring the Cessna off the water.

That morning, Pop told Howard the good news that they were going home. Howard sensed the excitement and spent much of the morning running through the cabin and barking. That, coupled with the two Benadryl tablets Pop had given him for his allergies, caused Howard to become sleepy. That was for the best, as he'd waited until the last minute to break the bad news—Howard was going to fly.

The basset hated flying. The moment Pop began to walk him down the dock, he dropped his hind end and hunkered down. He became dead weight, and ultimately, Pop had to use all his strength to pick him up, carry him to the plane, and hoist him aboard.

It was the moment of truth. The smell of smoke was strong now, and the decision to leave appeared to be a good one. The Cessna float plane seemed to struggle, but it rose into the sky just above the tops of the pine trees that would be in flames by the end of the day.

As Pop flew southward, he realized the wildfire was only one ridge away from roaring toward the cabin. If he hadn't taken the flight to assist the local authorities, it was possible he and Howard would've died.

Feeling better now that he was airborne, he checked his gauges and chatted up his passenger. A gust of wind slapped the Cessna in the side, causing its fixed wing to waver. Pop held on and maintained control.

"Old boy, I don't see any fires up ahead. What we just left looked more like Hell than Tate's Hell Forest."

Pop began to lower his altitude to get a better look at Franklin County, which spread out ahead of him along the coast. There was one area that appeared to be smoldering well to his east toward Alligator Point, but other than that, the ground didn't appear to be disturbed. The Gulf of Mexico came into view, as did Saint George Sound.

He began his descent, flying across Highway 98, over Hidden Beaches, and toward The Cut. Before he landed, he wanted to encircle the island to observe the damage.

Pop was puzzled. He could see the outline of Dog Island, but to the west, St. George Island seemed considerably shorter and The Cut was much wider. He immediately feared that a tsunami had in fact hit the islands, or that the undercurrent pulled away the beaches.

He slowed his airspeed and made a wide left turn as he moved over the enlarged gap between the two islands. He banked left and pressed his nose to the glass while firmly holding Howard in the copilot's seat.

Pop gasped and shook his head in amazement at what he saw.

CHAPTER 45

The Darién Gap
Colombia, South America

Bear struggled to drop the AV-280 Valor between the trees overhanging the crash site of the Starhopper. Despite the wide swath of jungle that had been crushed below, the tree canopy remained for the largest part of the area that contained the wreckage.

To Bear's credit, he didn't complain or spew out any sarcastic one-liners, which were his trademark. He knew how important this was to Gunner.

"Hang on, guys. I think I've got the angle right this time," said Bear, who'd manipulated the tilt-rotor's descent to an angle that was considered dangerous by the designers at Bell and Lockheed Martin. Of course, they'd never consulted an expert pilot like Lieutenant Barrett King. Hands-on experience was far more valuable than computer-simulated flights.

"Um, we hope so," said Gunner as a palm frond was shredded by the rotors. He glanced at Cam, who put her index finger to her ear and twirled it in a circular motion, indicating they were crazy to attempt this.

Bear corrected the aircraft back to a stable position and gently dropped it to the jungle floor, using two fallen black palms as landing skids. As he powered down, he looked through the external cameras to ensure the trees would hold them in place.

"I think we're good," he muttered through the comms.

"You think?" asked Cam, her voice unsure.

"No. I'm positive," replied Bear. He stood and performed a quick

214

visual inspection through the windows. Suddenly, he wasn't so sure. "Um, hang tight while I take a look."

He opened the door panel of the aircraft and slowly lowered himself onto the trunk of the fallen palm tree. After studying the jungle floor, he walked around until he was satisfied.

"It's a solid landing, guys. That said, I wouldn't mind makin' it snappy."

Cam turned to Gunner. "Did you find the body bag?"

He held up a nylon bag with a zippered closure. His mood was glum, but his intentions were good. He didn't want to dishonor the memory of Chief Rawlings by leaving his body to be fed upon by the creatures of the jungle. The man was a hero and deserved a proper burial.

Gunner gave Cam a thumbs-up and the two exited the Valor. All three of them carried their sidearms, and Cam, who would handle perimeter security, carried a rifle too.

Bear and Gunner led the way to where the famous astronaut's body had been left a few days prior. The lush tropical vegetation had begun to grow, already staking its claim on the remains of the Starhopper.

"Some of the body parts that we saw the other day are missing now," observed Bear.

"I was afraid of that," said Gunner. "That's why I wrapped him and placed his body on that piece of the outer shell. I hoped it would minimize the number of animals that could reach him."

"I've got movement!" exclaimed Cam. "Three o'clock, in the trees."

Gunner pulled his weapon and turned his body to the right, searching for the possible threat. The movement was imperceptible, but there. It was his old friend the anaconda.

"You've got good eyes," said Gunner.

"It's amazing how well they work when you're half-scared out of your wits. Every movement sends a shock through my body."

"I don't get you, Cam," said Bear as he waved to Gunner to continue. "You can take on a cartel and wipe the floor with 'em, but this place has you scared."

"I was okay about the whole thing until the jaguar almost ate us," she said.

"Jaguar?" asked Gunner as he stepped to the side to avoid several scorpions being consumed by ants.

"Yeah, just another story to tell over beers at the beach," she replied.

"Good," interrupted Bear, pointing ahead. "It's just as we left it."

Bear picked up the pace and Gunner jogged to catch up with him. While the guys loaded Chief Rawlings's body into the white, nonporous bag made of heavy-duty plastic, Cam wandered ahead toward the crew module.

"Hey, do you think we should do anything with this part? I mean, is there a flight data recorder or something to bring back?"

Gunner and Bear had made their way back to the ground, each holding an end of the body bag. Gunner replied, "Let's just leave it. If we can get a message through to Ghost, I'm sure he'll advise NASA. I suspect hundreds of scientists will descend upon here within hours after his call."

As they walked back to the Valor, Bear commented about the communications satellites. "You'd think with the thousands of satellites that orbit Earth, we could get patched through to one of them."

Gunner shook his head. "You should've seen it, Bear. The smallest piece of debris would tear through those things. I mean, I get why they had me blast it. The trajectory was heading for a bull's-eye on our planet. However, the thousands upon thousands of meteors created from the asteroid crushed everything in their path."

Cam caught up to the guys and joined the conversation. "Satellites, internet, telecommunications, weather prediction. The list of things we'll have to do without for a while is long."

"It may not seem that important under the circumstances," began Gunner, "but during my Earth science studies, I relied a lot on information transmitted back to Earth from satellites. They measure gases in the atmosphere, including ozone and carbon dioxide. They're also used to measure the energy Earth emits from volcanoes or tectonic plate shifts."

"Earthquakes, pole shifts, stuff like that, right?" said Bear.

"Exactly," replied Gunner. "I imagine the world's governments will focus on reestablishing communications networks. The warning systems I just described will take a back seat."

"That'll open us up for more threats from natural disasters."

Gunner grimaced and looked toward the sky. Like so many others, he took for granted the importance of technology in their lives. From hurricane warnings to volcanic activity, the planet would be more vulnerable until the technology was reinstated.

This thought led him to ask, "Cam, does this dark site in Costa Rica know we're coming?"

"The Navy lieutenant referred to it as a lily pad, but it's basically the same thing as the dark sites we've used on missions elsewhere. But, to answer your question, um, no. They don't know we're coming, so we need to play nice when we get there."

CHAPTER 46

Unknown Location
Costa Rica, Central America

It was dark as Bear navigated their aircraft toward the coordinates on the GPS screen. The AV-280's navigational panel provided a variety of colors and lights that illuminated the concerned look on Bear's face. Gunner shared the same concern.

"Are you guys sure you got the coordinates correct?" he asked, looking first to Bear and then back to Cam, who sat quietly in the dark.

"Give me a minute," said Bear. "They call it a dark site for a reason."

"Not because it's dark and can't be seen, goober," said Cam. "We ran into this in Myanmar, remember?"

"That's right, Bear," added Gunner. "It took a while for their radar to identify our code being sent by the transponder. If they're not expecting us, they may not trust the signal."

"And not turn on the landing lights," interjected Cam.

Suddenly, a ring of bright green lights illuminated together with smaller white lights that formed a large H in the center.

"Bingo! It's a heliport," said Bear.

He navigated the Valor over the H and quickly brought the tilt-rotor aircraft to an abrupt landing. Ordinarily, a heliport was required to have unobstructed approach and departure paths. This landing area would never have been deemed safe by the Federal Aviation Administration.

Within seconds after they landed and Bear began shutting down the aircraft, the heliport lights were extinguished and the trio was in the dark again.

"Jeez, that's some welcome," said Bear until he stopped his thought. They were now surrounded by flashlights attached to automatic weapons pointed at the doors and windows of the Valor.

Gunner unbuckled his harnesses and stood in the cockpit. "You wait here. There's no need to spend any more time than necessary. I'll get our fuel and try to see if they have comms to get me through to Fort Belvoir."

"Sidearm?" Cam suggested.

"No. Either they'll believe me when I explain what's going on, or they won't. One gun would just get me killed if these guys are trigger-happy or on edge."

Bear left the pilot's seat and assisted Gunner out of the Valor. The armed security personnel quickly repositioned to have numerous flashlights lighting up the door, with accompanying red dot lasers from their sights trained on Gunner's chest. He looked down and immediately raised his arms.

Gunner decided to play with the armed security force. He said in a robotic voice. "My name is Major Gunner Fox and I am from outer space. Take me to your leader."

Cam could be heard giggling in the background as she and Bear exchanged high fives.

"Hands up, smart guy!" shouted one of the men. He stepped forward into the beams of the flashlights. "I'm Captain Don Ruiz. Pal, if you're not Gunner Fox, I'll execute you myself."

"I am, so relax," said Gunner. He looked down at the red dots wiggling across his chest and torso. "Do you mind telling your people to stand down before somebody's nervous, sweaty finger lights me up?"

Captain Ruiz gave the order and walked closer to Gunner. He studied his face through the limited light. Gunner remained stoic with his arms raised while the captain slowly walked around Gunner to examine his body. Then he looked toward the Valor. "Major, welcome home. You look a little worse for wear."

"Yeah, it was a rough ride, an even rougher landing, but it was the inhospitable Colombian drug cartel that caused my face to look like a pizza that fell facedown onto the floor."

The captain laughed. "We've got someone who can look at that for you, sir." Now that the captain was aware of who Gunner was, his tone of voice and attitude changed.

"That won't be necessary, Captain. I'd like to make a call back to the States, and my team would appreciate anything you might have to eat or drink besides water and protein bars."

"Don't say another word, Major. We can help you on all of the above. In fact, we've got extra bunks for you and your team to rest. They're not fancy, but you don't have to worry about mosquitoes or any other jungle inhabitants that lurk around at night."

Gunner thought for a moment. He was exhausted and he was certain the others were as well. He'd give anything to sleep in his own home, if it was still there. But if it wasn't, he'd be able to deal with it better after a good night's sleep.

"You know, Captain, I don't think you'll have to twist our arms. We promise not to be in your way."

"You'll not be a bother," he said. "Truthfully, it's kind of boring out here. We act as a staging area for drug raids into Panama or Guatemala and to assist CIA efforts to destabilize the government in Nicaragua. At the moment, everyone is a little preoccupied with more important things."

Gunner turned and addressed Cam, who was leaning through the door in an effort to eavesdrop. "Cam, come on out. We're gonna rest for the night and get some food. We'll leave at first light."

"That's a good decision, Major. Global positioning satellites have been destroyed, and their relays are sporadic, so you'll find difficulty relying upon them for navigation. Are you comfortable with visual navigation?"

"Not a problem."

"Good, then welcome to a place you'll never see, or speak of, again."

Gunner laughed as Cam and Bear joined them. "That works for us."

PART FIVE

May

CHAPTER 47

Defense Threat Reduction Agency
Fort Belvoir, Virginia

Ghost disconnected the call, leaned back in his chair, and allowed the back of his head to thump the padded headrest. His eyes closed and he let out a sigh. Finally, after a brief moment to reflect on his conversation with Gunner and Cam, he managed a smile. The Jackal, who'd remained vigilant throughout the process, looked like she'd been right alongside Gunner throughout the entire ordeal. Ghost began to wonder if she'd need medical attention. She immediately assuaged his concerns.

"Sir, what he's been through is extraordinary. I mean, this is the stuff movies are made of."

Ghost raised his eyebrows and pursed his lips. "Yet it's just the beginning in many ways. Cuccinelli, this day may go down as my best, or my worst. Perhaps both. But it will certainly be my most memorable."

The Jackal attempted to bolster his confidence and demeanor. "Sir, I don't see how this can be viewed as anything but fantastic news. Gunner made it home. He survived the attack on the asteroid and made the perilous journey. Of course, the loss of life of Chief Rawlings and the others is regrettable, but it could've been avoided except for the Russians."

"That's the problem," said Ghost. "You know how these things go. At first, there will be a celebration for Gunner, one that he'll want no part of, I can assure you. Then the investigative teams will descend upon the Darién Gap to pore over every broken palm frond and piece of metal. During that time, some eagle-eyed do-gooder will

225

find a body part that sparks questions of foul play. Suddenly, a hero becomes a suspect as the investigation turns from crash site to crime scene."

The Jackal nodded. "Sadly, that's how these things go. What are you going to do?"

"Well, for one thing, I can't hide Gunner's return, although I can delay it somewhat. Giving him a day or two to decompress will prevent him from shooting some poor bastard from CNN who ventures onto Dog Island in a canoe with a cameraman."

The Jackal started laughing. "I can see that happening."

"Oh, make no mistake, it will. And if he doesn't shoot the reporter, one of his pit bulls, Cam or Bear, will do it. Trust me, they're fiercely protective of their friend."

The Jackal stood and stretched her back. She was tired, but very much alert. "Okay, here I go again, with my FBI hat on. As is always the case, the less said, the better. Neither you nor Gunner should speak to anyone about what happened in space. Make them ask. You can't get hammered for perjury if you keep your mouth shut."

"That's true, but a lie of omission is a lie nonetheless. Isn't that what Colonel Robinson and our recently departed mission director Mark Foster were guilty of?"

"Yes, sir, and neither civilian nor military justice will ever convict or punish Colonel Robinson of anything."

"Gunner Fox might," added Ghost.

"True, but he's the one who deserves to administer the appropriate sentence. He was the one who suffered because of the wrongdoing."

"Cuccinelli, you heard his description of what happened aboard the Starhopper. He's capable of doing that and more to Robinson."

"Yes, but nobody will ever know it was him if we keep the truth among our core group."

Ghost smiled at the young FBI agent. He promised to think of a way to keep her around. She was more than a computer specialist. Her analytical mind could be applied to virtually any operation he put a team through.

He took a breath and leaned onto his desk with both elbows. He tapped his fingers on the phone next to him. Traditional telephone landlines, especially those maintained by the military, remained open and functioning. He'd need to call Washington first. The Pentagon was back to full operations now that the asteroid threat had ceased. Today, the president and his staff would be returning to the White House to begin the arduous task of helping its citizens and rebuilding the damage.

"I'm screwed either way," bemoaned Ghost. "If I tell the truth, I betray Gunner and what he's accomplished. If I disclose what happened aboard that spacecraft, I set off a diplomatic firestorm with the Russians, who are at this very moment stalking our East Coast with nuclear-armed subs. If I engage in a cover-up, when it comes out, all of us will face the scrutiny of congressional hearings and the media."

Cuccinelli sat back down and interrupted him. "Sir, you're making the assumption that someone will find evidence that raises the specter of foul play. May I remind you that the Starhopper crashed back to Earth four days ago. During that time frame, Major Fox reports that the jungle wildlife has eaten most of the remains, and the decay of other evidence has accelerated due to the environmental conditions. I've been involved in crime scene investigations as part of my training when I was getting started with the bureau. Under the best of circumstances, a corpse has rotted so badly by the fourth day that it is very difficult for forensic experts to identify a cause of death. Keep in mind, the initial teams assigned to this crash site are scientists who are untrained in forensics. Even if they find any parts, they'll most likely handle them improperly."

Ghost breathed a sigh of relief. The Jackal was right and he simply needed to stick to the story. "You know what, I agree. What happened in the Starhopper needs to remain in space, or buried in the jungle. This is a moment to celebrate a hero's triumphant return."

He took a deep breath and reached for the phone.

CHAPTER 48

Over the Gulf of Mexico

Bear cruised at five thousand feet above the turquoise waters of the Gulf of Mexico at a cruising speed of three hundred miles per hour. It was almost noon when the white sand beaches of the Florida Panhandle came into view. As the minutes passed, the trio's level of chatter increased.

"I have to admit, I'm a little nervous," said Cam.

"About the scrutiny we'll face?" asked Gunner.

"Nah, I can run and hide from that, although you can't, mister space cowboy superhero."

"Stop that, Cam," Gunner ordered playfully. "You know that all I wanna do is grab a beer at The Tap Room and throw down a dozen on the half shell."

"Two, Major," added Bear.

"Each, right, big guy," said Gunner, who bumped fists with his pilot.

"I'm afraid to see the damage, especially to Dog Island," continued Cam. "What if it was wiped out by a tsunami like we feared?"

Nobody spoke for a moment, during which time Bear furrowed his brow while he studied his instruments. "Um, you know, guys, I'm not sure we have the fuel to make it all the way to Maxwell. I don't want to have to ditch this beauty somewhere in South Alabama."

Cam leaned forward from the seats immediately behind the bulkhead. "Doesn't our flight path take us directly over Tyndall? Just drop us down there and let the Air Force worry about it."

"Guys!" exclaimed Gunner. "Have you both forgotten about our cargo? The drug money?"

"Oh, sweet Jesus," said Bear. "We can't go back to Maxwell or any other federal installation unless we want a one-way ticket to Leavenworth." The United States Penitentiary in Leavenworth, Kansas, was a frequent destination of military personnel who committed serious crimes.

"We gotta dump this load somewhere and come back to get it," said Gunner.

Bear slowed his airspeed and looked toward the Gulf Coast. The distinctive geographic feature of Apalachicola jutting out into the Gulf where the river emptied came into view to his right. He gripped the controls and began to veer the Valor toward the east.

"What are we doing?" asked Gunner.

Bear set his jaw, a look of determination coming over his face. "We have to make another stop."

Gunner looked through his side window, and the barrier islands came into view. "No, Bear, we can't land on Dog Island."

"Yes, I can. It'll be a piece of cake."

"You know what I mean. It's not about whether you can. You shouldn't."

Cam offered her opinion. "Hang on, Gunner, think about it for a second. The island was probably evacuated, so it's not likely we'll be scrutinized. Secondly, this bird has Navy markings. People might think it's part of a Coast Guard relief effort or something. They don't know any better."

Gunner thought for a moment and then began to nod his head. "At least we have an explanation. But, Bear, in and out, okay?"

Bear didn't respond, simply smiling as he guided the tilt-rotor aircraft into position to ease onto the beach to the west of Gunner's home.

"Hey, is the pass between the islands bigger, or is that my imagination?" asked Cam.

Gunner looked to the left while Bear continued his descent. "It sure does. Hurricanes have done this in the past. There must have been some tsunami-like waves."

Cam turned toward Bear. "Do you have eyes on the house?"

"Um, yeah. But, um, you're not gonna believe this."

Cam and Gunner both pressed their faces against the small windows of the Valor. His house was in plain view and appeared to be unharmed. On the bayside, Pop's seaplane was safely tied off at the dock. It was what lay on the other side of Gunner's home that left them astonished.

"Is that an oil barge?"

"A big one," replied Cam.

"It's gotta measure two hundred feet."

Running perpendicular to the beach was a thirty-five-foot-wide articulated oil barge that had run ashore and beached a hundred yards from Gunner's property. The four-story-tall tug sat on the Gulf of Mexico side of the beach, and the vast length of the barge itself stretched past Gunner's house toward the bay. It blocked the only road leading to Gunner's property and the west end of Dog Island.

Bear let out a laugh as he gently dropped the Valor on the narrow stretch of beach on the west side of the house. "There is a bright side. Nobody will be able to bother the Valor. We're completely cut off from the rest of the island."

"Guys, if that ship had been a few hundred feet in this direction, it would've wiped out the house."

Gunner shook his head in disbelief. Then a smile came over his face as Pop and Howard came running down the beach toward them.

CHAPTER 49

Gunner's Residence
Dog Island
The Florida Panhandle

They say families give you two things—roots to ground you and provide stability, and wings to allow you to come back together quickly after being apart. Gunner threw open the door of the Valor just as the rotors stopped turning. His feet barely touched the sand as he raced down the beach to greet Pop and Howard, who despite his stubby legs and hefty torso, managed to beat Pop to the tearful reunion.

Tears of joy flowed as the Fox men hugged, examined one another, and then laughed about the ordeal they'd all been through. Howard barked, howled, and ran in circles, enjoying the moment until he couldn't dance anymore. After accepting some hugs from Cam and Bear, he flopped in the sand, panting.

"I knew you'd find your way home," said Pop.

"I owe it all to these two," said Gunner, hugging Cam and Bear around the neck, who graciously accepted their friend's thanks.

Pop looked toward Saint George Sound and then turned back to the group. "Everyone, there's so much to discuss, but I want to tell you that a Coast Guard vessel came by a little while ago and tied off at the dock. I assumed they were here to look at that thing." He pointed his thumb over his shoulder at the beached tanker.

"Yeah, how are they gonna move it?" asked Gunner.

"No, I mean, I don't know. They were here to deliver several two-way radios and a secure satellite phone. I told them thanks, but they were probably worthless, but supposedly the military has managed to launch new satellites into space already."

"Really?" asked Cam.

"Yes. According to the Coasties, the Space Force had planned for this contingency. As soon as NASA gave them the all clear on the meteor storm, rockets lifted off from Texas and Florida to deploy new surveillance and communications satellites."

"Good for them, right?" said Bear.

Gunner put his arm around Pop's shoulder and led him toward the plane. "Did they say anything else?"

"No, but there was an envelope that read *eyes only*."

"What did it say?" Gunner asked casually.

"I didn't open it!" protested Pop.

Gunner laughed and rolled his eyes. "Pop, what did it say?"

He was busted. "Um, well, if I had opened it, it might've said that you were to remain at home and have no contact with the outside world. That you'd be visited in due time. Something like that."

"Anything else?"

"Yeah, it was signed off with *phone home, Ghost*."

Gunner stopped just short of the plane and looked to his friends. "He's trying to shield us from something."

"I bet we're in trouble," said Bear.

Cam slugged him. "I knew we should've taken this thing to Maxwell."

Bear shot back. "We couldn't, Cam! Remember the money?"

"What money?" asked Pop.

Gunner led Pop to the open door of the Valor. He pointed to the bags, grain sacks, and duffels full of cash. "That money."

Pop began pointing at the bags, his lips whispering as he counted them. "How much is it? A hundred thousand?"

Gunner chuckled and squeezed Pop's shoulder. "A lot more, Pop. Listen, we have something we have to do, and obviously, we need to be quick about it." He turned to Bear and Cam, who joined his side.

"We've got a dozen bags, all equally full," said Cam. "How do you wanna do this? A quarter each?"

"Sure, except I wanna give two of my bags to Chief's family. I'll use the third to pay off Pop's mortgage and mine."

Bear agreed. "Same here. The way I see it, Chief Rawlings is the guy who taught you how to survive space. I'd trade two of my bags for what that man did for you."

"What are you gonna do with the third?" asked Gunner.

"You know, it's time for me to settle down. I've got to quit shacking up with women, you know, sponging off them." Bear turned in a circle and admired the beautiful gulf beaches. "Maybe I'll find a spot down the street. You got any black folks in your neighborhood?" He began laughing. The three friends had always been color blind in their relationship.

"Okay, for the first time, I agree with Bear."

"What?" asked Bear as a grin consumed his face. "Pop, you're a witness. She agreed with me!"

"Shut up!" Cam tried to punch him again, but Bear dodged it. "I wanna do the same and, if you and Pop don't mind, maybe I'll find a spot on Dog Island, too."

"Just like family," said Pop.

They retrieved their gear and a bag of money. Bear calculated that they could fly to Chief Rawlings's home town of Victoria, Texas, deliver the body, and make a quick stop at Lackland Air Force Base in San Antonio for fuel.

Gunner said he'd make the call to Ghost to clear it first, but he planned on omitting any mention of drug money. Cam agreed to stay at the house with Pop to fend off any unwanted visitors, like the media or the CID, the Criminal Investigation Division of the Army.

As they were getting ready to take off, Gunner said to Pop, "If you happen to get into town, a cold beer would be nice when we get back."

"And oysters, too!" shouted Bear.

"Say no more, boys. I'm on it!"

Cam and Pop stood well back from the Valor on takeoff as the tilt-rotors whipped the fine sand into a stinging frenzy.

CHAPTER 50

May 2, 2019
Gunner's Residence
Dog Island
The Florida Panhandle

There's nothing like an oyster roast on the beach. Gunner and Bear
had returned from Texas, where they spent an emotional couple of
hours with Chief Rawlings's family. Upon their return to Dog Island,
the group enjoyed a couple of beers and then slept 'til way past noon
the next day.

Pop and Cam had taken Gunner's boat into Apalachicola in
search of Oyster City beer and a bushel of oysters. There were
roughly a hundred oysters per bushel. A bushel would typically feed
six people, but when they considered that Bear was one of the four,
they knew they needed enough for six.

That afternoon, the group enjoyed the warm sun, cold beer, and
comradery as they prepared the beach for the oyster roast. Bear set
six masonry blocks in place and found a large piece of half-inch-thick
metal from the wreckage of the oil tanker. This would create their
flat-top grill.

As the sun began to set over what was left of St. George Island to
their west, Gunner built a roaring fire using driftwood and pieces of
wooden docks that had found their way on shore.

"I think it's hot enough," said Pop, who was supervising the entire
operation, along with Howard, of course. Howard wasn't allowed any
oysters, but he did enjoy the cans of albacore tuna that Pop had
stockpiled for the disaster. "Sprinkle a few drops of water on the
metal to make sure it's hot. If it sizzles, we're golden."

The sizzling of the salt water gave him his answer and, with Cam's help, he dumped half the oysters on top of the metal. Finally, he took one of the wet burlap grain sacks that used to contain the money, soaked it thoroughly in water, and draped it over the oysters.

"Eight minutes for a light roast, right, Pop?" asked Gunner.

"Yessir. When they're done, we'll let that first batch cool and then start another when we're ready."

Gunner raised his beer. "Here's a toast to Chief Rawlings and the fallen," he began as everyone raised their glasses. "They were heroes who died saving the world. We ask God to hold them gently in His hands, and to let them soar above the clouds to the Heavens they loved so much. Godspeed, Patriots!"

Everyone clinked their glasses and drank the warm beer.

Off in the distance, the rhythmic thumping of a helicopter's rotors could be heard approaching from the mainland. As it drew closer, the sun provided Gunner a better look at it.

"Black, no markings."

"That's odd," commented Cam.

"Depends on who it is and what they want," he surmised.

The chopper approached but remained a respectful distance away from them. It gently set down near the Valor, where it planned to stay, as evidenced by the engine being shut down.

Gunner breathed a sigh of relief and finished his beer. "If it was trouble, they would've done their signature *circle the prey* swoop around us. I'll be right back."

He walked away from the curious group, who watched intently as Gunner approached the helicopter. Just as he arrived, the door swung open and the copilot hopped onto the sand to assist two passengers as they exited.

Ghost and the Jackal had arrived at Dog Island.

Gunner broke into a jog and extended his hand to shake his former mentor's. Then the men exchanged a bro-hug. He tried to shake hands with the Jackal, but she immediately hugged him instead. It was a touching, genuine gesture that surprised Gunner at first, but then warmed his heart.

"You two are late for the party," said Gunner with a chuckle.

"In more ways than one, Major," said Ghost. "You're looking good."

"Yeah, better than a couple of days ago, anyway," quipped Gunner. "I hope you like oysters and beer. Besides a bunch of canned goods, that's all we have to offer."

"Sounds perfect!" the Jackal responded for them.

Gunner appreciated her enthusiasm, but his focus remained on Ghost. He sensed the two of them hadn't traveled all the way from Fort Belvoir on a social call.

After Pop was introduced to the newcomers, and the remainder of the oysters were shared with them, the group made their way inside the house. After they discussed the challenges America faced from the catastrophe, Ghost got to the point.

He explained the decision he'd made regarding the events that had taken place in the Starhopper. Gunner and the group completely understood the need for keeping what happened under wraps.

Next, the conversation turned to Heather's death. In a strange twist of irony, Gunner, the one person who was most affected by the secrets held by Director Foster and Colonel Robinson, was the voice of reason in determining what would happen next.

"Here's the thing, I never truly had closure on what happened that day at the ISS. In my gut, I felt that something was misleading about the story NASA fed the media and Congress. I admit that I was bitter for a long time over it."

"Rightfully so, son," said Pop, who was hearing some of these revelations for the first time. He'd grown agitated as the details came out during the conversation, but Gunner held his hand several times to reassure him.

Gunner continued. "Now I see it from a different perspective. As much as I hate to say it, there are bigger things at play here. What happened to Heather years ago has been avenged. I did it myself. The cover-up must continue, just like the melee and resulting deaths in the Starhopper must remain buried in my mind. Let all of the astronauts, American and the others, be remembered as heroes for the part they played. For me, it's enough to finally know the truth and that those responsible were dealt with."

He sighed and furrowed his brow. He had one more thought. "However, there's the matter of Colonel Robinson. If the Jackal's theory is correct, he may have murdered or at least arranged for the killing of Foster. He took it too far just to protect his reputation or save his ass from the cover-up. What can be done about that?"

The Jackal responded, "I can plant the seeds of suspicion with some of my friends at the bureau. Let them quietly look into Foster's death. Once they know the *who* and the *why*, putting the pieces of the puzzle together are much easier."

"That'll work out for the better," said Gunner. "I'm in a pretty mellow mood right now. It may not be that way if I ever cross paths with the colonel."

Pop grabbed the one-gallon brown jug of Hooter Brown ale and topped everyone's glasses. They clinked them together and took a sip.

Ghost exhaled and leaned forward in his chair. "Let's move on to the next order of business. Two things. Bear, you can't keep the Valor. I borrowed that from the Navy and they want it back."

"Oh, come on. That's twice I got to fly one of those birds, and let me tell ya, they're the bomb."

"You're such an idiot," chastised Cam. "In what world do you think the military's gonna let you have your own personal aircraft, especially one like the AV-280."

"The other thing is the drug money." Ghost dropped a bombshell that caught them all off guard. The looks on their faces probably confirmed the seasoned operative's suspicions.

Gunner began before being cut off by Ghost. "Wait, Ghost, it's not—" Visions of the bundles of cash right over their heads in the loft filled his head.

"Not another word, Major. I've been around this business a long time. While it was admirable that you burned down the compound in the Darién Gap, and all of the drugs with it, as you so meticulously described, it was reasonable for me to assume that there was money hidden there as well.

"The bottom line is this. I don't care what you did with it—good, bad, or indifferent. For my part, and the Jackal's, we don't want to know anything about it. And, now, or in the future, when the opportunity arises, do what you must, but know that I can't protect you from that."

The trio exchanged glances.

Ghost continued. "A marginal kill? I can keep you from being run through the court system like others. But profiteering is another story. Are we clear?"

Everyone nodded their acknowledgment.

"Good. Now, I have an offer to make you."

CHAPTER 51

Gunner's Residence
Dog Island
The Florida Panhandle

When Ghost commanded Air Force special operators from nearby Hurlburt Field, the missions they undertook were sanctioned by, and largely directed by, the Pentagon. He would never forget the day when he was called to Washington and then, within seconds of his arrival, he was whisked away by helicopter to Fort Belvoir. Hours later, and without the benefit of consulting with family or friends, his life changed forever.

He was no longer active-duty Air Force. He was technically unemployed. Certainly, he was very well compensated by his handlers. He was assured that he'd never be subjected to an audit nor would his bank accounts be monitored by the IRS. For so long as he performed his duties as requested, he would have an interesting career and a lucrative one as well.

Ghost was admired within the dark ops community. He was not only revered for his successes, but also for his ability to spot new talent. Approaching a member of the military about quitting their career and joining the most secret of secret units was not as easy as it might sound. The timing had to be perfect, and the level of allure had to be enticing enough to convince a person to cut off ties with society, as well as family, if necessary.

He turned to Gunner and asked, "What do you know about the *Activity?*"

Gunner's eyes grew wide and he glanced at Cam and Bear. They'd discussed this topic before, albeit briefly. He casually responded, despite his inner excitement, "The Army's Intelligence Support Activity unit, often referred to as the Activity. Highly secretive. Top-notch operators. I ran across some of them while I was in Afghanistan."

Ghost looked to Cam. "Major?"

"Sir, I recall that the Activity was formed after the Iranian hostage crisis decades ago. At first, Army special ops, namely Delta, were rumored to be given self-contained missions. By self-contained, I mean without the knowledge of anyone other than those who worked within the close confines of the Activity."

"How about you, Lieutenant?" asked Ghost.

"Same as Gunner and Cam, but I'll add they were unique in that they had their own charter and structure. You know how the military is—chain of command and all that. Only, they never went outside the Activity for help. They have their own intelligence divisions, aviation support, classification names, etcetera. Truthfully, though, everything I've just said is rumor. You know, locker-room talk and such."

Ghost stood and walked around the living area. He glanced at the Jackal and then over to Pop. "Sir, I'm sorry to ask this of you, but I need some privacy. Would you mind giving us a little time to speak alone?"

Pop was a good soldier and understood. "Nope, not at all. Howard needs a walk to relieve himself of his dinner. We'll stroll around by the sound and check on the dock."

Gunner stood and gave his father a pat on the back. "Thanks, Pop."

After a minute in which Howard needed some coaxing to leave, the group of five was alone again.

Ghost returned to the conversation. "What I'm about to discuss with you rises to the highest level of our nation's intelligence classifications. The Activity undertakes missions that are not given according to presidential directives. They're not subject to oversight by congressional intelligence committees because virtually all Activity is self-contained by its own secretive multimillion-dollar budget tucked within the Department of Defense.

"This level of secretiveness is designed to shield Congress, and any administration that occupies the White House, from scrutiny when missions go south. Within Washington, and around the world, so little is known about the Activity that the enemy doesn't even consider whether their operatives are inside their borders.

"The reason that I'm telling you all of this is because I've been tasked with reconstituting a unit that was mothballed years ago after the war in Afghanistan came to an end. It will be a small close-knit group of operators and key support personnel, but it will also have the benefit of other assets used within the Activity.

"Each of you passes the requirements of being mentally and physically sound, mature, competent and, above all, willing to go the extra mile on every task. These operations are demanding, challenging, deadly, but in the end, rewarding."

Ghost paused, so Gunner began to ask some questions. "Are you saying we'd be going back to Afghanistan or the Middle East theater?"

"No, not necessarily," replied Ghost. "You'd go where the situation dictates. But I will say this. Because of how you handled yourself on the NASA mission, and with your Earth sciences background, I imagine that when a catastrophic event presents itself, you'll be called upon."

"Who will we report to?"

"Me. Nobody else."

Gunner looked to the Jackal. "Are you in?"

"Yes, Major. Well, I am if you guys are."

Ghost discussed the Jackal's role. "We're entering a new era of warfare, whether it be against terrorists, rogue nations, or mother nature, as Gunner has experienced. The team I want to assemble around you will have a particular experience in intelligence gathering as well as covert operations.

"The unit that we'll be reconstituting chased al-Qaeda all over Afghanistan and took out famed drug cartel leader Pablo Escobar."

Cam had a question. "Sir, with the broad range of activities, pardon the pun, we're gonna need access to a wide variety of tools—weapons, transportation, communications, and identification."

Ghost assuaged her concerns. "Major, our budget may not be as big as the Defense Department's, and you may not have multiple branches of the Armed Forces to call upon for assistance, but let me assure you of something. You will want for nothing. The *accountants*, as I call them, have the ability to requisition anything you need to accomplish your mission. No questions asked."

"How about backup?" asked Bear. "Who's gonna watch our six?"

"Each other," replied Ghost. "Plus your support team at Fort Belvoir."

"Do we get an increase in rank and pay?" asked Bear.

"You're retiring from the Air Force and will receive the benefits afforded you based upon your service. After that, your pay from the Activity will make your head spin. Finally, there are the spoils of a successful mission, when available."

"I understand," said Bear. "So, can we keep the Valor? It's not bothering anybody over on the beach."

"No, Lieutenant, but any mode of transportation that you can pilot will be yours as needed. You just can't bring it home with you."

"Where will we be based?" asked Cam.

"Technically, Fort Belvoir, but you will be stationed in your home."

Bear looked to Gunner. "Well, unless he objects, Cam and I are planning to find a place here on the island."

Ghost thought for a moment. "If you do that, it helps us logistically. We might be able to assist you with the purchase."

Gunner looked at the Jackal again and smiled. "What do you think?"

"Well, it beats working for the FBI. But then again, I don't have to risk my life like you do. I will make you this promise, though. I will be there day and night to protect you any way I can."

Gunner looked to Cam and Bear. "Any more questions?"

They both shook their heads.

"Whadya think, Gunner?" asked Ghost.

"Sir, would you give us a moment to talk? I'm sure Pop would like to exchange some war stories with you guys."

Ghost and the Jackal excused themselves and joined Pop outside on the beach. While they were gone, Gunner hoped to have a serious discussion with his friends in order to make a smart decision. His hopes were dashed when Bear started the conversation.

"Hell yeah! I'm ready to jump on board the crazy train."

Even Cam got in the act. She reached her arm up as if she were pulling the rope of a train whistle up and down.

"Woot! Woot!" she hollered as Bear walked around the couches bellowing, "Choo! Choo!"

Gunner shook his head in disbelief at the comic relief exhibited by these two. He saw pitfalls in the proposal, but the upside potential was great. Gunner was not a rule follower, and most of these types of operations required operating outside the box. The trip to the asteroid proved that.

The three of them took a few minutes to discuss the risks, the pay, and the autonomy. It was agreed that the prospects of getting hurt were high, but they always were when they were deployed on a mission. In fact, operating outside the normal rules of engagement might make their tasks safer, so the autonomy and secretiveness was a key.

As for the money, they'd most likely kept close to a million dollars of the drug cartel stash. Only Bear was likely to blow through it, which would be more difficult for him if he was confined to Dog Island and under his friends' watchful eyes.

This was an important decision, and Gunner needed a clear head. He left Cam and Bear to talk about the opportunity between themselves as he quietly slipped down the stairs and into the cool night air.

CHAPTER 52

Gunner's Residence
Dog Island
The Florida Panhandle

Gunner walked toward the west end of Dog Island, which had become his place to relax and reflect. He needed to get away for a moment, taking this opportunity for the first time to consider what he'd been through over the last several weeks, or years, for that matter.

Despite the fact that she was gone, Gunner was feeling a newfound connection to Heather. It was if she were there, even though she couldn't be. The two of them had such a close relationship that they easily finished each other's sentences and oftentimes made the same comment simultaneously. The two of them were always on the same page.

After her death, a void was left in Gunner's heart and his mind. His partner, his soul mate, had been stolen from him and replaced with anger toward anyone he deemed remotely responsible. As a result, the closeness they shared had drifted out of his consciousness and was replaced with bitterness, sorrow, and self-pity.

Until now. It would take Gunner years to fully process and recount the events that led him into space. One thing he knew, however, was that the connection he had with his wife while she was alive had become a part of him again. Now he could call on her for advice. Or to lend an ear. Or simply walk with him on the beach. *Their beach.* The home they'd dreamt about together until they brought it to a reality.

"Woof! Woof!"

Howard was hollering for him. Because it was dark now, he couldn't see his best pal, so Gunner began walking back toward the house. Within ten seconds, Howard was by his side, soaking wet from playing in the gentle surf. His tail was wagging and beating against Gunner's calves as they walked together.

"Buddy, I was talking to your mommy. She said she misses you, too."

Howard looked up and appeared to smile. His head snapped toward the water and paused.

"What is it, old boy?" asked Gunner.

Howard barked twice and walked into the water until it sloshed against his belly. Gunner waded in and saw what had grabbed his attention.

He gently nudged Howard back toward the beach and retrieved a bottle bobbing in the waves lapping against the shoreline.

"Whadya know, Howard. It's a message in a bottle. See, it's got a cork in it." Gunner held it down to the basset's level so he could sniff it. "Do you think we should read it?"

"Woof!"

"I don't know, Howard. I feel like we'd be intruding. Why don't we take it home and put it on Heather's side of the bed? She'd probably think something like this is romantic, wouldn't you agree?"

He barked again and then ran ahead as Ghost and Pop approached. Gunner knelt down to the water and rinsed off the sand. He tucked the bottle in his left arm and hugged it against his chest, where his heart was beating rapidly.

Pop led Howard back to the house, leaving Gunner and Ghost alone.

"Well, Gunner, what are your thoughts?"

"You know, when your life is turned upside down like mine was after Heather died, you really don't know what to do. Everybody says you gotta move on, but it's not that easy."

Ghost understood. "Some people never move on."

"I can imagine. Together, the whole world revolved around us. I never expected to live my life without her, and when it happened, I was at a loss."

"You never quit, Gunner. You didn't run away. I watched your career from a distance. I kept tabs on you, and you never knew it. I watched you pick up the pieces."

Gunner laughed. "And here we are. Ghost, a month ago they were within an inch of kicking me to the curb. I could've lost everything over that test flight because I didn't give a shit anymore, truthfully."

Ghost stopped them and turned to Gunner. "That's changed now, hasn't it?"

"It has, and I'm not totally sure I can explain why. It's as if I'm whole again, because I can feel Heather here, and here." He pointed to his head and tapped his right fist against his heart.

"Listen, I'm not trying to lead you into a place that I don't think you're ready for. If anything, now more than ever, I think you need to join me on this new mission. We can do great things together. I've known that since the day you arrived at Hurlburt Field."

Gunner chuckled and looked toward the house. Cam and Bear were leaning on the rail, staring at the two men as they spoke.

"Well, I'll have a couple of very disappointed friends up there if I say no. What's this new team or unit called?"

"Gray Fox," replied Ghost.

"Wait, like the one in Afghanistan. They were the best."

"And you will be, too. Gray Fox is being resurrected for you, Gunner."

"I'm honored."

Gunner turned to the house and hollered, "Hey, guys, can you come down here!"

Like two little kids who'd just been given permission to go play outside, Cam and Bear practically knocked each other over to race back into the house and within seconds emerged on the beach.

When they arrived, Ghost gathered them all together, but he looked to Gunner. "When the time comes, will you be ready to answer the call of duty and go where your country needs you?

"Yes, sir, *send me*," replied Gunner, repeating the secretive motto of the Activity he'd heard in Afghanistan.

"Me too," said Cam.

"Ride or die," added Bear.

"We stick together," said the trio in unison.

And, with that, *Gray Fox* was reborn.

THANK YOU FOR READING ASTEROID: DESTRUCTION!

If you enjoyed it, I'd be grateful if you'd take a moment to write a short review for each of the books in the series (just a few words are needed) and post it on Amazon. Amazon uses complicated algorithms to determine what books are recommended to readers. Sales are, of course, a factor, but so are the quantities of reviews my books get. By taking a few seconds to leave a review, you help me out and also help new readers learn about my work.

And before you go ...

SIGN UP for Bobby Akart's mailing list to receive special offers, bonus content, and you'll be the first to receive news about new releases in the Asteroid series. Visit: www.BobbyAkart.com

VISIT Amazon.com/BobbyAkart for more information on the Asteroid series, the Doomsday series, the Yellowstone series, the Lone Star series, the Pandemic series, the Blackout series, the Boston Brahmin series and the Prepping for Tomorrow series totaling thirty-eight novels, including over thirty Amazon #1 Bestsellers in forty-plus fiction and nonfiction genres. Visit Bobby Akart's website for informative blog entries on preparedness, writing, and a behind-the-scenes look into his novels.